Buried Fire

JONATHAN STROUD

Corgi Books

For Gina, with love

Under the old king's barrow, in a hollow place hidden from the winter mists and the summer sun, a dragon coils.

Round and round a hoard of gold its long length stretches, pin tail to razor snout, plugging the airless space like a giant bung. The old king, who had once sat proudly in the centre of his gift hoard, now lies in a corner, a clump of bones swept into the shadows and forgotten.

In the darkness, nothing stirs. The dragon lies as still and silent as a graveyard skull. For a thousand years or more it has never moved, not an inch. But its mind is burning.

The fire is barely a needle prick in size – a blood-red point glowing in the dark, a tiny flame of anger, lust and greed, squeezed almost to nothing. There is no air in the barrow, but the dragon does not need it. The flame of its mind feeds off its own white fury, and burns, burns, burns down the endless years.

Far overhead, in the bright, green world, little things with hasty bodies live and die. But here in the stillness, change is banished, for the dragon has learned to ignore Time.

To do this, the dragon compresses its mind clean of its memory. It allows the pressure of the earth to squeeze out all traces of the life it has left behind.

One by one, across the centuries, it purges its

thoughts; they rise, coiling and uncoiling, through the dead ground like bubbles in the sea. At last, almost imperceptible except where they shift the dew, they emerge from the earth and hang above the grass until the breezes drift them away.

The ground where the discarded thoughts appear is thickly grown with foxglove and harebell, and home to a large company of brightly-coloured lizards and little birds. Eager for strange knowledge, their quick eyes watch from hidden places, waiting with a silent hunger.

Only rarely – once, twice in a millennium – does the dragon notice the sagging earth pressing down upon its back. Then the red point flares with sudden anger, and far above, the earth quivers.

Long centuries pass.
The barrow flattens under the weight of grass seeds.
The dragon lies still.

DAY 1

1

The boy was asleep in the hollow on the hilltop when the dragon's thought came up from the ground and enveloped him. It rose through his body slowly, like a giant soap bubble, with its oily surface quivering and glinting in the sun.

As it spread out across his chest and stomach, the boy stirred uneasily, but he did not wake. His face had time to grimace briefly – then the bubble crept up across his throat and over his face, and the sound of his breathing was suddenly cut off.

Still it rose, a vast translucent dome, until the boy was swallowed whole. A book lying open on the grass beside his hand burst into flame as the thought engulfed it.

Time passed. The sleeping boy slept on in the afternoon sunlight, with a burning book beside him. It burnt unsteadily, with a jittering green and yellow fire, until it was reduced to a fine white ash. A light breeze blew across the hollow, but could not reach inside the dragon's thought, and the pile of ash lay quiet upon the grass. The boy lay like an embalmed thing, steadily breathing the thought inside him.

Quick movements stirred the grass across the hollow. Tiny lizards, flecked with green and orange scales, pushed their way up between the gorse stalks and the early heather. With eager, darting movements, they scuttered ever nearer to the bubble, until one by one, and in ever greater numbers, they passed through its surface, out of the natural air. Small tongues flickered, drinking in the essence of the fiery thought, while the boy's clothes singed around the edges and his face grew pale.

Time passed.

Into the nowhere of his sleep came a red stillness.

It brought with it a sudden hunger, a sharpening of senses and a new keenness of desire. He felt as if he hadn't eaten for a month, a year, a hundred years, though his midday sandwiches lay heavily inside him.

The redness was all around. It had a pink tint, like a strong light showing through flesh.

And it burnt his eyes. All about him everything was aflame – the trees, the rocks, the earth, the sky. Though his eyes were closed tight shut, the heat from the burning world set them both on fire.

Then, just when it seemed to him that his whole face must burn away, the terrible heat died down and his eyes opened. He saw a sky blistered with a savage sunset that seemed to set the world alight. Dark things circled beyond the clouds. A smell of chemicals and cave water stung his skin and his ears caught the sound of gold melting through the mountains. His mouth tasted of cast-iron.

It seemed as if days passed, and nights; the sun moved at a bewildering speed, striping the unknown landscape with zebra shades while his eyes and the eyes of the dark moving things above him watched it all unblinking.

Now he seemed to move
with a lightning movement,
and he was in a different place,
where tall pillars were arching to a point,
and tiny things were running, screaming,
scattering,
leaving an explosion of gold on the marbled
floor beneath his descending claws.

Another movement, and now
a pitch black stillness, of which he is a part.
A red gleam on a wet stone floor,
and a breath
so slow, it ceases;
drawing out an impossible span
years long.
And now

The blue sky lightened towards evening and a wind
sprang up, blowing south-easterly over the hilltop
from Fordrace and the Russet Woods. The dying sunlight shimmered on the bubble dome, and the torpid
lizards, lying head to tail in a perfect circle against the
inside of the bubble's rim, twitched uneasily.

Then the bubble was caught in a stronger gust. It
rose further from the ground, and was lifted free at
last, to be blown across the hollow and over the ridge,
west towards Little Chetton and the sun. The lizards
scattered, the ash dispersed on the winds, and only the
boy was left, sleeping on the grass, with scarlet weals
upon his eyes and cheeks as white as death.

Fifteen minutes later, a cooler breeze caught his
face, and Michael MacIntyre awoke.

The Reverend Tom Aubrey was a busy man. Before the afternoon was over he would have to chair three parish meetings, attend one Women's Institute coffee circle and inspect the leaking pipes in the Sunday School boys' lavatories. And he was too hot to relish any of them. The simple fact was that summers and dog collars did not mix. The tight white ring constricting his throat was a perfect trap both for sweat trickling down and for heat rising up. It rubbed and it itched and it grew dirty with a speed that rather annoyed the Reverend Tom.

He sat in his chair in the small white study behind the vestry and scratched the back of his neck with a deliberate care. On the desk in front of him a thick pile of ecclesiastic correspondence stared up at him accusingly, demanding to be read. His eyes flittered across the top sheet, glazing as they went. Behind him, the voices of the workmen in the churchyard, and their radios and spades, drifted in through the blinds along the slats of sunlight. The Reverend Tom sighed, and his sigh became a yawn.

There was only half an hour before the church finance meeting, and he had yet to read the warden's notes on the subject. With a reluctant hand, the Rev. Tom flipped through the papers looking for the report. As he did so, his eyes accidentally rose a little, and caught sight of himself in the study mirror, framed between the rails of cassocks and robes that he seldom wore. He looked at the reflection and wondered what Sarah would think if she saw him now. Handsome? Possibly. Dishevelled? Certainly. In need of a shower and a change of clothes? Yep.

There was a knock at the door. The Reverend Tom lowered his head and interested himself in the topmost paper. "Come in!" he called, in an otherwise-engaged sort of voice.

"Tom—" The church warden, Elizabeth Price, put her head round the door. "The top workman wants to see you – if you're not too busy. Are you too busy, Tom?"

"Far too busy," said the Reverend Tom. "I'll be right with him. What's it about this time?"

"Not sure. They've found something. Won't tell me what, but they've all stopped work, so you'd better come and look."

"More tea all round, no doubt. OK, let's see what it is then."

They took the long route through the nave, since the side-door was blocked with the workmen's things. St Wyndham's church was never warm, but Tom could still sense the mid-afternoon heat pressing down remorselessly from outside. Strong cones of stained-glass sunlight speared down from the windows every ten strides along, filled with silent spirals of wandering dust. A line of poetry came ridiculously into Tom's head. He said,

"Love bade me welcome: yet my soul drew back,
    Guiltie of dust and sinne,

9

only it's dust and skin in this place. It's a wonder we don't choke."

There was an old woman in the church, sitting in the final row of chairs before the doors. Tom eyed her cautiously as he approached. He had been at St Wyndham's three months; it had taken him less than three days to recognise and dislike Mrs Gabriel. As ever, she wore her thick red shawl and a look of disapproval. Tom adopted a genial smile and made a forlorn attempt to pass her by.

"Are you not ashamed, vicar?" She was looking straight in front, towards the distant altar. Tom and Elizabeth halted.

"Ashamed, Mrs Gabriel? What about?" asked Tom, though he knew full well.

"Of the sacrilege going on in this ground." She did not turn to him. "It wouldn't have happened in the Reverend Staples' time, nor in the Reverend Morrison's."

"Mrs Gabriel, we've talked about this before," Tom began, but Elizabeth interrupted him.

"I'll just go ahead and tell Mr Purdew you're on your way," she said, and disappeared hastily through the West Door. Tom looked after her enviously.

"The churchyard is a holy ground," went on Mrs Gabriel, still gazing straight before her. "Though I don't expect that word to mean much to you, young man. People had expectations when they were laid there, no matter how long ago. Now you're digging them up."

"Mrs Gabriel," said Tom, shifting from one foot to the other, "there really is no need to be concerned. I've told you about this already. The church foundations are slipping a little on the north side. It's nothing dangerous at present, but we must shore them up. That's why the men are digging here. And because no one was buried on the north side in the old days, there's very little chance of disturbing anybody's rest.

He took a deep breath, wondering if he'd won. For the first time, Mrs Gabriel turned her head towards him. "I still say—" she began, but Tom had had enough.

"I'm sorry, Mrs Gabriel, but I must fly. I've a meeting very shortly. See you on Sunday, I hope." Tom gave a brisk smile and made off, leaving the old lady sitting alone in the church. As he opened the door, he heard her final sally.

"I don't know, vicar. You'll find an excuse to dig me up when I'm gone."

I think there's very little chance of that, Mrs G, thought Tom, as he went outside.

Fordrace parish churchyard stretched in an unbroken ring right around St Wyndham's, and was itself surrounded by an ancient stone wall. On three sides of the church, the grounds were wide and sunny, and filled with a higgledy-piggledy crop of well-tended gravestones. But to the north of St Wyndham's was a narrow strip of grass cast in almost permanent shadow. A path ran through it, close to the side of the church, and one of the four old yew trees grew stunted beside the wall. There were no gravestones here, and no evidence that it had ever been used for that purpose, in all Fordrace's long and quiet history. It was a slightly cheerless spot, and if it weren't for the church's sagging foundations, Tom would have been quite happy to leave the place undisturbed.

Tom walked around the corner and out of the searing heat, which in all directions drained the colour from the yellow-red rooftops of the village and the blue-green bulk of the Wirrim. The shadowy side of the churchyard was littered with piles of earth and scattered work tools, and the red-skinned workmen sat on the stone wall in the fringes of the shade, stretching their legs out into the sunlight and taking great gulps from Cokes and Fantas. Elizabeth and the foreman were standing beside the trench. It ran along almost the entire length of the church wall, practically obliterating the path, and ending under the green-black leaves of the yew.

Tom came over to them, smiling at the workmen on the wall. One of them grinned back.

"Hoy there, vicar. We've got a real wonder for you this time!"

"Found a skeleton, Jack?"

"Better than that, vicar. You'll wet yourself, you will."

"Not a chance. Found something good, Mr Purdew?"

The foreman was a thin man with a face turned to leather by long years in all climates. He reminded Tom of the Bog Man he had seen in the British Museum before he came to Fordrace. There was the same sad resignation about Mr Purdew, who at that moment was staring doubtfully into the trench with a cigarette hanging almost vertically from his lip. Elizabeth looked up at Tom, her eyes gleaming.

"Depends how you mean good," Mr Purdew said. "It'll be a devil to shift, that's certain."

"Just look at this, Tom!" Elizabeth was grinning with excitement. "We'll all be in the papers tomorrow!"

Tom climbed a ridge of dirt to the edge of the trench and looked.

"Good Lord," he said.

At the bottom of the trench was a large stone cross. Still caked in orange clay, it lay at an angle to the trench walls, its shaft extending away from the yew tree, and with its left arm still buried in the earth.

"I think it's very old," said Elizabeth breathlessly.

Tom nodded. It was ancient. You could tell by the shape. It was not like the simple Latin cross, with the three short arms and one extended out into the shaft. It had a circle as well, surrounding the centre, and joining each of the four arms with arcs of stone shaped like the handles of giant cups. That style was called the Celtic cross, though Tom had a vague idea that it wasn't just the Celts who used it. Moreover the whole front of the cross seemed carved with ornate patterns, caked with clay, and impossible to make out.

"Good heavens," said Tom, at last. "Mr Purdew, this is a marvellous find."

"Aye, I suppose you'll be wanting us to shift it out of there, will you?" Mr Purdew flicked ash from the end of the cigarette with a quick purse of the lips.

"Well, we must call the archaeological authorities

over at all speed," said Tom. "But yes, with their blessing, we must get it out."

"And I suppose you'll be wanting us to extend the trench and all," continued Mr Purdew, gloomily running a hand through lean hair.

"To uncover the rest of it; yes, of course. Hold on, I've got to have a closer look." Tom crouched on the edge of the trench and swung himself in, landing heavily on the packed earth beside the buried cross. Taking his handkerchief from his pocket, he dabbed eagerly at some of the encrustations of clay on the centre of the cross. Before long his voice rose out of the trench.

"It might be Celtic, or Anglo-Saxon; I don't think the Vikings came this far west, did they, Elizabeth?"

"No way near," she replied. "What do they look like, Tom?"

"Long and sinewy carvings. In the centre at any rate. They wind all over each other. It might be an animal of some kind. Yes! There's a claw."

"Sounds Anglo-Saxon to me. What do you think, Mr Purdew?"

"I think it's going to be the devil to shift it. Can the lads go home, vicar, if you're going to be down there all afternoon?"

"Mr Purdew, I'm sorry! I'll leave you to it. We've got to have this out today!" The Rev. Tom thrust his claggy handkerchief back into his pocket and straightened up. Then he gave an oath. "Oh damn! I think one of the arms might be off. The one that's still in the clay. I can see a ragged edge just here." He ran his finger between the hard wall of the trench and the stone. "Yes. Damn."

"It's bound to be down there," said Elizabeth. "Come on up, Tom. Let's get the museum on the phone."

Tom left the cross reluctantly and walked back along the trench to the far end, where a steep ramp led back to ground level. His heart was dancing now. Let Mrs Gabriel chatter how she would – nothing like this had ever happened in the Reverend Staples' time, nor the Reverend Morrison's. It was Tom Aubrey, new vicar of Fordrace, who had dug here – and if this didn't wake the village up a little, he'd be very much surprised.

Michael had woken up. There was a pain in his mouth, and a worse one in his eyes. His whole body felt raw, with the faint tingling shivering of a fever. He tried to open his eyes, but a piercing light blinded him and he screwed them up tight shut.

"Bluh'ee heh" he said, and afterwards "Chrith!" when he realised his tongue had swollen so much that he could hardly speak at all. It was like the feeling you got when you burnt your tongue on soup – sore and clothy all at the same time. Michael groaned, with a mixture of pain and panic, and tried to sit up. But his body resisted with a lancing arc of pain, and he subsided back onto the grass.

Bloody hell, he thought. What's happened to me?

Then the answer came to him. I've got sunstroke, he thought. Oh God.

He lifted a weak arm and put his hand to his forehead. Sure enough, his skin was red hot but very dry. I've sweated all the water out of me, he thought again, till there's none left at all. Now I'm overheated, and I'm going to die.

He tried to remember all the little he had ever known about sunstroke. Stephen had suffered it once, on the first day of the holiday in Tenerife. He had been out on the beach all day without his sun hat and though Michael had been very young, he had never forgotten the embarassment of Stephen vomiting up all over the hotel lounge.

Well, he hadn't been sick yet. That was a good sign.

He recalled Stephen having a cold bath. Michael had had to run to the bar to ask for a box of ice. Stephen had shouted and struggled, all red in the face, lying in the bath with his clothes still on.

Delirium. That was another sign. And he hadn't got that yet.

But he was red-hot, and weak, and he'd been out in the sun all afternoon long, like Stephen had. It was sunstroke for sure. And God, his eyes hurt!

Time to move. Michael forced himself to concentrate. He had to get home quickly, for an ice-cold bath. Or he might die.

And home was not near. It was out of the Pit, and across the high ridge of the Wirrim and down almost two miles to the cottage, where his brother and sister might or might not be home.

Never mind. Concentrate. Move. Slowly, his eyes still tight shut, Michael rolled himself onto his side, and then onto his front, until his face touched the cool grass. Which smelt – faintly – of something chemical.

The scent made him nauseous. (Oh God, that was the first sign of sunstroke!) Frantically, he levered his head and chest off the ground with his hands flat and his elbows shaking. Then he was sick.

When it was over, Michael felt a little better. He remained with his arms locked, his eyes closed, wishing he had positioned his hands a little further apart. Then he bent his knees, moved to a crawling postion, and tried to stand.

He managed this with a surprising lack of difficulty. The strength seemed to be returning to his body. For a minute or two, he stood with his head bowed into the fresh breeze across the head of the Pit, willing it to cool him, but feeling the blood throbbing in his temples and behind his eyes like a salt tide. Then, covering his eyes with cupped palms, he tried opening one eye.

The pain was so intense that he cried out, and almost fell. Instead, he was sick again, which dulled the agony, and gave a chance for despair to rise up within him.

Oh Christ, he thought, if I can't see, I can't find my way out of the hollow. And I can't get down the hill. I might as well be blind! Oh God – maybe I am! He felt a tightening of the chest and a spasm in the bowels. Not that it'll matter much – I can't get home to have my bath, so it's all over.

The image of the unreachable bath overwhelmed Michael with grief. He bent over, with his hands clamped on his knees, and began to cry. The great washings of tears gave his eyes the first relief since he had awoken. The salt water bathed his eyelids, stinging and cooling them all at once. Yet, as they issued from the corners of his eyes, he experienced an odd sensation, which made him frown even in his pain.

There was a tiny spitting noise, a low angry hissing, as if a stove-hot saucepan was being dunked in sinkwater. And as his burning tears fell onto his cheeks, Michael felt jets of hot air erupt from between his squeezed eyelids and rise up on either side of his head.

There was no doubt of it. His eyes were steaming.

"My Go'," groaned Michael, "Woth ha'en'eng oo me?"

For Stephen MacIntyre, the day had gone downhill since breakfast.

The key to this had been his sister's mood. It had swung from sunny prospects to darkest gloom with the speed and variation of a berserk barometer. Outlook had become definitely unsettled. At breakfast, she had been an administering angel. She had cooked it, which was rare, and included black pudding, which was rarer. All through the meal, she had chatted happily, without any sign of what Stephen called her 'martyr business'. She had even left the table without hinting once about the washing up, which so startled Stephen and Michael that they had done it automatically.

By mid-morning things had changed. For a start, Sarah's hay fever had started up again and put a dampener on her mood. Then, in the midst of her snuffles, she had rung the estate agency, and had a tense conversation with her boss that left her smouldering. After that, she had prepared a briefing for her new client, concerning a property in a northern fold of the Wirrim towards Stanbridge. At ten, she had driven off to collect the keys and make the tour. At eleven thirty, when she returned, she was in the blackest of moods, the visit having gone badly. By now, her hay fever was worse than ever. Then she shouted at Michael for resting his trainers on the kitchen table, and at Stephen for walking in at the wrong time to enquire about lunch.

"I only asked if you felt like any," protested Stephen.

"So I could make some for you while I was about it," Sarah yelled.

"I was going to make some for you, actually," said Stephen mildly, and not altogether truthfully.

"But he won't now," predicted Michael.

"I don't want any, anyway," said Sarah, looking frazzled.

"Fine," said Stephen. "How was the house?"

It had been the wrong thing to say; he realised that now. Well, he'd probably realised it at the time, sort of, but perhaps he'd hoped that his sister would be less than predictable. She wasn't. When the resulting fracas was over, no one was speaking to anybody. Sarah ate her lunch in her room. Then she emerged with an announcement.

"Tom's coming over for dinner." She spoke it like a challenge. "So don't mess the house up."

"Oh right," said Stephen.

"The Pope," said Michael. "Let us pray."

"Oh shut up," said Sarah. "If you don't like it, you can go out. I don't care."

After the door had slammed, Michael and Stephen sat for a moment in contemplative silence. Then Michael said, "She's right. It's too good a day for stewing here. I'm going up the Wirrim. See you later."

And out he had gone, taking a couple of apples and a novel from their grandmother's bookshelf. For a demure old lady, she had been unusually fond of what she called 'racy' fiction. First Stephen and now Michael had found benefits from her collection that their grandmother would hardly have expected.

Stephen had stayed in the cottage through the hot afternoon, until Sarah, in a suddenly busy mode, had begun hoovering. That was the last straw for Stephen. The rigid drone and the fraught atmosphere finally drove him out of the house and onto his bike.

Outside, the heat of the summer rose from the garden and hovered in a flickering haze in front of the heavy beech trees and the laurel hedge. Stephen's watch read five thirty. Up on the Wirrim, Michael would be getting fried to a crisp, unless he had the sense to keep in the shade, which Stephen thought doubtful. For a moment, he was tempted to follow the lane to the right, to the bridleway which led by steep degrees to the quarries under the lip of the Wirrim, but the pressing heat bore on him strongly. Far too much like hard work, thought Stephen as he turned the bike towards the Fordrace road.

*

The village of Fordrace was clustered around a compact green, beside which, in all seasons and even in the height of summer, a sizeable stream ran, heavy with the rainwater dropped on the Wirrim's ridge. To the north, a thickly growing beech and oak wood, locally known as the Russet, stretched along the foot of the Wirrim's nearest curve. To the east and south lay ancient croplands, some still marked with the strip patterning of the medieval farmers, and all at this time heavily blanketed with wheat. The village itself had expanded little over the centuries. It still retained its ancient visage, except for one small estate of cramped redbrick houses, behind the Parson's Pub, which had been built in the early eighties and regretted ever since. The church of St Wyndham stood overlooking the green, with its Olde Mill (now a tea-room), its millpool, and its collection of glossy well-fed ducks. Elsewhere, a 19th century schoolhouse, a small library and two general stores completed the picture.

Stephen knew it very well, without feeling quite at home there. He had been there many times in his early childhood, on visits to his grandmother, and from those far-distant days some memories remained: the general store (particularly the penny sweet bags), the ducks, and the dusty boredom of the inevitable Sunday morning services. But then his parents had moved far away to the north, taking Stephen and Michael with them, and their visits to Fordrace had almost ceased. Sarah had not gone with them. She had chosen to go to live with granny, looked after her in her illness, and found herself a job. Stephen could still remember how pleased she had been with this independence.

And now we're lumped on you again, he thought, as he cycled down the hill. And aren't you glad!

Stephen tethered his bicycle to the wooden signpost on the fringes of the green. Without any particular purpose, he wandered across it, dodging squalling toddlers and their over-heated parents, until he came to Pilate's Grocery and General Store. The cool interior beckoned him.

"Yes sir, what can I get you?" Mr Pilate was the kind of shopkeeper who wished his customers to be as efficient as he was himself. The three walls of his Grocery and General Store were teetering from floor to distant ceiling with jars and tins and boxes and hanging objects, all meticulously ordered and arranged. It reminded Stephen of an Egyptian temple, with its coolness and its dark, and the hieroglyphic columns of Heinz and Baxters rising austerly into the shadows.

Stephen made a spur of the moment choice. Mr Pilate reached behind him with blind assurity and picked up the chocolate and the can from the icebox, smiling all the time at Stephen as if waiting for the real order, the order that would make his time worthwhile.

"Anything else, sir?" he asked, which meant, 'You're not seriously expecting me to be satisfied with that? Look at the choice on display, think of all the hours I've spent ordering this down from Stanbridge, placing them in neat rows on your behalf, and now you're waltzing in here asking for a Snickers and a Fanta, and you're not even concentrating. I deserve better than that, surely.'

"No thanks," said Stephen. "That's all."

Mr Pilate gave a little sigh, and thumped out the paltry sum on his old cash register.

"Then that will be fifty-seven pence," he said. "Sir."

Stephen handed it over and took his goods. As he received his change, Mr Pilate said abruptly, "Well, you're my last customer. I'm closing early today. Off to the church."

"Why," asked Stephen. "What's happening?"

"They've found an old cross in the churchyard. Buried there. Very old, they say. Museum woman's over now, and they're due to lift it out shortly. Huge thing, apparently. Needs a crane."

"Sounds worth seeing," said Stephen.

"Whole village will be there, most likely." Mr Pilate raised the hatch in the counter and emerged. "Your friend the vicar's been bustling about like a blue-arsed fly. Very pleased with himself, he is."

"He's no friend of mine," said Stephen. "You must be thinking of someone else."

"Don't you get on? He's pretty thick with your sister, isn't he?"

Even in the coolness of the store, Stephen flushed. Mr Pilate's teeth gleamed in the dark as he shepherded Stephen towards the door.

"I won't say anything against him myself. He's young. And maybe a little eager. Our blood runs slow and thick in these parts. He'll learn."

"Goodbye, Mr Pilate," said Stephen. He walked out onto the green, and leaving the grocer locking up behind him, set off towards the church. Its tower was bathed in evening pink, and a large group of people were thronging against the boundary wall. A yellow breakdown truck with a winch and crane had been reversed up the lane, and now stood with the crane's arm extended out into the churchyard.

By the time he had crossed the green, Stephen had drunk his can dry. He lobbed it into a bin and squeezed himself into the nearest gap in the crowd. The crane's arm was positioned with its horizontal bar over the side of a long trench. Three thick metal cables had been lowered into the depths. Several workmen stood around the hole, and Tom Aubrey was standing close by them, talking animatedly to a man with a notebook and pen.

He's loving it, Stephen thought. He'll be insufferable for weeks now.

At that moment, a short stout woman appeared up a ladder from the trench, climbed heavily to her feet and began barking instructions to the workmen standing round. Stephen turned to a man standing next to him.

"What's going on?"

"Looks like they're going to raise it. About time too. I've been waiting here all afternoon. That woman wouldn't give permission for ages, but she must reckon it's safe now."

"Hope they don't drop it," said Stephen.

The man nodded. "Yeah. That bloke there's from the Herald, he is."

"Have you seen it?" Stephen asked.

"Yeah, took a look earlier. Must weigh a ton. It's got an arm missing, but other than that it's in perfect nick, which is why they're all so worked up."

The man's voice trailed off, and Stephen realised that the hubbub of the crowd had died away and a stillness had descended. In silence, the workmen climbed out of the hole, Tom and the reporter moved back to a safe distance, and the archaeologist gave a last frowning inspection to the cables. Finally she moved away. Expectancy hung in the air.

The foreman nodded. A man in an armless denim top vaulted over the wall, pushed his way through the crowd and made some professional adjustments to the winching system on the back of the truck. Everyone waited. Stephen noticed that a metal trolley, like the sort driven around in large stations, only thicker and heavier, had been brought to stand on one side of the trench. It was covered with plastic sheeting.

"When you like, Charlie," the foreman said, and spat his cigarette behind him into the trench. The man by the truck nodded and flicked a switch. With a low smooth whirring, the drum on the truck began to turn and the metal cables were drawn upwards. First they went taut, then there was a moment of stress, and a slight increase in noise from the rotating drum.

The crowd was silent. The only noise was the hum of the crane motor.

Now the cross appeared from the trench, caked in earth and longer than a man. Its bulk was securely looped by cables in three places, twice along the shaft and once on its vertical arm. Orange clag clung to it everywhere, making the outline irregular and lumpen. One arm was missing, its shoulder abruptly broken off beyond the stone ring. As the cross rose through the air, Stephen was fleetingly reminded of those rescues where helpless bodies are winched by helicopter from some cliff face or upturned boat. He was suddenly aware he was holding his breath, and that the same mood was shared by the rest of the crowd. Everyone was silent, sober-faced. Even Tom's smile had turned into an anxious line.

After two minutes of smooth whirring, Charlie flicked the switch again. The cross hung above the trench, two feet above ground level. Without a word, he pulled a lever, which swung the crane arm slowly to the left. At first, the arm moved too strongly. The cross was jerked violently in mid-air; it swayed back and forth with alarming swings. One of the loops of cable slipped a little, towards the end of its arm. With his face white and his eyes staring, Charlie slowed the rate of movement. Slowly, the rocking of the cross became less and less until it was almost imperceptible. By now it was over the trolley, scraping clear of it by a few inches only, and still no one had said anything.

"All right Charlie-boy, lower away," said the foreman. His voice was hoarse with relief.

Charlie released the cables and the cross sank down upon the trolley. The motor cut off. A collective sigh of released tension rose up from the crowd. Stephen realised that his t-shirt was slippery with sweat.

Without a word, as if released from a spell, the crowd began to disperse. Across the wall, Tom was clapping the foreman on the back and the workmen were cracking open cans of beer. Stephen quickly turned away. After all the tension, he had a sudden overwhelming need to move. Two minutes later, he was back on his bike and pedalling hard.

5

Michael opened his eyes. The pain which had blinded him an hour before rose up again, but less insistently, as if it had lost heart.

Slowly, his squint relaxed and he looked around him for the first time. He was still sitting at the bottom of the hollow; all around him were the clumps of bracken, the scattered rocks and the tufted grasses. A couple of clouds hung in tatters in the sky. It was just as it had been when – an age ago – he had put his book aside and closed his eyes. Just as it had been, and yet everything had changed too. The whole world was tinted with a reddish hue. Where the grass was once a sun-dried yellow, it was now dull red. Where the sky had once been blue, it was now a grey expanse like beaten metal, flecked with a pinkish tinge. All the summer's variety of colour seemed to have been leached away.

Michael held his head in his hands, pressing gently on his boiling eyelids with fingertips which flinched at the heat. He looked again; the view was the same. Everything seemed oddly flat, like a bad painting with no real perspective. It lacked the normal depth which he had never really been aware of before, but which now, in its absence, he missed with a sharp pang. He wondered vaguely whether it would be dangerous to descend the hill with his vision in this state. But it didn't matter. He was already wrecked.

In fact, his condition puzzled him. Physically, he felt

27

a little stronger, which was odd, for the day was hardly any cooler and the sun still beat down. A sudden increase in energy, flowing upwards through his body, had cleared his head, and stopped his shaking.

He got to his feet and began to climb warily out of the hollow. Everything still looked flat. Once or twice he misjudged the distance of a rock or tuft of earth and slipped, but his sight was not as treacherous as he had expected and he soon gained the top of the rise. There, he paused to take stock.

He felt fine. Full of beans in fact. The climb had done him good. If only his si—

A rabbit ran across the opposite end of the hollow, over the back of the ridge and out of sight. Michael froze where he stood, his heart thumping in his chest.

The rabbit's movements had been those of a ghost's.

It had been fast, and he had caught only a second or two of its sprint across the grass, but he had seen enough to realise he hadn't seen it properly at all.

He had seen through it.

Although well out in the open, it had been almost invisible in the red-grey twilight of his gaze. He had caught its rabbit's outline, the shape of the ears, the flash of feet. But where was its solidity, where was its substance? He had seen the grass behind its body as it ran. And what was that crystal brightness lodged up where the head should have been? That hard-edged shape, which erupted from the dullness of the red-grey world with the impact of a pearl in mud?

Michael shook his head. Sunstroke. Remember – Stephen had been delirious too. It made no difference. He had to get home. Hastily, he turned away from the hollow, and began to negotiate the rise, walking east along the Wirrim, between the holes and crevices of old mine workings, and here and there the upraised mounds covered with short grass.

Five minutes later, he saw something which convinced him he had finally gone mad.

Two figures were approaching along the path which curved in an elegant descent down the combe to Fordrace. They were several hundred yards away when they came in view, walking together and holding hands, though their lower halves seemed curiously dim. Michael found he couldn't focus on their legs at all, but this was almost irrelevant beside the horror and wonder of their heads.

The figures had the heads of sheep.

They each had a sheep's pointed ears and blunt, curved, foolish snouts. They also had a general air of sheepiness, placid, amiable and somewhat stupid. And yet, aside from this, Michael had never seen anything less like sheep in his entire life.

The heads were formed of a glorious patterning of moving lights, scintillating like a fish's scales or the facets of a diamond. As they drew closer, their surface was revealed to be a flowing current of changing colours, which swirled and disappeared and reappeared again in a never-ending motion. A bright nimbus blurred the outline of the heads, but even so, they seemed sharper, more real and three-dimensional, than anything Michael had ever seen before. He stopped and gazed in stupefaction.

"Nice evening," said the left-head.

"Hallo," said the right-head.

A man's voice. A woman's voice. They passed close by him, Michael smelling a perfume in their wake, hearing the crunching of their boots on the stones of the path; hearing, as if in a dream, the left head say to the right head, with his sheep's mouth close to her sheep's ear, two words of human sarcasm.

"Friendly bloke!"

Michael looked after them with his mouth open. He blinked once. And, as if a veil had been removed, the picture was changed. The sky was blue again, the grass was a familiar parched yellow-green; and the two figures were suddenly a rather ordinary man and woman, walking along with their heads too close to mind the view.

Then Michael began to run, careering down the slope in a terror that gave no thought to path or precipice. He ran unblinking, ferns lashing at his legs, until his eyes began to smart at the buffeting air and filled with tears. Then he tripped on a root edge, sprawled forwards blindly, and tumbled over and over down the hillside, until the crashing bracken slowed the fall and closed over him at last.

When Mr Cleever called in at the church, Tom was standing in his shirtsleeves and open collar in the vestry, washing the last of the clay from the surface of the cross.

It had taken a lot of effort for eight workmen and

one vicar to wheel the trolley around the side of the church and in through the West Door. In fact it had been, in Mr Purdew's words, a devil of a job, but Mrs Troughton from the museum had insisted on it. She had wanted the cross safely under lock and key before she left for Stonemarket, and no amount of groaning or swearing had changed her mind. Now here it was, and Tom had been quietly studying his spoils.

"Good heavens, Reverend, washing your own floor?" said Mr Cleever, as he stepped into the nave. He smiled, widely.

"Just getting this clay off, Mr Cleever." Tom was suddenly conscious for the first time of the rivulets of orange water trickling over the flagstones. "I wanted to see what the designs on our treasure were."

"Quite. Do you mind if I have a peep? The whole council's buzzing about it, and I simply had to come and look for myself. It sounds most exciting."

"Of course." Tom stepped back, wiping his hands on a towel.

He watched Mr Cleever come forward, aware, as he always was, of the fluidity of the movement, and the controlled strength. The parish councillor was a large man – tall, with receding hair and light blue eyes and a smile that grew from unpromising beginnings to spread across his face like a Cheshire Cat's. It was a memorable smile, which made regular appearances in all his many dealings as councillor, youth group leader, and chairman of several local societies. It carried about it an air of energy and firm resolve, and was much admired about the village.

Tom often felt a certain reservation concerning Mr

Cleever, which he knew was defensive, and was guiltily conscious might be envy. He felt it now. 'Just like
him to turn up here,' he thought. 'Why can't he wait
till tomorrow like everybody else?'

Mr Cleever halted on the other side of the trolley,
his eyes fixed on the great prone cross which lay
between them, glistening with water along all the
diverting, interlaced, spiralling whorls of rock.

"Well, well," he said. "Well, well." And that was all
he said for a long time. Tom tossed his sponge into the
bucket and stood there with him, gazing at the
Fordrace Cross.

At first, the complexity of the style had confused his
eye, but as he had run his sponge along the furrows of
the surface, and the Wirrim clay had been gradually
dislodged, so the design had been revealed.

The focus of the carvings was the centre of the cross,
within the circle where the four arms met. There, an
ornately curling animal was depicted, writhing in on
itself in endless folds and curves. So stylised was the
beast that there were only a few recognisable parts of
its anatomy scattered here and there among the rib-
bon-like meanderings of the body. There was a leg
stretched out towards the stump of the cross's left-
hand arm, with two long curving claws like a bird's
splayed out in defence or attack. There was another
foot and claw near the base of the circle, and what
might have been a tail of sorts, which was split into
several spindly spines or barbs radiating outwards in all
directions, but which still interlaced neatly with the
arcing tendrils of the body. All this was very abstract,
and it was only by the head that Tom could tell he was

32

looking at an animal at all. The head came down at an angle, gripping part of the body in its open mouth. There was one large eye, a long snout and lots of sharp teeth.

It's not a vegetarian, thought Tom.

Outside the circle, the cross was covered with a series of weaving lines which ran up and down the shaft and the two remaining arms. Every now and then small branches arched off into slightly bulbous points which Tom suspected might be leaves or buds. On the shaft, these intertwined over two long thin spears, which crossed in the middle, and whose points almost touched the circle's edge.

Just outside the circle, at the three points where an arm or shaft emerged, the plant stems diverted to leave a small gap, in which was carved an abstract symbol. The one at the top was a triangle, while the one at the base was a series of wavy lines which joined to make a shape a little like a wonky crown. The symbol on the right-hand arm was unmistakably an eye.

"Magnificent," said Mr Cleever.

"It is superb," agreed Tom. "I wonder what age we're talking."

"Oh, I should think Celtic, almost certainly." Mr Cleever spoke with conviction. "The circle suggests that. But the style is very unusual. I've never seen anything quite like this before, even in London." Mr Cleever was chairman of the Fordrace and District archaeological trust, and sometimes organised Outings. He touched the edge of the cross with a tender gesture. "Delightful delicacy. Carved with great skill."

"Rather puzzling symbolism," said Tom. "All this business up here round the circle."

"Yes, what do you make of it?" Mr Cleever asked, looking up at the vicar with eyes that were half appraising, half amused. Tom caught the humour in the glance and felt his chest tightening with annoyance. He turned to the cross again.

"This beast in the circle," he began, "might represent the devil, I suppose. He's often represented as a dragon or serpent. Some of the crosses in Northumberland show him that way, if I remember."

"Well, they're often depicting Norse Myth as much as Christianity," interrupted Mr Cleever. "But there is a confluence of ideas there, I admit. So you think this is Old Nick, do you?"

"It's an obvious interpretation," said Tom. "Perhaps too obvious for you, Mr Cleever. As a humble man of the cloth, my thoughts do tend that way, more's the pity." He cursed himself inwardly for getting riled so easily. "So the circle – and the cross, of course – serve to hem him in, keep him trapped."

"That's good. I like that," said Mr Cleever.

"As to these symbols here, the eye and the triangle and this thing here, I've no idea at all. The eye could be Vigilance, perhaps, if we're talking about means of restricting the Enemy; this thing might be a crown but why would that be? The triangle? Don't know."

Mr Cleever smiled. "It is certainly all very mysterious." Again there was the hint of wry amusement which so irritated Tom.

"What's your theory?" he asked, refusing to dance to the councillor's pleasure any longer.

"I just wish we had the other arm," said Mr Cleever. "It's a very great pity it's missing, a very great pity. Do you think it's down there still?"

"Almost certainly," said Tom. "I'd lay my dog-collar on it. Mr Purdew's men had a look, but it was getting late, and the ground's probably shifted in all the years it's been down there. We'll have a look tomorrow, if the men from the museum don't move in first."

"What men?" asked Mr Cleever, sharply, but at that moment there were footsteps along the nave, and Elizabeth Price approached, carrying her briefcase.

"I'm off now, Tom," she said. "Gosh, it's hot in here. Hello, Mr Cleever. What do you think of our prize?"

"It's quite fantastic, Miss Price, and very important, and all due to our good Reverend here."

"Hear, hear," said Elizabeth. "Well done, Tom. Listen, your friend Sarah rang just now. She says you're late, but you're not the only one because Michael hasn't come home either. He's been out on the Wirrim all day. If he's not back soon she's going to get worried, but if you're not back soon she's going to get angry."

Tom looked at his watch in a manner he hoped was not too flustered. "Drat, I *am* late. Thanks, Elizabeth. See you tomorrow."

"No problemo." She was making for the door. "I'm going for a swim – I'm boiled. I thought churches were meant to be cool. Don't forget about the museum woman, Tom. She's coming at eleven. See you tomorrow. Goodbye, Mr Cleever."

Tom watched the door shut behind her, then looked

at his watch again. He had to move. Then he realised that Mr Cleever was looking at him quite closely.

"Pleasant young woman," Mr Cleever remarked. "Now, Reverend, who are these people from the museum? They're not going to threaten our claim, are they?"

"I shouldn't think so, Mr Cleever. There's little doubt it's a religious artefact, found on church land."

"There's always doubt when museum authorities get involved, take it from me. You'll have to watch them, or they'll whip it."

"There is some talk of taking the cross for examination at Chetton. Temporarily, I believe."

"I bloody knew it!" Mr Cleever's face went red with fury, and Tom noticed with surprise that his fists were clenched. "I'm sorry, Reverend, but I've had run-ins with these people before. We'll all be kept out of the equation. There'll be months of study in some antiseptic backroom before we can get a look at it again. Absolutely bloody typical."

"Really, I'm sure it won't be that bad," said Tom, though the thought of losing his glorious prize was hitting him hard. "If the worst comes to the worst, the bishop—"

An abrupt and tumultuous ringing filled the church, jarring his senses and stunning him into silence. It took him a moment to realise the source, which was nestling against a rafter in the side aisle.

"The fire alarm!" he said. "But there's no fire."

"It must be faulty," said Mr Cleever, whose rage seemed to have been dispelled by the interruption. "You switch it off; I'll check the rest of the building."

Tom did what he was told. The alarm refused to believe it had made a mistake at first, and kept starting up again whenever Tom switched it on. "Faulty battery," suggested Mr Cleever when he returned. He had found no sign of fire in the church.

"It must have responded to the heat that's built up here this afternoon," suggested Tom. "First time it's happened."

He tried switching it on again. This time, the alarm was silent.

"Well," said Mr Cleever. "Another conundrum to ponder over. I won't keep you any longer, Reverend. I know you've an appointment."

Tom looked at his watch grimly. "Yes, Mr Cleever, I really must dash. Come back and look again tomorrow, if you like."

Mr Cleever was gazing at the cross again. He looked up with a vague expression, as if out of a dream.

"Thank you, Reverend. I shall. Good evening to you."

He walked out quickly, and Tom ran to check the windows of the vestry and offices. He was late for Sarah yet again, and Sarah would not be pleased. He wondered if Elizabeth had said why he was delayed. It was a good excuse, but his communication with Sarah hadn't been of the best recently, much to the amusement of her delinquent brothers.

Oh well, thought the Reverend Tom, as he ran down the nave to the West Door, with his keys in one hand and his jacket in the other. Wait till she hears about the cross!

Sarah sat in the half-darkness of the living room, gazing through the open windows out into the dusk. She had been still for so long that she no longer felt distinct from the grey-black patches of shape and shadow which surrounded her. Only her anxiety defined her and gave her form.

Beyond the windows, dusk was closing in upon the hidden perils of the Wirrim; the holes, the deep workings, the unmarked crags and crevices, the treacherous high pastures which led by easy steps to sudden cliffs or falling-places. It was from one of these that Sarah had once seen a sheep's corpse, its red-white tatters hanging limply on a distant ledge.

Never once had it occurred to her to doubt the intuition which had grown by imperceptible degrees throughout the afternoon. She remembered it too well; it was only ten months since the night when black ice on the moorland road had passed her brothers into her care, and two hundred miles away she had woken up crying.

The fear had been stronger then, sharper; this was a more insidious dread, hazy and indefinite, but focused without doubt on Michael.

Night was falling, Michael was missing and Tom still hadn't come.

Outside, a burst of laughter from the Monkey and Marvel echoed derisively round the hollow room. Instinctively, she shuddered.

Suddenly the light came on, making her blink and shake her head. Stephen had emerged from the kitchen where he had been making a sandwich.

"Don't worry, sis," he said. "He'll be all right. Honestly."

Sarah said nothing. Stephen planted himself nearby, and adopted another tack.

"You'd better watch out. Tom'll break his vows."

Sarah scowled. "What?"

"You look good." Stephen clarified himself from the depths of the sofa. It was true. Sarah's camisole and shorts were well-chosen and worn better. But she was not to be distracted.

"A lot you know," she said grimly, looking out of the window.

"It was a compliment! You've done well!" Stephen shrugged to himself. "He's often late, isn't he?" he added, as he picked up a magazine.

"Who? Oh, will you shut up about him? I'm more concerned about Michael. It'll be dark soon."

"Sarah, it's mid-summer. It won't be dark for hours. He's gone out for a long walk and he'll get back when it suits him. He's probably done the Wirrim Round or something. Quit your worrying. Anyway, it's probably for the best."

"And what does that mean?"

"Well, you know."

"I don't at all. What do you mean?"

Stephen shifted with the edgy feeling of one who has strayed the wrong way. "All I mean is that I may not get on with Tom sometimes, but Michael doesn't get on with him a lot more often than I do."

Sarah had stiffened at the window. "That's not true. Tom likes Michael."

"Oh rubbish. But anyhow, Michael doesn't like him. That's probably why he's late back. And you said you didn't care anyway."

The atmosphere deteriorated into an icy impasse, during which Stephen read the magazine unconcernedly and Sarah forced herself to make a drink. Ten minutes later, when the sky was a cold dark blue behind the black bulk of the Wirrim, the Reverend Tom Aubrey's car was heard approaching down the lanes.

"Sorry," said Tom, as Sarah wordlessly held open the door. "But I've got an excuse. Hello Stephen."

"Hi," said Stephen.

"How are you, Sarah?" Tom kissed a half-proffered cheek.

"Worried. Michael still hasn't come back."

"Ah, I was going to ask about that," said Tom, wishing he had. "How long's he been up there?"

"Days," said Stephen. "He went out last Tuesday with a weird haunted look and a loaded shotgun. And he had a noose around his neck too. Do you think Sarah's right to be concerned?"

"Since lunchtime," said Sarah. "And I'm not being stupid. He's missed two meals by now."

"Well, I'm sure you've no need to fret," said Tom, his own news frothing about impatiently inside him. "He's just exploring somewhere, or he's gone over to Little Chetton to the pictures. Bags of time before you need start worrying. It won't be really dark for ages."

"I'm with you on this one, Tom," said Stephen.

"But wherever he's gone," Tom went on, slipping into an easy chair, and pulling Sarah onto the armrest beside him, "he's missed the action. Fordrace church was the place to be today. You'll never guess why."

"I know why," said Sarah shortly. "Your friend Elizabeth told me about it. She sounded very out of breath."

"Oh." Tom felt the annoyance of an expected revelation spoiled. "Well I won't bore you with it then."

"You can bore me with it, if you like," Stephen suggested aimiably. "How old is it?"

"Celtic, we think."

"How old's that?"

"Well over a thousand."

"Not bad. That must be older than the church."

"Well, there's been a religious settlement here longer than the present church. And that's 11th century. I'm a bit hazy on the details, but Elizabeth is going down to research it a bit. I'll need to know, now that I'm a celebrity vicar."

Sarah rose from the armrest suddenly. "It's getting dark. I want you both to go looking for Michael."

"Oh, come on, Sarah!" cried Stephen, and Tom frowned.

"I've only just got here—" he began. Then he stopped. Footsteps had sounded on the gravel outside; slow footsteps, dragging in the dirt.

Sarah slammed the porch light on in the same motion as she wrenched open the door. Still halfway down the drive, a white face was bathed in yellow light.

"Hello Sarey. You couldn't put that light out, could you?"

41

Three pairs of eyes stared at Michael as he entered the porch. He was moving slowly, with his neck and shoulders slumped forwards, and his hands shook as he grasped the doorframe. Under the yellow porchlight, his face was bleached, and the rings of his eye sockets were a ghastly mottled red. Worst of all, his eyes were screwed up tight, but his mouth was smiling.

"Hello Sarey," he said again. "Are you alone, or is the Pope with you? Sorry if I don't kneel, but I don't quite trust myself just now." He stumbled into the house, feeling for the light switch as he did so. "It's a bit bright, but I feel great, really I do. Just sunstroke, like Stephen."

Wordlessly, Stephen took his brother by the arm, and guided him over to the sofa. Michael almost fell in it, with a sigh of satisfaction.

"That's better," he said. "Now all I need's a bath." He began laughing gently to himself. Sarah stifled a sob with her hand.

"Call a doctor, Sarah," said Tom, and his voice was hard.

Sarah didn't move. "Why's he laughing?" she said. "What for?"

"Look at his eyes." Tom was bending down close to Michael. "You should call a doctor, straight away."

"He says it's sunstroke," said Stephen, who didn't like the vicar's tone of voice. "He was up there too long. You know what a day it was. Shouldn't we cool him down?"

"He's not overheated." Tom straightened suddenly. "Sunstroke doesn't look like this. I'm not as unworldly as you think, Stephen."

"What do you mean, Tom—" Sarah began, but Stephen interrupted her.

"How the hell should you know what sunstroke looks like?" he shouted. "And whose house are you in to start making dirty insinuations?"

"It's my house," said Sarah. "Shut up, Stephen."

There was a high laugh from the sofa. A voice said, "This is all delightful, but please could someone run me a bath?"

A silence followed for a brief space; then Tom spat out his pent up breath.

"If you won't call the doctor," he said, "I will."

While Tom was dialling, Stephen grabbed Sarah by the arm in a grip which made her gasp, and bent his head close to her ear.

"He thinks Michael's been taking something," he hissed savagely. "Drugs or something. Did you hear it in his voice? Tell him he's wrong, Sarah."

His sister said nothing, but her shoulders began to shake. Stephen did not relax his hold.

"It's like him to make insinuations like that. Who does he think he is? He's got no say over what we do. Anyway, there's no way Michael would do anything like that. No way. You know it's wrong. Tell him so. Tell him he's wrong, Sarah, or I'll make him regret it."

"Oh God, what's the matter with him?" Sarah said. "Why won't he open his eyes?"

There was a flurry of movement from the sofa. Michael was propping himself up with one arm, with his chin resting on the back of the sofa, facing into the room. His face was still screwed up tight; his lips were pulled up, revealing his teeth.

"Because, Sarey, I don't quite trust myself. There's nothing wrong with me, but I've seen a few funny things, you see, and I don't want to startle myself again. But that's all it is – Stephen doesn't talk much sense, but he knows that much. There's no truth in anything the Pope might say. I tell you though, I'd love to see what he looks like. I'd tell you what he's like inside, just by looking at him."

Sarah was crying now, quietly, her shoulders shaking. Stephen tried to put his arm around her, in an uncomfortable gesture, but she shook it off as Tom came into the room.

"Doctor's coming," he said. "Oh Sarah, this'll sort out. Come here." He hugged her; she responded distractedly.

Stephen drew near his brother and looked closely at his clothes. For the first time, he noticed faint black marks all over his shorts and T-shirt. He frowned and sniffed, and the tang of smoke came faintly to his nostrils. Burning.

"Jesus, Mike," he whispered. "What the hell have you been up to?"

The prone figure extended a questing arm and touched the front of his t-shirt.

"Stephen," he whispered, "I swear to you, I did nothing today but sleep up on the Wirrim. I'll show you the place if you like. But something strange has . . . I'd tell you first of all of them, but I can hardly bear to share it . . ." His voice drifted off. Stephen bent closer and caught up his hand as it went limp.

"You can tell me, Mike. Quick, they've stepped onto the porch. What is it, Mike?"

For a moment the silence made him afraid. But then his brother's voice came back, stronger than ever.

"I was just thinking. I'd better look. I'll have to sometime. And it should be you, Stephen. There's no one else I'd rather try. It's been a good few hours, maybe it's gone."

"I'm sorry," said Stephen, "but I don't understand."

"You don't need to, not yet. Look, don't take this wrong; just back off a little from me. I don't want you too close when I open my eyes."

"I thought the light was too bright—"

"I can open them easily enough, Steve. I've been wanting to open them properly all the way down. They've been aching for it. You can't guess how much they itch. But I was too scared. I opened them just enough to feel my way. And – thank God – so far, everything's looked OK."

"So what's the problem?"

"No one was in shot. That's the crucial bit. Make or break. The rest of it only changes slightly. Right. I'll do it. Just look at me. That's all I want you to do."

Stephen stayed where he was, kneeling on the carpet two feet from his brother. Michael did not seem delirious exactly, but nothing he said made any kind of sense, although he was evidently in no doubt about his logic. Stephen had an uneasy feeling that this was what madness looked like, head on. Michael was shaking all over. His hand, resting on the sofa seat cushion, was gripping hard, locked white. His eyelids twitched, twice, and the flushed skin around them seemed to shudder. Stephen knew he was summoning the courage to look, and that for an instant, his courage was failing him. Instinctively, he reached out and squeezed his hand.

"It's all right, Mikey," he said. "You know it's me."

Then Michael opened his eyes, and although Stephen didn't know what he had been expecting, he found himself rigid with tension as he looked into the normal eyes of his brother; brown-irised, wide-pupilled, slightly redder than usual maybe, but ordinary eyes nonetheless.

This qualified as a relief. He breathed out, and smiled foolishly, and Michael, whose gaze had been locked into his face with an iron concentration, smiled too.

"It's OK," he said slowly. "Thank God."

Then he blinked, and to Stephen it almost seemed as if something had shifted, deep under the surface of his brother's eyes, as if for an instant a curtain had been drawn back, and he was looking at two glass marbles, with thin red swirls locked in their centre, rotating rapidly within.

It was a moment's image only.

Then Michael screamed.

DAY 2

The phone rang, scoring deeply into the surface of his dreams, but it had to ring many times before it clawed deep enough to reach him. His eyes were still clamped shut, fogged round with sleep, as his faltering hand brought the handpiece to his ear.

"Sarah?" he said, "What's he done now?"

"Sorry, Tom—" Another voice broke in, calm but urgent. "Sorry Tom, it's Elizabeth." Elizabeth Price? What time was it?

"I'm sorry to wake you. But it's important."

"What time is it?"

"Five thirty. Tom, you've got to come down to the church right away. The police are here."

"Police?" Tom struggled into a sitting position. The dawn light was already glowing round the edges of the curtains with its unearthly paleness.

"There's been a break-in. Someone's stoved the side-door in."

"What!" Tom was sitting on the edge of the bed now, rubbing the side of his face which itched with anxiety. "What have they taken?"

"Nothing, so far as I can see. But you'd better get down here."

"Right." It took him two minutes to get dressed, pulling on the same trousers he had removed only three hours before. What sort of swine would break in to a church? Nothing taken – that was a relief . . . but no, they'd have scrawled on the walls, or pissed on the altar or something. Bastards. The Reverend Tom slammed his door with a crash and ran wet-foot over the dew-sodden Rectory field to the church wall. This he vaulted, and thirty seconds later he was standing in the Norman side-arch, viewing the broken door.

Elizabeth was beside Constable Vernon, who was crouching next to the splintered wooden door and squinting at it with a professional eye.

"What's happened here, Joe? What's the damage?"

"If you're talking about the door, they must've hit it good and hard." The constable grunted dismissively and stood up. "They've snapped the bar straight in two, with a blow from the outside. You didn't get round to furnishing a lock, I see."

"Well, no I didn't, Joe." Tom fingered the long white splinters protruding from the bar. "It's done the job for centuries." Tom did not exaggerate. The beam had rested in metal clasps on the back of the door, sliding back and forth into the hollowed sockets of the stone arch, till it was smooth as marble and black as soot. And now it was split like matchwood.

"I can't find any damage in the church," Elizabeth said from close beside him. "My first thought was that they were after the cross, but of course it's just too heavy."

The cross. Tom went cold. The events at Sarah's had driven yesterday's elation clear from his mind. He had forgotten the cross. It could be no coincidence, no coincidence at all. She must have missed something. He ran down the nave and into the vestry, footfalls rebounding off the vaulted ceiling. There was the stone laid out on the trolley, but all around it the flag-stones were laced with thin brown stains.

"Oh God," thought Tom. "What have they done?"

Then he saw the bucket, and the dirty water, and yesterday's sponge caked with clay, and he sighed at his foolishness.

Elizabeth was right behind him. "It's all right, Tom," she said, putting a hand upon his shoulder. "The cross is fine."

So it was. In the half-light of the church, the shape of the stone was muffled, its carvings a sworl of shadows, but it was definitely whole. Tom touched the shaft of the cross.

"So what did they want?" he said. "What's the point?"

Elizabeth considered him. "You looked wrecked," she said. "Didn't get much sleep?"

"As a matter of fact, no." It came out too sharply, and he saw the warden flinch.

"I'm sorry, Liz," he said quickly. "I had a terrible night. Sarah's little brother has been playing the fool up on the Wirrim. Came home high as a kite. Screaming, burbling nonsense, the usual stuff."

"Heavens, Tom, will he be all right?"

"Not if I had my way he won't be, the little idiot. Sarah's just not tough enough on them. Swears he's never done anything like it before. She's blind to their faults, I'm afraid."

"But is he all right?" Elizabeth's tone of voice forced Tom out of his absorption and he met her gaze.

"Sorry, yes. The doctor was a bit confused. Never seen symptoms quite like it, apparently. But it wasn't

51

sunstroke, which is what the boy was claiming. Temperature was fine, pulse rate fine, all the usual things. Just very red and blistered around the eyes. No one's sure why, but he'd obviously been up to no good somehow. Still, he was safe in bed, and sleeping, by the time I left. Which was late."

Elizabeth nodded. "Go outside. You need some air. I'm going to phone the bishop; it's about time he heard about this."

A great weariness came over him as he stepped out, into the freshness of the day. A faint smell of smoke hung in the air, reminding him of the autumn to come. A host of birds were trilling with irreverent zest among the branches of the yew, and his eyes wandered to the giant hole cut in the graveyard soil, its edges wet with morning. Joe Vernon was sitting on another of Mr Purdew's trolleys, talking into a radio. Presently, he snapped it shut and walked over to Tom.

"Well," he said, "it must have been done sometime before half past four, since that was when Tony Hooper noticed it, on his way in to work. We may get more information; someone may have seen lights on in the church or something."

"Not that there's any evidence they went inside the church at all," he continued, as Tom offered no comment. "Perhaps it's just some stunt, though it seems a pretty crazy one to me. Are you all right, Reverend?"

Tom was staring out in front of him, looking at the hole in the earth. Slowly, Joe Vernon followed his gaze, across the mound of earth to the corner of the hole closest to the yew tree, where the branches spanned out over the diggings. The neat squared corner of Mr

Purdew's trench was gone. Soil had been ripped away from the side of the hole and had fallen to the bottom where the cross had lain. It was as if a huge bite had been taken from the earth, exposing the tangled roots of the yew tree which jutted out like a chaos of ligaments or veins. PC Vernon walked across to the lip and looked down.

"Nothing there," he remarked.

"I bet there isn't," said Tom, so quietly that the policeman failed to hear. "I bet there isn't."

"There's been a lot of activity on this side of the trench," said PC Vernon. "Sure this wasn't done by Purdew's boys?"

Tom dumbly shook his head.

"In that case," the constable went on, "we'll have to add this to our list of mysteries. I wonder what they were after."

Tom felt sick.

Then Joe Vernon sniffed, and bent his head closer to the trench. "Another thing I can't understand," he said, "is why they should bother to burn it."

Wordlessly, Tom came to stand by his side. The roots of the tree which protruded from the ground had been scorched and twisted by an intense heat, and the soil exposed by the night's digging was blackened and blistered with the corruscating touch of fire.

"How are you, Mike?" Stephen stood at the end of the bed, holding a tray. "I've brought orange juice, water and sweet weak tea. A choice fit for a king."

Michael was sitting up in bed, plumped up against pillows, with a dressing-gown draped over his shoulders. Sarah had pulled open the curtain furthest from the invalid, and he sat in the dark half of the room. He waved a hand regally.

"I might try the water. Not the juice. My tongue's raw." His voice was thick and clotted, and when he stuck his tongue out at his brother it was an angry red, and scored here and there with thin white sores.

"Your tongue is foul."

"Thanks. Think I'll ever kiss a girl again?"

"Again?"

Michael gingerly took a sip of water. Stephen passed to the window and looked out. Sarah was walking down the garden in bare feet, carrying peelings to the compost heap. There were coils of mist hanging in the shaded meadows beyond the garden, and behind the cold hump of the Wirrim, the early sun burnished the sky. Another hot one.

"I'm pleased to see you can open your eyes this morning—" Stephen said. Sarah was tapping the box empty over the compost heap, stretching out awkwardly with one foot raised to balance her. "—without screaming like a bloody pig." He felt his anger beat hot against the pane.

"Stephen—"

"That was quite a performance you put on last night. You managed to screw us all up before you went to bed. Well, I can tell you pal, that after you were tucked up nice and cosy, Sarah cried for – oh just a couple of hours, and had a blazing row with Tom, over the little matter of whether or not you habitually took drugs."

"Stephen, you know that's crap—"

"Do I? Last night I was ready to kill Tom for his suspicious little puritan mind. But this morning – well, sorry mate, but I'm not so sure. Did you see Sarah's face this morning when she came in to see you? Or did you not dare open your eyes?"

"I saw it."

"Did you? Well so did I. And I'll tell you what I read there, shall I? For all that she fought your corner, and sent Tom away with a flea in his ear – in the end, Michael, she's being worn down by sheer lack of alternatives. And this morning I feel the same way."

He had turned now, and was facing his brother. Michael's face was hidden by shadow.

"So tell me," said Stephen, "what else is there to think?"

There was a long silence. A door slammed somewhere below. Michael was motionless, propped up in the bed. From along the landing corridor came footsteps. The door opened, and Sarah looked in, her face lined and heavy. She had put her shoes on, and was carrying her work bag.

"How are you, Michael?" she asked, and her voice was toneless.

"I'm fine. Really, I'm fine." He leaned forward urgently. "Sarah, I'm sorry about last night. I know it's strange and I don't understand it myself; but I swear to you I haven't . . . taken anything. I swear it. Stephen told me you stood up for me. Thanks."

Sarah looked at him for a moment. Then she turned to Stephen, who was standing mute against the window.

"I'm going to Stanbridge. The number's on the table. I've several tours to make, so I may not be back till six. Dr Pandit's number's there as well. Will you need anything else?"

"No. That's great," said Stephen. "Thanks."

"Right." Sarah went out. They heard her footsteps recede, and presently the front door close. The car started and pulled out into the lane, its busy noise quickly fading into the silence. Michael had slumped back on the pillow. Stephen was staring at an unpreposessing bit of wardrobe. Somewhere in the centre of the room, their gazes bisected each other and went on.

"Open the other curtain, please," said Michael.

The room was filled with light. Michael flinched, but he didn't move. His face was clear again, the redness had faded, and he looked well.

"I'll tell you what happened," he said, looking at his brother for the first time. "But you must promise not to tell anybody."

Stephen shrugged. "All right. But I'm not the only one you're going to have to convince."

"Maybe. The point is though, something strange

has happened to me, and you're the only one I can trust to tell. I have to be able to trust you."

Stephen slapped his hands against the edge of the windowsill. "I've said yes, haven't I? Get on with it."

"OK." Michael breathed out hard. "The first thing is, it was like I said. I went up on the Wirrim to read. I didn't go anywhere else. I just climbed up the Burrway to the top, walked along till I got to the Pit and sat down there. Then I read the book for an hour or so until I got to the bit with the sauna."

"What does that prove?" Stephen was aware that his hostility was increasing all the time that Michael was speaking. It did so because he did not expect the truth, and that pained him and fuelled his anger.

"Just listen. I read up to there, and then since you said that was the only bit worth reading, I lost interest, and felt a bit sleepy. So I settled back for a nap."

"In the sun?"

"Yes, that's why I thought I had sunstroke when I woke up."

"The doctor said—"

"I know what the doctor said. I've got ears, haven't I? I know it wasn't sunstroke now, but at the time, it was the only obvious thing. Something happened to me while I was asleep, Stephen."

"What?"

"I don't know. But I can tell you the result. Something's happened to my eyesight. There's nothing else wrong with me, and even my eyes feel fine this morning, but that's where the change is. The only difference is that I can control it this morning."

"Michael, you're not making any more sense

than you were last night. What happened to your eyes?"

"Looking at you now, like this, there's no problem. Nothing wrong. But if I do this—" He paused. "God, Stephen, you should see yourself. You look beautiful, out of this world."

"Right, that's it." Stephen straightened himself. "I'm going to beat a little sense into you, you drugged-up little rat."

"And if I do this," Michael continued, uncomprehending, "you're back to normal again. Your ordinary self. It's wonderful." And Stephen, in his uneasiness and disgust, saw that tears were running down his brother's smiling cheeks. He cursed and dropped into the bedroom chair.

"Tell me," said Michael, "was there any change in me just then?"

"No, you seemed quite continuously mad," replied Stephen flatly.

"What about last night, when you were close to me? When I screamed."

"Your face contorted, as faces do when they're barking."

"What about my eyes? That's what I'm interested in." Michael was sitting on the end of his bed now, leaning forward earnestly, with an air of scientific interest. Stephen frowned. He seemed reluctant to answer.

"Come on – you did see something. What was it?"

Stephen breathed out slowly. "Yes," he said at last. "I did see something." He paused. "I thought – and don't think I'm in any way supporting you – I thought I saw a movement in your eyes. In the centre. Just before you flipped."

"Yes!" Michael clapped his hands. "That's what I was after. When I woke up, I couldn't open my eyes for a while. Later, I found I was seeing things in a different way. Everything was washed out, like it was painted in red watercolours. There were red flecks all over the sky, the rocks, everywhere. And it was all 2-D – I'd lost the perspective somehow.

"But that was just the start of it. I'll tell you what really freaked me, and why I couldn't bear to open my eyes. It was the rabbit, and the couple, and then you."

Stephen hid his head in his hands.

"It's like you're not solid, as if all living things are ghosts. I sort of see through you, except for where your head should be, and that – that doesn't look like you at all."

His brother made an unintelligible sound. Michael lay on his back, looking up at the ceiling.

"It's as if your head has become a jewel, a precious stone carved in a shape unique to you. I've only seen a few of you so far, but I'll bet everyone is different. Your head is – can you guess? Well, it's like a horse's. A horse's head made of gemstones. They move all the time, spiralling full of colour as you breathe. A horse! Who would have guessed that? But it makes sense, as I realised when I thought about it last night. It's got your wildness there, and your stubbornness too. I'd know I could depend on you, even if you weren't my brother, just by looking at it. It's weird. It is you, even though it doesn't look like you. Sarah's one is different. She's a dog of some kind. I'm not good with breeds, but when you think about it, she has got all the nervy faithfulness of one of those red setter things, hasn't she? So it reflects a kind of truth, though it startled me at first. I'd love to have seen the Pope's face too, but I hadn't cracked it then.

"It was only this morning that I've been able to control it. Yesterday my eyes kept changing automatically; that's why I thought I was mad. But now, it's just like when you hold your finger right up to your face, so it all goes blurred, and then you suddenly focus on it. It pops into view. Like magic. And Stephen, you can't know how beautiful it is."

Stephen was resting his chin on his hands. After a pause he said, "I wasn't around in the Sixties; and I've never been to San Francisco, but you sound to me like you've missed your time by thirty years."

"You fool!" Michael sprang to his feet, stood in his pyjamas on his bed and kicked the duvet savagely towards his brother. "Do you think I don't know how ridiculous I sound? I ought to have known better than to try and tell you, you stubborn horse-head, but I know something that'll convince you all right. What is it we've never sworn by?"

"No." Stephen looked up, his face blanched. "You wouldn't. Not for this crap."

"Maybe now you'll give me the benefit of the doubt. I swear—"

"Don't you bloody dare!" But Michael was already spitting the words out through gritted teeth.

"I swear. On the graves of our parents I swear that all I've said is true."

"You little shit!" Stephen launched himself towards his brother. Michael leapt back off the bed on the

60

other side, and pointed his finger towards him like a dagger to the face.

"That's how serious I am!" he shouted.

"My God." Stephen's hands fell to his sides. "If you're lying . . ."

"You know I'm not," said Michael. "And if you want to see where it happened, I'll take you to the place."

It was twelve o'clock by the time Mrs Troughton had been convinced of the theft. Despite Tom's insistence that the churchyard desecrators had dug at the precise edge of the trench where the missing arm of the cross would have been, she was resolved to check this for herself. To this end, Mr Purdew had been summoned, his cigarette drooping more dejectedly than ever, and the earth around the roots of the suffering yew tree had been scraped clear for a further foot in every direction. Nothing was found, and, at the warden's behest, the roots were covered over again. There followed a dismal half hour in which Tom was sandwiched between police constable and archaeologist, discussing the crime from every possible angle. Mrs Troughton, who was in a wild state of fury, took immediate exception to Tom's comment that such a theft was inexplicable.

"You do realise," she said, glaring through glasses in Tom's direction, "that this cross is utterly unique. It is clearly of very early Christian date, and may represent a fusion of Saxon and Celtic art unlike anything found before. Who knows, vicar – your little church may stand on a truly ancient site! For even a fraction of the cross to be stolen is an absolute tragedy, and may stop us from decyphering the primitive symbolism on its carvings!"

"There's no firm proof that the missing piece was ever down there," Tom said. "But even if it was, the bulk of the cross has not been touched, and will still be a monument to the early Church. I just don't understand why anyone should try to steal the one arm. Why not take the rest as well?"

"It was too heavy," said PC Vernon, and wrote this down in his book.

"Obviously," said Mrs Troughton.

"But why bother scrabbling round in the dirt in the middle of the night just to pinch a piece of stone, which must itself have been too heavy for anyone to lift without help?"

"Maybe," said PC Vernon, "they're going to ransom it."

Tom didn't know quite how to answer this, though in fact he thought it wasn't such a stupid idea. It was better than any of his own, which were laced with confusion. His head was awhirl with disordered objections to the events of the morning. Even if a ransom was far-fetched, there was no other conceivable explanation for the theft, except plain malice. But malice would have led to vandalism, and the rest of the cross had not been touched. And what was all the scorching in the trench? You didn't use a welding torch to shift earth. Tom gave up. It made no sense.

By the time Mrs Troughton had made an ill-tempered departure, Tom was unable to string a coherent thought together. His mood was not improved by the arrival of Mrs Gabriel in his office to complain about the further desecration.

"It's your example they're following," she said, "and thank you no I won't sit down. You started this, vicar, and who knows if there isn't worse to come. Already they've breached the church!"

Tom sighed; to his ears came the accusing sound of Mr Purdew's workmen, mending the door.

"To move the cross!" Mrs Gabriel shook her head at the thought. "Maybe it was there for a reason, did you think of that?"

"Mrs Gabriel, you do not go round burying crosses six feet underground for a reason. And even if someone did, it's been there for hundreds of years and it's time it was found and restored. The people of this day and age would like to see it and enjoy it. They can get spiritual comfort from its antiquity."

"For some people the splitting of the cross would give greater comfort," said Mrs Gabriel. Tom frowned with bewilderment.

"What do you mean? The cross was already split," he said.

"Maybe, but now it's split and separated," said Mrs Gabriel, with firm conviction. Tom felt he was missing something.

"I know it is a great shame, and was a wicked act to steal this relic," he said, "but Mrs Gabriel, we still have most of the cross, and can raise it in the churchyard. It won't be moved, I assure you."

"That will do no good," she said, and turned to the door. Tom straightened himself and addressed her back with as much dignity as he could muster.

"Mrs Gabriel," he said, "is there something that I don't know? Which you could tell me?"

Her voice came from beyond the door. "What do any of us know about this Church, or its history? Least of all you, young man."

The door shut. Twenty minutes later, Tom was walking through the doorway of Fordrace library.

Vanessa Sawcroft rewarded Tom with a wide smile of welcome as he cautiously approached her desk, wondering not for the first time how she managed to wear her grey twill suit in the throes of midsummer. The library windows were open, but the air was sluggish and smelt of lilac and leather. Ms Sawcroft, a spare, neat woman in her fifties, wore her shirt done up to the neck and her hair in a crisp grey bob, which shimmered slightly as she moved. She fixed Tom with an efficient eye.

"Hallo," said Tom. "I was wondering—"

"You look awfully tired, Reverend," she said.

"Call me Tom," said Tom. "Yes, I am rather. We've had some trouble up at St Wyndham's. There may have been a theft."

"I'm sorry to hear it. Have you come to drown your sorrows in literature?"

"Something like that. I'm after your section on local history."

"Over there on the third shelf. Anything in particular?"

"Church history, local legends, that sort of thing."

"It's all there."

Tom took himself to the shelf indicated, which was pleasantly sited by a high window in a remote corner. A wicker chair with a green cushioned seat awaited him. Scanning the shelves, he plucked from them a pamphlet published by the Fordrace Women's Institute, entitled 'Our Church and its People', and two glossy books about the parish churches of Hereford and Worcester, which would include St Wyndham's.

Neither of the glossy books told him anything he didn't know. His church was Norman, built in the 11th century, quite possibly on a Saxon site. It was named after a minor saint whose exploits were obscure, and had maintained its backwater feel throughout the centuries. It had an attractive tower, a notable mahogany pulpit (which had been brought to the church from Palestine in the 14th century by a benefactor knight), a walled-up prayer room above the chancel and lots of rural peace and quiet. Even this information was out of date, thought Tom. The prayer room had been opened and made safe several years ago, and as for peace and quiet, there was little of that about at St Wyndham's this morning.

The pamphlet was mainly a dreary catalogue of Rotary Clubs, Benevolent Funds and coffee mornings, all of which Tom knew only too well. He flicked his way impatiently from page to page until, under a passage entitled 'Our Rich Heritage', a short paragraph caught his eye.

Although our village's grand tradition
of Christian worship has marched forward

triumphantly through the centuries, there are strong folk traditions in our area, which have persisted despite the best efforts of our enlightened ministers to discourage them. Today they are mostly quaint superstitions which harm nobody, but this was not always the case. Fordrace was once a local centre of one of the witch scares which so troubled our ancestors, and exorcism in the old days was common.

And that was all. 'Strong folk traditions . . .' Tom frowned. What exactly was he looking for? It was difficult to know. If Mrs Troughton was correct, his church was possibly of great historic significance, and he should certainly know more about its background than he did. Fine. But then there was Mrs Gabriel. A silly old woman for sure, but she evidently attached more significance to the cross than the purely archaeological, and in the light of the theft – that inexplicable theft – it suddenly seemed a very good idea to try and scratch the surface of these 'quaint superstitions', whatever they might be.

At the back of the pamphlet was a short bibliography, which included the following entry:

For some details of local lore, see 'Legends of Fordrace and the Wirrim' (1894) by Harold Limmins, a local teacher and scholar. Published a hundred years ago, this remains the only work to address this subject in any detail.

That was more like it. Tom looked at his watch. He would ring Sarah soon to check on the boy. But first . . . He got up from the wicker chair and began scanning the rows hungrily. From an adjacent row, Ms Sawcroft, laden high with books, smiled over at him.

"Having any luck, Tom?" she asked.

"I'm homing in," he replied, and went on searching.

The Wirrim that morning was at its most beautiful. The rounded folds were splashed over with an easy sunlight, which fired the grass slopes and the stone walls' broken chain with a tint of gold. Only the steepest valleys on the southern side remained in shadow, where cold streams plummeted in thin cascades a step at a time, and each step was a hundred feet. The air blew fresh and strong, and clouds fleeced comfortably in the sky, casting teasing shadows on the bright earth.

Stephen and Michael climbed, each consumed by his own thoughts.

Stephen hardly registered the view at all. The ease with which his brother had sworn the forbidden oath had shocked him, and made him deeply ill at ease. He was prepared to follow where Michael led – he owed the oath that much. But when Michael's imagination dried up, and his lie was left exposed, Stephen had no idea what he would do. A good beating was in order, but that would probably upset Sarah even more than

Michael's behaviour had in the first place. She had set a lot of store on her family's mutual support in the last few months, and Stephen and Michael had done their best to be restrained. But now – Stephen kicked out at a pebble on the path – his restraint was hanging by a thread.

Michael picked his way around the jutting stones of the steep path with unconscious skill. Almost as soon as he had made his declaration to his brother – a declaration that was both justification and challenge – he had begun to regret it. He did not regret the savagery of his oath, for his word was true; nor did he regret, exactly, showing Stephen the special place. It was more . . . well, he was not at all sure that Stephen really deserved this knowledge. As the morning wore on and they climbed higher, he felt a gnawing certainty grow in him that he should have kept his secret to himself. It was his own weakness that had done it, his weak-willed need to share; but how could he share something as strange and singular as this, even with his own brother? Stephen had no hope of understanding, he had no gift. He was just a common boy, special only for the hidden beauty of his face.

Twice, on the early stages of the trek, while they were fringing the Russet and keeping to cattle paths and easy walk-ways, Michael had lagged behind his brother and turned the sight on him behind his back. Both times the outline of a horse's head, resplendent with pulsating life, had appeared to him, and suddenly, Michael had known what he was looking at.

It was his brother's soul.

What else could it be? It was no aspect of his physical state, that was for sure, yet it seemed to coexist with his physical body. It was constantly swirling in upon itself, like magma beneath the earth, or – Michael smiled at the simplicity of the analogy – like soup in a pan just before boiling. It had a thousand colours, lit by an inner light, and what he marvelled at most of all was the fact that it reflected Stephen's emotions. The whole thing was swirling with anxiety, with streaks of red, and darker thoughts. Once, when Stephen tripped on a tree root, and Michael heard his voice curse loudly, he saw a brief swirl of angry purple burst up from inside the soul and fade away.

There was no question; it was a beautiful sight, and Michael could have gone on watching it all day and never switched back to the boring old colours of the summer. Yet he had to switch off, or risk losing his footing in the red-grey half-light.

How stupid he had been to tell him. He could have been the only person in the world to know . . . and now he had sworn an oath Stephen would force him to justify. There was no way out. Unless . . . Perhaps he could persuade him to forget about it, treat it as a joke? Maybe, but it wasn't likely.

"Stephen—" His brother stopped and turned, and his look killed the words dead in Michael's throat. There would be no going back. Not now.

He smiled sheepishly at his brother and shrugged. Somewhere at the back of his eyes, something was aching.

"Well," said Stephen. "Shall we go on?"

Mr Cleever was standing at the door, and in the act of ringing the bell, when Sarah turned the car into the drive. He turned and beamed at her as she halted and got out.

"My dear, what perfect timing. I was just resigning myself to a long walk back again."

"Didn't the boys answer, Mr Cleever?" Sarah fumbled in her handbag with what she was conscious was a fluster, found the keys and unlocked the door. "Please come in."

"Thank you, Ms MacIntyre. I don't think Stephen and Michael can be home. I rang twice."

"They should be here. Michael's not well." She plumped the handbag down on the dresser and hurried to the foot of the stairs. "Michael? Stephen?" She called up, but the house was silent.

"All gone," said Mr Cleever beamingly, and then, as if it were a statement; "Boys."

"Yes." Sarah was disconcerted now, and angry. The job in Stanbridge had gone tolerably well, and she had been happy to return home early and attend to her errant brother with Stephen's help. Now it seemed that they had both gone walkabout. This was too much to endure; she could not bear it. "Would you like some tea, Mr Cleever?" she asked.

"Thank you. May I sit down?"

"Oh, of course, please." Mr Cleever sat in an ample

chair, and while Sarah made the tea in the kitchen down the hall, regaled her with small talk about the interminable dealings of the Geological Society and the Parish Committee on Education.

"I cannot think," he concluded, "how things can have become so lax in these areas. Children can only suffer when taught with such moral looseness. Thank you, I will take sugar."

He sipped his tea. Ms MacIntyre seemed discomposed.

"My dear," said Mr Cleever, setting down his cup, "you are not happy. I will not ramble on any longer. What is the matter? If I can do anything, you may be sure I shall, if it is in my power."

"It is too stupid," said Sarah, her feelings welling up all of a sudden. "Really, I am embarrassed to talk about it." But Mr Cleever, with gentle sympathy, elicited the information he desired.

"It does seem highly singular," he said, when she had finished, "that Michael should . . . stray off the path so suddenly. After such a careful upbringing as he has enjoyed in your hands."

"It has never been enough," said Sarah. "He misses his mother."

"Of course he does, but you could not have done anything differently in all the time you have been here. You have been absolutely admirable. Where did you say Michael said he had spent the day?"

"Up on High Raise, on the Wirrim, he said. Why, is it significant?"

"Not really. I suppose he may have hiked across from Little Chetton. There are buses there to

Stanbridge. Sarah – I may call you Sarah, mayn't I? –
are you all right?"

"Sorry, it's just so close in here—"

"Say no more, we'll go into the kitchen. It'll be cooler there."

So it was, and Sarah cooled herself quickly by drinking two glasses of iced water. Mr Cleever, however,
declined a glass himself, and still seemed flushed by the
time he made his kind proposal.

"Sarah, my dear," he said, "you know, I expect, that
I am Fordrace youth group leader. In this role I have
dealt, on occasion, with children who are under the
wrong influences, and I think I know the signs pretty
well. There may be nothing in it. His denials, however strained, may be true; that is certainly what we
should hope. Even if they are not, by acting now we
can turn it into a minor aberration. If you think it a
good idea, why not send him over to me, on some pretext or other, and I'll have a look at him and maybe
have a quiet chat. It comes easier from some one less
close, you know."

Sarah agreed to this with relief. It seemed very sen-
sible.

"But where has he gone now?" she asked.

"He won't come to any harm, I'm sure of it. Besides,
you say Stephen will be with him, and I'm sure he's a
good pair of hands."

Sarah supposed he was. But then Mr Cleever gave a
little exclamation. "Good heavens, I'd clean forgotten
what I came to talk to you about in the first place. It's
two things, really. Firstly, I want to speak to you in
your capacity as estate agent. You still work for that big

72

firm in Stanbridge, don't you? Good. Well – I have an estate! It's a farm, actually. Hardraker Farm, not too far from here. Do you know it?"

Sarah did. Mr Cleever seemed pleased. "Good, that's what I hoped you'd say. Now, I don't actually own it, but I'm the executor of the estate. The previous owner, Old Mr Hardraker, died a few years ago, leaving the place in a dreadful state. He can't have worked it properly for thirty years, and it's in appalling disrepair. I've tried to find a new tenant, but no one will take it on, and it's completely deserted now. However, it does cover a lot of land, and now that I've been given leave to sell it, I'd like to get a valuation."

"I'd be glad to see it," said Sarah. "If you want to make an appointment—"

"Yes, that would be delightful. I'm a little busy over the next few days, but I shall ring you next week to arrange something. Thank you, Sarah; that's a weight off my mind. Now, the other thing. It's no less important either."

He paused, appearing to sort delicate words into the correct order in his mind. His smile, when it came, was a little pensive.

"It's about the Reverend Aubrey. About Tom."

Sarah waited, holding her glass with both hands.

"I know that you and Tom have – an understanding," Mr Cleever began slowly. "You must know him better than the rest of us. After all, it's been only a few months since he came here to St Wyndham's, and the pressures of modern pastoral work have kept him very busy . . ." He trailed off, as if unsure of himself.

"Are you saying he doesn't spend enough time with his parishioners?" asked Sarah, crisply.

"Not at all, not at all. He is, by all accounts, very industrious. Only – and I speak as a former church warden here, with some first hand experience – he is a little inclined to . . . go his own way. Perhaps he doesn't confide enough with those of us who are there to help in his ministry."

"Really, Mr Cleever, this is ridiculous. I am sure Tom does everything properly—"

"Forgive me, Sarah. This is not what I meant to say. He does confide in us, quite regularly, and certainly has a close understanding with Miss Price. They make a very good team. No, what I wanted to ask you was whether anything has been pressing on his mind lately. He seems a trifle distracted."

Sarah didn't know of anything that might be the cause. She wasn't sure she had noticed it herself.

Mr Cleever finished his cup and flexed his fingers. "Of course. It's probably nothing at all – just my imagination. I'm sorry to have brought it up, only as parish councillor I need to be aware . . . Give my regards to Tom, when you see him. I've not called in on him today – I thought he'd have enough to do, what with the outrage this morning."

Sarah wanted to know what outrage this was.

"Oh, you haven't heard? I thought everyone knew by now. No, there was a break-in at the church last night. They believe the lost fragment of the cross was dug up and stolen. And they have no idea who did it, or why. Very vexing indeed. Well, it is a long walk back and I must be going. I'm sure Tom will fill you in on

the dreadful business when he has time. Don't forget
to send young Michael over when you see him. I'll see
what I can do. Thank you very much for the tea, my
dear. Goodbye."

After only a few minutes, Tom's quest ended in success.
To the left of the main shelf he spotted a small book-
case with a glass front, marked REFERENCE ONLY
and filled with large, old, battered volumes. And there,
between 'The Stanbridge Fire of 1823 – a personal
memoir' and 'Fordrace Farming', he discovered a
small green-spined volume, with thick, rough-edged
leaves. Opening it on the title page, he read:

LEGENDS OF FORDRACE AND THE WIRRIM

by Harold Limmins Esq.

Coalgate Hill Publishers, Taunton

There was no date, but Tom already knew it was a
19th century printing. He returned to his seat and settled down with satisfaction. Turning to the next page,
he was intrigued to find, beneath a Latin dedication,
several patches of handwritten notes. They were written in faint blue ink, in a tight, ordered script. The first
one said:

Willis' theories of W.low, worm etc. p.51

The next one, a little way down, read:

The Pit. Early refs. Dangers etc. p. 68

The book was printed with very small, close type in long thick wodges of text, and it made Tom's eyes ache to look at it. Without any system whatsoever, he moved through the book, dipping in here and there, whenever one of the reference headings, which were placed in the wide margins for ease of understanding, caught his fancy.

Harold Limmins Esq. wrote in a slightly fussy style, very much that of the opinionated amateur scholar. He carried a lot of information about Morris Men, May Dancing on Fordrace Green (which had been banned midway through the 18th century on account of the 'excessive drunkenness attending the revels') and a strange Spring festival called 'Furring the Root' which was still performed in March in his own day. Tom enjoyed the accounts of these folk customs, many of which he had never suspected, and he had quite forgotten the vague purpose of his reading by the time he came upon another patch of handwriting, scratched tightly in the margin in faint blue ink. Just below the side heading 'The Wirrim; Geology and Etymology' were the scathing words: 'The old fool, what does he know?'

Tom had no idea how far Harold Limmins' knowledge stretched, but the passion of the sentence was clear. It was page 51, and the inked handwriting was the same as the notes at the front. Something had greatly angered someone, and on this emotional morning, that interested Tom. So he looked to the nearest main paragraph heading and began reading from there.

It read:

The Wirrim itself is a ridge of limestone and Carboniferous shale extending for five miles above the Russet countryside between Hopalming and Stanbridge. In width it is narrow, rarely reaching as much as three quarters of a mile broad, and sometimes, where the side valleys and mining operations have strongly cut away, a mere five hundred feet across. It runs East-West, with its main indentations in the Eastern half. The village of Fordrace is cradled in one such, where the Wirret Stream runs south from High Raise. It is a sheltered spot, south-facing and hemmed in on three sides by the Wirrim's arms.

Since earliest times, the Wirrim has been the focus for Man's energies in this area. Open-cast mining (for coals and limestone) began in the later stone age, particularly on the Northern side above Little Chetton. Early settlements existed near the summit of the ridge; there is a bronze age site to the south of the depression named Wirrinlow, where bracelets and pottery shards have been found. A sword was discovered there in the 17th Century. No sign of the buildings remain, but the top of the hill is dotted with some fourteen burial mounds, and various holes and hollows, of which Stoker's Hole and Wirrinlow are the largest. It is possible that some of the hollows are the traces of sunken burial mounds or barrows. Others may be geological sinkholes or ancient quarries.

Etymologies: Some controversy exists over the peculiar names of the Wirrim region, but it is generally accepted that 'Wirrim' itself derives from the Anglo-Saxon 'wergend' (gen, pl. 'werian'), meaning 'defender', since the ridge would be protection both from enemies and, in the valleys below, from the harshest weather. 'Wirrinlow' thus stems from the Anglo-Saxon 'werian-hlaew' meaning 'defenders' mound', suggesting it was once a raised point and may well have sunk. ('Hlaew' in Saxon may mean mound, cave or barrow.) The etymology of Fordrace is obvious: the village is sited at the fording point of a strong stream or 'race'.*

It was here that the ink message in the margin pronounced its scathing message. The asterisk referred to a footnote at the bottom of the page. This read:

*A dissenting view has been offered by Mr Arthur Willis, a local folklorist and archaeologist, whose theories are recorded here for the sake of completeness. He argues that 'Wirrim' derives (by a somewhat tortuous process) from the Anglo-Saxon 'wyrm' meaning 'serpent' or 'dragon', and that 'Wirrinlow' is hence a derivation of 'wyrmhlaew', or 'dragon's mound'. This, while barely possible, is strained beyond belief by his contention that Fordrace stems from the Anglo-Saxon 'fyr-draca' or 'fire-dragon'. A case, perhaps, of a gentleman's obsessions overcoming his objective intelligence.

Tom could just make out, very faintly, another ink marking here. He angled the page towards the light and traced the words. It said: 'Limmins and Willis, both fools – but Limmins blessed because ignorant.'

Tom stopped reading and gazed meditatively towards the ceiling. The library was very quiet and Ms Sawcroft was nowhere to be seen. No doubt about it, there was something here, some issue which Tom did not understand, but which caused passions to flare. What was it? Why should words matter enough to deface a book? He sighed. It was more than probable that the ink writing was very old – perhaps a hundred years or more. There was no chance of it having any relevance today. The whole thing was pointless.

He should go back to the church. There was more than enough to do there. And ring Sarah. He really must do that. The library, and this book, were just a waste of time . . .

A woman carrying a bag of books entered the library and went over to the desk and rang the bell. After a pause, Ms Sawcroft appeared from a back room and came hurriedly over to renew the loans. Tom shook his head to dispel the mood of weariness and indifference which had drifted over him. Yes, he would go, and soon, but not before checking the other reference highlighted at the front of the book. Let's see . . . Page 68 . . . He turned the thick, clothy pages in his hand, slowly, carefully, until he came to the place he sought.

This was side-headed: 'Wirrinlow – historical references and traditions' and was fairly brief. Tom read on:

> The hollow known as Wirrinlow has likewise appeared several times in local history and folklore, where it has a dubious reputation. The first reference is in a 16th century pamphlet kept in Hopalming museum, entitled 'Sprites and othere Visitations'. According to this, 'Marjorie Favvershame did, upon the 14th April 1583, receve upon the Wirrinlaw, also knowne as the Pitte, an unholy visitation, which lefte her frothing and nere dead. Aftere six days, complaining shrilley of devilles and impes around her, she was removed to Hostone Priorie, where latterly she died.'

Beside the passage, the writer in ink had been at work again: 'She had not the will.'

Tom frowned at this. It was quite beyond him, but the tone of it he did not like. Suddenly he realised how uncomfortable the library had become. The woman at the counter was complaining loudly to Ms Sawcroft about an overdue fine, and the heat in the room had grown intense, an uncomfortable heat which made his neck and wrists sweat and stilled even the buzzing of the bluebottles by the window. Tom got up and opened the casement wide. Fresher air wandered in. He perched himself on the window seat and read on quickly. The book continued,

One hundred years later, at the end of the 17th century, the Fordrace Parish Records mention the names of two parishioners, Tobias Thomson and George Pole, who died of exposure while sheltering in Wirrenlowe Hollow in Midwinter 1692. Oddly, their remains were interred outside the churchyard in the common ground.

Not long after, the Stanbridge Chronicles record one of the last known outbreaks of Witch Fear in England. In a tragic episode in 1734, two women of a farm near Fordrace were pursued by a mob to the summit of the Wirrim and beaten to death with sticks. Their bodies were thrown into the Wirrinlow and left as carrion. The Chronicles explains the matter thus:

'These women were accused of witchcraft

and idol-worship, and of coming of a long line of idolators. One of these, Meg Pooley, had been seen flying over the Wirrim; this same Pooley was likewise accused of firing her neighbour's barn. Both she and the other, Mary Barratt, were also said to have looked upon their neighbours with an evil eye and stolen from them gold and precious things. The Justice could find no witnesses to the women's deaths and was forced to abandon the inquiry.'

A line in Fordrace Parish Records, written in an unknown hand, seems to refer to this incident: 'Pooly and Barat – returned to The Pitt, their proper place.'

Thereafter, Wirrinlow fades from the local traditions, except from an aside in Rev. Colver's 'Memoirs' (1825):

'There was at this time, a fading flame of folk memory, which ascribed to areas of the Wirrim an unsavoury reputation. In particular, the region about the barrows on the summit, called by some The Pit, was largely avoided by the common man, and those who went there were looked upon with grave suspicion. I encouraged, in my sermons, strong scepticism on the subject of demons and fairies, and I fancy I have been largely successful in this endeavour, for I have not seen evidence of such belief for nigh on twenty years. But the details of these dark things, I was unable to discover.'

The Rev. Colver seems to have been justified in his belief, for there are no further records of such obscure beliefs that this author can find. We must assume them consigned to history.

Here the chapter ended. Beside it was one character, heavily scored on the paper: !

It seemed to Tom that this was written in felt-tip pen.

He closed the book. There had been no mention of the cross, and no concrete information of any kind. But he knew now that there were hidden traditions of the Wirrim, which were closely tied to death and superstition. And it could well be that they continued in some form to the present day. Could there be any connection with the theft, and the witterings of a sad old woman? He himself knew of the Pit, a large hollow on High Raise, popular with picnickers and ramblers. He had heard no ill of it, nothing to reflect its seemingly chequered past.

A slight cough disturbed him from his reverie. Ms Sawcroft was standing near him. She was still wearing her grey twill, yet was unflushed in the heat.

"It's early closing today, Tom." She smiled at his confusion.

"Sorry, Ms Sawcroft, I was miles away."

"It's closing time. Did you find anything of interest?"

"A few scraps. Nothing much."

She eyed the book resting on his knee. "Was there anything you were after in particular? I know my way around these parts, you know."

Tom was about to answer her question with some vague nicety, when from thin air, he asked, "Arthur Willis. Do you have anything by him?" As she hesitated, frowning, he added, "I'm not sure if you will. In fact, I'm not even sure he was published. But he was a local writer, referred to in here. Late 19th century, I think."

"I don't think so . . . Let me check."

She returned to the desk to consult the computer file, and Tom replaced the book in the Reference cabinet. When he had done so, he found her shaking her head and smiling.

"Sorry, I can't help you. No Arthur Willis here, although there is an Alfred Willis – 'The Gardener's Scourge: My War against Greenfly' – and I don't imagine you were after him."

"No," said Tom. "I wasn't. Is that just this library, or might there be something elsewhere?"

"That's the Central Library records for the county. You'll have to go further afield for it, if it exists."

"Right. Oh, is there a book of local biography?"

"Yes, in reference again. But it's closing—"

"I'll only be a moment. Sorry. I'll just take a quick look."

Tom hurried over to the shelves and almost immediately found the county 'Dictionary of Biography'.

Ignoring the bustling sounds from the desk, he flipped the pages until he came upon what he sought. There was a photocopier beside the desk, and he made a copy for 10 pence. Ms Sawcroft eyed him with calm impatience.

"He did exist," said Tom. "Sorry to hold you up."

"Don't worry. It's always good to find what you're looking for, especially when it's a hard chase. I'll put the book back for you. Thank you. You'll find the door's on the latch."

Back in his office, Tom cast his eye over the photocopied sheet. The entry was brief.

WILLIS, Arthur James (1841–1895)
Folklorist

Born Fordrace; educated at Stanbridge and Oxford; taught abroad before returning to Fordrace in his thirties. Spent years researching local traditions of the area; his theories were notable for their cavalier mingling of historical and legendary material, which garnered the derision of his rivals. He was a flamboyant character, legendary for his intemperance and professed paganism. His only published work, 'The Book of the Worm' was printed privately, in an unfinished state, by friends after his death. He died in a house fire, at his home at Crow Wood, Fordrace.

Tom tossed the paper onto his in-tray and stretched himself. There were a hundred and one things to do, and he still hadn't spoken to Sarah. He leant over and picked up the phone. It would be as well to check that her intemperate brother hadn't had any more visitations.

14

High on the Wirrim, two boys stood on the lip of a hollow, scanning the clusters of stones, the purple harebell wedged in corners, the alien brightness of coke cans and crisp packets dotted here and there among the grass.

"The Pit," said Stephen. "So it happened here."

"Over on the far side, beyond that stone."

"Right," said Stephen. "I see."

"Look," Michael snapped at him, "I know you don't believe me, and I don't care. Too bad. So just leave out the sarcasm." He sat down decisively and rubbed his eyes. Their aching had got worse the higher he went; a dull pressure which flared angrily whenever they moved. It made him irritable, a feeling which was worse now that he had made the climb, and knew that it proved nothing.

"I don't quite know what you were hoping this proved." Stephen casually echoed his thoughts. "I should give you a hiding for this; but frankly I can't be bothered." He half-walked, half-cantered down the slope and into the hollow, and wandered off across it, leaving Michael sitting.

"What proof can I give you, you idiot?" he said under his breath, and with this exclamation, he felt the pain in his head flare, and his eyes refocus.

The earth was red, like old blood or weathered brick. It seemed to radiate a heat he could not feel from a centre somewhere deep below the surface, a hidden bruise beneath the skin. Stephen's soul moved across that skin, its pale lights fluttering and winking with their small foolish anger. The glow around its form was weak and feeble beside the livid red of the waiting earth. It made Michael laugh to see its frailty, and he saw the horse head look back at him, stare, and turn away.

Then it seemed to Michael that the earth was clear as glass beneath him, and that somewhere fathoms down through all that redness a thing was rising. Up it came, slowly swirling, coiling, curling, a ball of movement underground. He saw the red strata of the rock below distort briefly as it passed across them. And he felt its purpose.

Stephen was standing in the centre of the hollow when he heard his brother laugh once, gutterally; a harsh sound. He turned with a start, but Michael was staring down into nothing, and with an exclamation of disgust he resumed his fevered thinking. His brother was either lying or mad, and he could do nothing about it whichever it was. He was stupid to have come.

Then he heard Michael calling for him to wait. He ignored the urgency in the voice, and kept walking.

But footsteps came running behind him and a slight fear entered his heart and made him turn.

"Michael, keep away. I've had enough. Just piss off."

"Stop! Stop here and listen to me. Listen, Stephen, I've got proof." Michael's face was flushed, lit up with joy and expectation.

"Don't give me any of that crap."

"I've got proof, I tell you. It's coming."

"What? You've flipped. Just keep away from me. Look, keep your hands off!"

Michael had grabbed the front of Stephen's shirt, wrenching it towards him with clenched fists. Stephen caught both wrists and tried to wrest them loose, but Michael's grip was iron-strong. His face was locked in a grin of fierce effort, and for the first time since the scream the night before, Stephen grew scared. He punched upwards between his brother's arms, catching him on the side of the jaw. Michael's head jerked back and he swore savagely, but he didn't loose his hold. Stephen hit out again in blind panic, then closed, locking Michael's head from the side and dragging him down with him to the ground. They rolled there, gasping and swearing. Stephen was the stronger, but Michael was possessed with a wild energy and gave no quarter.

At last, driven to desperate lengths, Stephen managed to land a punch below his opponent's ribcage. While Michael was foaming and gasping for breath, he wrestled himself free and sat squarely on his chest, gripping his hair with both hands.

"Now," he snarled, "I really am going to kill you."

But Michael gazed up through half-closed eyes and

laughed at him, and something rose swiftly from the ground and engulfed them before Stephen could think or move.

He fell through the earth, into a secret place where a restless power awaited him.

He came to a halt with the soft slowness of a stone dropping through syrup. It was cold around him, the slow remorseless cold which over many nights will shatter solid rock without a sound. But somewhere close a fire burned.

He felt bones underfoot, and hard cold things, which had once been beautiful under a warm sun. Up ahead was an abyss of black. Nothing moved, but he felt something offered to him, and acceptance surge in his breast.

Then he tried to step forward, and something snagged his foot. He looked down, and saw among the bones his brother lying under him, smiling up in vindicated triumph. And with that, a bubble of fear came vomiting up from inside his stomach, and he was lifted by that fear up and away with vicious speed, up and out through the cold earth until the sun broke suddenly on his back once more.

But the air was thick and acrid, and his eyes were blind, and his skin stung him.

Then Stephen, with a soundless cry, flung himself to one side, out into the summer air. And the lizards scattered.

"Well," said Michael, "you really messed that up."

Stephen was lying on his back in the grass of the hollow, with his mouth open and eyes blinking. It took him a moment to realise where he was, or recognise the figure who stood over him.

"Mikey, your nose is bleeding."

"Yes. You punched me, remember."

"Did I? Sorry, Mike. Hey, Mike, I feel wonderful."

"Well you've no right to. You should have stayed where you were. What made you go tumbling off? God knows what that's done – you were hardly in there a moment. There's no way you can have absorbed anything."

"I don't know. But listen, Mike – was that what happened to you before?"

"Of course. I didn't know until now, because I was asleep then. But I recognised the feeling when it passed through me. You've cocked it up big time. You should have stayed in there longer."

"I don't know; it didn't feel – but I feel great now."

"Well, you won't have the sight. Remember the state I was in afterwards. You've got to pay for these things, Stephen."

"You seem to know an awful lot about it all of a sudden."

"I don't have to prove it to you any more, do I?"

"No. But I'm just as confused, only – God, where the hell did it come from, Mikey?"

"It rose up. That's all I know. Now, if you feel so great, how come you're still lying there?"

"I'll get up. Give us your hand."

Michael extended an arm and pulled Stephen to his feet. He stood there for a moment, shaking gently, blinking round like a man with a fever risen out of bed.

All of a sudden, without warning or any pain, his focus changed. He cried out as he saw his brother in another shape.

"My God!" he cried. "Michael – you're beautiful!"

Michael started and clutched at him. "You can't," he hissed. "Not as easily as that! You're lying!"

But the dragon's thought flowed through his brother's veins like wine, filling him with a high and giddy exhilaration. He stretched his arms out wide, his fingers splayed in the air; then he spun around, taking in the world with savage, greedy eyes. At the third spin of his feet, he lost his balance, teetered wildly for a moment and fell heavily among the heather, laughing even as the wind was driven from his body.

"Oh, Michael," he said, sitting up slowly between gasps, "how can you, how can you be so – serious? Smile for me! Have you looked in a mirror? Did you know that you're a cat, Michael? Your hackles are up, Mikey, swirling blue and exploding like fireworks. You're not happy, are you, not at all, but it's you all right. You're summed up perfectly!"

He laughed again, leaning back in the gorse and gazing up at the two-tone sky, where the flat slab of space seemed underlaid with red and the clouds were flecked with grey.

Michael watched with an impassive face. "You'll be able to control it in a little while," he said. "But you'll be sick first." He frowned. Cat-souled? Could that be right? He felt his own solitariness, his watchful caution. It might be true.

For nearly five minutes, Stephen lay on his back and burbled softly, his body shaking and twitching with little repressed tremors of delight. Michael watched him, almost unconsciously changing the focus of his eyes. Stephen's form blurred and his horse-like face appeared, gazing up amid the heather, with its fluid surface spiralling with colour. The colours welled up from within like eruptions under glass, spread outwards across the surface with an eager haste, and were swiftly drawn in again. The intensity of movement was greater than before, the colours brighter and more varied, though there seemed a slightly lurid sheen to them which had not been there before.

'It'll be too much for him,' he thought. 'He'll be sick soon.'

And with that to comfort him, he rose, and left the burbler lying, and went to the ridge to look out across the valley.

The afternoon was old, and the sunlight which had bathed the countryside all day was showing the first signs of retreat. The pale blue of the sky was sapped of colour, and the furthest hills and fields were faint under a distant veil. The air was still. He shifted his focus automatically, and saw the colours darken. The sky changed to its reddish tint, the fields to a rusty brown, the coppices and skirting of woodland a dull dark brown. The people below – and there were some, out in the furthest fields – suddenly sprang into prominence. He had hardly been aware of them before, lost like ants in the vastness of the scene. Now, the brightness of their souls revealed them: they glittered like tiny moving jewels.

How delectable they were. But what was it that made them shine so? And if they sparkled like that when they were so far away, how bright would they look when all collected together? Michael wished he was on the crowded green at that moment, to see for himself.

A sudden noise behind him reminded him of Stephen. He waited a little longer before going back with a sympathetic face.

Even after the nausea, Stephen still wore an expression of delight, though the lines in his face were etched with weariness. He could no longer see, except for a searing light which pained him, but instead of keeping his eyes shut, he rolled them up so that only the whites showed. It gave him a very unpleasant aspect, which Michael lost no time in pointing out, but Stephen only replied, "I can't help it. I can't shut them. The urge to look is too strong, but it hurts me when I do. This way, it pains me least."

Michael helped him stand, took his arm around his shoulder and set about guiding him from the Pit. His brother was still shaking like a panicked rabbit, but he walked easily, sensing where to place his feet with a surprising confidence. After those last words, Stephen kept silent as they took the path downhill, and Michael did not break in upon it. A mood of anxiety and envy had come upon him. When the bubble had encased them, its taste and feel had been familiar, but he had known, with as much certainty as if he had been told, that its purpose was with Stephen, and that Stephen had in some way rejected it. Stephen had only been immersed for a minute or so -- and that he should have received the gift despite it, Michael resented deeply. They descended the Wirrim without words.

By the time they got to the cottage, it was nearly seven. The sky was lit with a pale evening blue in which cold stars already shone, and shadows were gathering under the elms outside the gates. Here, they loitered.

"Damn. The Pope's here," said Michael in a low voice, surveying the small car squeezed into one corner of the drive. "Now what do we do?"

"Not much we can do, is there? I need to sleep."

"We can't have them seeing you like this. That'll confirm all their prejudices. Depends where they are. Hold on, I'll see."

He left Stephen among the trees and moved off, keeping to the edges of the drive, where the gravel was sparse and overgrown with weeds. A minute later he was back, breathing heavily.

"They're in the sitting room. The Pope's yakking and Sarah looks angry. There's a storm brewing."

"Good. Maybe we can slip past."

"If we go round the back, we can have you in bed before the dust settles."

Michael led the way around the edge of the drive to the side gate. It opened with a squeal which made him cringe, and they passed though into the garden. The path ran down the side of the house, under the gaze of a small open window which belonged to the sitting room. From it came Sarah's voice raised in anger.

"We'll have to duck down low by the window," Michael whispered. "You go first and I'll say when."

Stephen inched his way along, feeling the pebbledash against his fingers on the right. As he drew close to the window, Sarah's words became distinguishable.

"Why don't you tell her about it, since you know each other so well! I've got more important things to do than waste my time listening to all this rubbish."

"Now look—" Tom's voice was heavy with annoyance.

"You've plenty of excuses to work late now. See if I care."

"This is ridiculous. What's put this into your head?"

"What are you waiting for?" Michael prodded Stephen in the small of the back. "She'd be better off without him, and you know it. Come on, let's go."

Stephen bent down, almost double, and scuttered sightlessly under the window. Michael followed him, and together they moved away towards the corner of the house. Behind them, their sister's angry voice continued to sound out into the dusk.

16

On his way back, Tom took a detour. He had wound down the window and his face was buffetted by the air of late evening, warm, scented and mazy with insects. His body seemed compressed with tension and anger; a jagged spring coiled in his chest, its end stabbing at his lungs and sending a sharp tightness out into his shoulders and arms. His foot hit the accelerator savagely; each curve of the drowsy lanes was a challenge to be snapped at. In such a mood, he could not go home. Not yet.

The road made a wide arc through the darkening fields, and flirted with the southernmost fringes of the Russet. For nearly all its length, the trees were banked on one side of the road only, their impassive columns buttressed against the strips of arable land. At one point however, the trees extended beyond the road to form a separate, isolated square of forest. This was Crow Wood.

Tom stopped the car. When he got out, he took two long breaths, leaning back against the warm metal. The sky was blending with the black leaves overhead.

He should have been more patient, shouldn't have got angry. Sarah was still upset about her brother, and rightly so. He should have spent less time talking about his own problems, and listened like a priest should. But to bring up Elizabeth Price, when he hardly knew the woman . . . Crazy! Where on earth had that come from?

He sighed heavily. Nothing seemed to be making sense any more. In the space of a day, everything had shifted. Nothing was right. Why break into a church? Why dig up an old stone? Why get worked up over an old cross?

Why spend hours in a library, when you didn't know what you were looking for?

No, but there was something to be found. Tom was sure of it. And he had one lead still to follow.

He must get some sleep. But first, to get rid of the tension, he set off at a run, following a beaten path into the trees.

Tom forced himself to run at speed. The tension in his chest pained him, but he ignored it, letting his arms and legs work to their full, and soon the ground was flashing past at a disembodied pace. His eyes were locked ahead, his body straining, and the residue of frustration and weariness was lost in the air behind him.

When, in a state of emptiness, he slowed, heart racing, breath jerking with life, he found he had come to the ruin in Crow Wood. There was a small clearing among beech trees, its floor pierced in many places with saplings and forest fronds and now thick with dusk. A wall of bricks, slightly taller than head height and punctured by the thin skeleton of a window, rose from the bracken on one side of the clearing. Another wall, at ninety degrees to the first, attained a lesser height and stretched into the darkness. The ground was ridged and tussocked with the chaos of fallen masonry.

Tom's shoes crunched on brick fragments. He walked into the centre of the dead house. The inner surface of the wall was jet black. White moths flew around his head, spreading silence with their wings. A lone timber, charred along one length, was propped against the wall. A beer can had been lodged carefully on top of it. Moving closer, he made out faint signs drawn on the bricks. He struggled to read them, his eyes screwed up . . .

The words had been scraped on the charcoal lining of the bricks, and showed through red against it: *Sandra 4 Lewis. 1979.*

Tom turned away. Alfred Willis had died here, a hundred years ago. He tried to imagine the smell of burning, the heat, the trees orange and red with flames, the sounds. But a hundred years of green silence covered those images and smothered them.

Tomorrow he would check the County Records. Somebody must have a copy of Willis's book. He would find it, read it, and then he would stop chasing shadows.

He walked back to the car and drove home slowly.

It took two minutes for Stephen to be spirited up to his room and put to bed. He was asleep almost immediately, his eyes closing properly for the first time since he had left the Pit. Michael went downstairs and made himself a sandwich in the kitchen. His eyes were burning fiercely. It had grown worse throughout the afternoon, and now they felt red around the rims.

Michael sluiced cold water on his face and blinked several times to make his eyes settle. Slowly, the heat faded, but a bottled-up desire remained. The urge to see – the other way – was very great. All day he had felt the pressure to use his new sight, and though he had mostly been able to keep this feeling under control, he would not be able to do so for long. Besides, he had only had Stephen to look at all day. Tomorrow, he would go into the village, and watch the people on the green. The anticipation of their jewel-like hidden souls made his heart ache.

Sarah came downstairs from her bedroom. She started when she saw Michael standing by the sink.

"So you're back, are you?" she said, tartly. "Where have you been all day?"

Michael made ready to unlock his excuses.

"I felt an awful lot better this morning. Stephen and I went for a long walk – I needed some air."

"Where did you go?"

For no real reason, a lie slipped out: "The Russet. To Thrush Bank and back."

"And where's Stephen?"

"Asleep. He's absolutely shattered. No stamina, that's his trouble."

"You should have left a note. You're both just bloody thoughtless."

"Sorry, Sarey. Sorry I've upset you."

He waited, hardly daring to believe it would be that

simple, but Sarah left it like that. She went to put on the kettle. Michael fidgeted a little.

"Sarah, I couldn't help hearing just now . . . I'm sorry you had a row. Are you OK?"

She sighed, flicked the switch and sat down at the table opposite him.

"Oh sure. It was my fault really. I was worried about you, and Tom's got a lot on his mind at the moment. We'll be fine tomorrow. It's just been a really crap day."

She gazed at the tabletop for a time. Michael found he had an overwhelming temptation to look at her with his other sight. From somewhere else came a doubt, a sense that to do so was an invasion of her private space. But he did it anyway.

Her soul was swirling slowly with a dozen shades of blue, shining and glistening with a beauty which lanced him through with guilt and shame.

"I'll make you a cup of tea," he said.

"Thank you, Mikey."

She drank it rapidly and strong. When she had finished, she looked up at him with an appraising eye.

"Michael," she said. "Could you do me a favour?"

"Sure."

"I was meant to go over to Mr Cleever's this evening, and pick up a series of council leaflets. I'm distributing them next week. I really don't want to go – you know how overpowering he can be. Do you think—?"

"Say no more. You'll have to tell me where he lives."

"Have you got lights for your bike?"

"Quit worrying, sis. I won't come to any harm."

Sarah watched him set off, pleased at his willingness to help. In truth, he did seem a lot better today, and hopefully Mr Cleever would be able to build on that with a few subtle words of advice. She tapped her empty mug with exasperation. Really, Tom should have been the one to do it, but the whole cross business was getting him too wound up. He needed to calm down and rest.

For that matter, so did she. Things would be better tomorrow.

Filled with his contrition, Michael was soon gliding down the hill like a ghost in the night, the beam from his front light casting the hedges into strange relief. A startled rabbit ran in front of his wheel and nearly sent him tumbling, but he stabilized himself and soon shot out into the deserted green, which was lit in places by orange light from the village windows.

Mr Cleever's house was a sizeable Victorian villa set back from the green behind a rose garden. His sizeable car was parked on the verge outside, and it was next to this that Michael left his bike. He walked into the garden under a kissing gate of climbing briars, and headed up the path. Ahead, thick curtains hugged against the glass of great bay windows, from behind which came forth music and light and the sound of voices. The sultry scent of ageing roses hung about him as he passed along the paving stones to the door and rang the bell.

There was a break in the flow of voices from beyond the window, then someone laughed, and the noise began again. Michael fidgeted on the doorstep, anxious to be gone. A sound of movement came from inside, and the door opened. Mr Cleever looked out, squinting a little as he adjusted to the dark, and broke into a wide smile of welcome.

"Michael MacIntyre, isn't it? An unexpected pleasure."

"Hello, Mr Cleever. Sarah sent me over . . . to collect some pamphlets . . ."

He trailed off, conscious of the intensity of Mr Cleever's gaze, feeling somehow a little foolish as he stood there on the step, still grass-stained from events on the Wirrim. I should have tidied myself up a bit, he thought.

"Pamphlets . . ." Mr Cleever seemed to have difficulty focusing on the issue himself. "Of course! She can't make it, then?"

"No, she's a bit under the weather."

"I'm sorry to hear it. Well, it's good of you to pop down yourself, Michael. Come in a moment."

"I don't want to bother you if you've got guests." Michael hesitantly moved into the house; Mr Cleever held the door ajar, and closed it as soon as Michael stepped through.

"Good heavens, no bother about it," said Mr Cleever. "Just some old friends. They can wait a minute. Straight down through the house, Michael, to the sitting room. I'll hunt out the pamphlets in a moment."

Michael walked down the narrow hall, with Mr Cleever close behind. The walls were white and adorned with prints of old engravings. They reflected their owner's archaeological interests – Michael caught flashes of standing stones, henges, forts and ruins. The floor was of black and white tiles; aspidistras in large vases took up position in tight corners; and the light was surprisingly poor. Somehow, it all gave off an old-fashioned aura which made Michael feel hemmed-in by history.

They passed a door which must have led into the front room. It had been pulled almost to, but the bright light gleamed round the cracks. A stream of classical music came from inside, yet it seemed to Michael that the volume had been turned low, and that the voices were stilled too.

There was a small sitting room at the end of the hall. Mr Cleever squeezed past Michael and waved him to a chair.

"The pamphlets are upstairs somewhere. I'll fetch them. Would you like a beer while you're waiting?"

Michael was slightly taken aback. It was not something adults asked. The only beers he had tasted were surreptitious ones, bought for him at off-licences by Stephen and some older friends. Still, Mr Cleever was a bachelor; maybe he didn't quite know the score.

He took advantage. "Yes please."

"Excellent." It was only while Mr Cleever was unearthing a bottle from somewhere in the neighbouring kitchen that Michael remembered that his host was sometime youth group leader of Fordrace, and had been known to campaign on the subject of underage drinking. "You old hypocrite," he thought, as he accepted the bottle.

"Won't be a moment," smiled Mr Cleever, and disappeared back into the hall. His footsteps could be heard ascending the stairs.

Michael sat back in his chair and sipped the beer. The sharp smooth earthy tang settled round his tongue and added to his general feeling of unreality.

He looked about him, taking little in, waiting for Mr Cleever to return. Above, there was the scuffled sound of movement, but his host did not reappear on the stairs.

An engraving above the fireplace caught his eye. It was the only picture on the wall, caught in an age-darkened gilt frame. It was of the kind he had seen in books, a three-dimensional plan of an historical site, only with odd perspective, and with little figures wearing the costume of another century. There were curly letters – A, B, C, D – next to important bits, and notes to these letters written in ornate handwriting at the bottom of the engraving, but they were too far away for Michael to read.

The site depicted was a burial mound, covered with grass and with its rim set about with stones. Half of it seemed to have fallen in on itself. Men in tall hats were standing on it, holding odd measuring devices. There was a smaller barrow in the background, and something dark flying in the sky. Michael had half a mind to get up and survey the picture at close hand, but indolence and the pleasant numbness of the beer prevented him.

On the mantlepiece below the engraving – Where on earth was Mr Cleever? – was a small object which caught the corner of his eye, like a sudden movement. Between a porcelain milkmaid and a drummer boy, both of which Michael considered quite naff, was a ceramic lizard.

It was maybe six inches long, coiled in upon itself, with a long green body and an endless tail, which wrapped the base of the model twice round. The head was raised slightly; the small red eyes, set back low upon the thin elongated snout, were half open, and gazed up as if considering the room with a cold appraising eye. The mouth was closed, but somehow managed to suggest a lot of teeth under its surface. It was distinctly ridged.

Michael looked at it for a moment, and then, for the first time in an hour or more, he became aware of an aching in his eyes.

There was no doubt that the model was very well made. It might even be valuable. The two eyes, which gleamed so, could well be made of garnet or some other semi-precious stone. Maybe – Michael thought – even ruby! Some of the larger scales on the back of the body were also gems.

All in all there was a definite beauty to it, and Michael began to wonder how it might look to him through his other sight. In its loveliness, it reminded him of the souls he had seen, only harder, more solid. He felt he might risk a look, just quickly.

From down the hall, and the distant room filled with unknown company, came a sudden laugh; a woman's, high and gleeful. Michael jumped and his whereabouts returned to him in a flurry. All at once he realised how quiet it had been before, and how close the room had got. There was a little sweat on his forehead.

He looked at the mantlepiece again. The model lizard seemed to have lost its sparkle. The eyes were dull once more.

Where was Cleever? He'd practically finished the beer. All of a sudden Michael was annoyed. Had he got the pamphlets or hadn't he? Had he forgotten him, or was he playing some kind of game?

Well, you couldn't do that to Michael any more, parish councillor, youth leader, archaeology chairman or not. If you kept him waiting, you paid the penalty, and the penalty was—

—Michael would take a peep at Mr Cleever's soul. See that private side, he would, and he would never know that he had had it done. Yes. A pompous old fool, Cleever, and a little slimy. What would it be? A warthog, or a dung-beetle? Michael grinned to himself, and all of a sudden, he heard returning footsteps on the stairs.

Now then.

Mr Cleever came back into the room. There were no pamphlets in his hand. Michael waited. Not yet.

"I have to apologise, Michael," Mr Cleever said (but he was still smiling). "The pamphlets your sister wanted aren't here yet. The ones upstairs are for a different area of the parish. Sometimes I don't know if I'm coming or going, what with all my different interests."

Pull the other one. What do you take me for? What are you after? You don't play with me.

"Oh," said Michael. "I see. Well, it was nice beer."

"You must send your sister my apologies. It must have been tedious for you. Did you notice that engraving, by the way? An original, you know. 17th century. Do you know where it's of?"

Who cares? Don't try anything with me. You turn out the light, I see in the dark.

"No? It's up on the Wirrim. The Pit, Michael. Do

106

you know where that is? Up on High Raise. I hear you go up that way sometimes."

So I do, stranger. And I do more than that. Things happen to me; things happen which make me different.

"Nowadays, the surface of the mound has entirely collapsed. There's some structural instability in the ground below, which has led to quite a sizeable hollow being formed. Very unusual feature. But then, the Wirrim's an unusual place."

He looked back at Michael, and rested his arm on the mantlepiece. Michael was motionless in the chair.

I should do it now. Look him right in the eyes. And do it.

Mr Cleever smiled suddenly. "You're different, Michael, but you're not unique. Go ahead, take a look. I won't mind."

And in that sudden moment of confusion and fear, Michael did what he had been plucking up the courage to do, and looked. But he lacked entirely the arrogant composure he had hoped for, and was instead smitten, for the first time since his awakening in the Pit, with a sense of desperate peril.

He looked. And saw.

Mr Cleever was not a wart-hog, or a dung-beetle. His soul hovered by the mantlepiece, its eyes fixed firmly on Michael, and in that vital instant he knew that it was returning his gaze, sight for sight, and that if he saw, it saw too. The eyes were small and red and sparked like gemstones, and bored into him with a hungry intentness of purpose which sent a sick feeling coursing through his stomach. These eyes were set in a surface as dark and thick as treacle, with just the thinnest streaks of colour and brightness fighting free of the broiling darkness, only to be subsumed again in a moment.

And the shape was that of a reptile. It had a long thrusting blunt snout pointing right at him, and there were teeth all along the side of it, sharp and horribly even. And in a strange way, it seemed to Michael that the smile was superimposed exactly on Mr Cleever's own ordinary smile, and that the two were in no way different. The head was quite smooth, except for two lumps high up near the back, close together and extending into the hazy light which surrounded the form.

Then the mouth opened, and Michael saw the red interior flare as Mr Cleever's voice said:

"I can see your fear. But I'm not your enemy, Michael. Far from it."

Michael's terror coalesced into a single word. Even as he swore, the bottle was falling to the floor.

His focus shifted. The human face reappeared, and the smile was the same.

The bottle smashed.

Now Michael was careering up the long dark hall, toppling an aspidistra from its marble stand and sending it against the wall in a shower of soil and pottery.

"Michael! There is no point running. What you see, you will become!"

That came from behind him. From the side, from the front room, a sharp oath and hurried movement; the door opened and someone came out at a run, but who it was Michael did not see. He was already past and wrenching at the handle of the front door. As he pulled it open, fingers clenched like claws on his jacket, but he ripped himself clear and was sprinting down the garden, his eyes burning with pain.

No one followed. He did not look back.

As he shot away into the darkness, heat hovered about him like a cloud.

18

At the cottage, Sarah had gone to bed. But Stephen had emerged, and was sitting in the kitchen finishing off a fried egg sandwich when Michael burst breathlessly in.

"In the words of the song," said Stephen, "I feel fine."

Michael dropped into the chair opposite. He was haggard and drawn. "Good grief," said Stephen, with his sandwich halfway to his face. "What's happened now?"

"It's not just us."

"Eh?"

"We're not alone in this. Cleever. He's one."

"He's what? – you don't mean—?"

"And there may be more of them. In fact, I know there are. I didn't see them, but they wouldn't have been there if they weren't, would they?"

Stephen shoved his plate to one side and held up both hands in an imploring gesture. "Start again," he said. "Tell it through slowly, and don't miss anything out."

"First, I'm locking that." Michael got up and turned the key in the back door. "Right."

"Michael, what's got into you?"

He told him. Stephen listened to the end without interrupting.

"I see," he said quietly.

Michael stared at him with a stricken face. "You see? Is that all you can say? Christ, Stephen, he read my mind! He read my mind! He knew I was going to look at him, and he answered me, and I hadn't said anything, nothing, only thought it! Oh God, he's probably reading it now. He knows what I'm thinking . . ."

"Calm down. There's no point panicking. We've got to think this through. We'll hole up here for a bit and work something out."

"When he said do it – when he read my mind – I didn't want to and I knew I shouldn't, but I couldn't stop myself. I couldn't control my eyes; it was like they were burning around the rims, and the burning was only going to stop when I made the change."

"Do you feel that way now?"

"No. It's OK now, sort of. Well, it's been getting worse, but nothing like it was when I was with him. He just stood there smiling, and my eyes flared." Michael shuddered. "You know how he smiles."

"I don't wonder you were frightened, Mikey. If his soul reflects his smile, I wouldn't envy the man who sees it."

Michael sat forward eagerly. "You think it's the soul too, then?"

"What else could it be? I get an awful feeling when I look at someone that way, Mike. I tried it on Sarah just now. It's like peeling off the layers and leaving them naked. You see too much."

"Yes," said Michael slowly. "That's what I feel . . . sometimes. At the same time, why not look, if you can?"

"We don't know. But I bet Cleever looks a lot."

"Oh shit." All of a sudden, Michael was overwhelmed with a terrible certainty. "He'll get me, Stephen. He won't let me go after what I've seen."

"Calm down. Look, a crocodile shape sounds bad, but that doesn't mean it's actually evil."

"This one was." Michael was in no mood for philosophising. "Oh shit, he'll come here for me, I know he will."

"He won't have the balls; but if he does, I'll see him off. He doesn't know about me yet, does he?"

"He won't care . . . Oh God!" Michael was struck by a sudden terror. "Have you shut the windows? The downstairs ones?"

"For Christ's sake, Michael. He's not going to come climbing in after you!" Stephen drummed his fingers on the table. "Anyway, Sarah shut them when she went to bed. Now let's just calm down and think. What was it he said when you ran?"

"He said I'll become what I see. Or saw. I don't know. I was too busy getting out."

"Yes, but 'become what'? What does it mean?" Stephen picked up his fork and tapped it against his plate. "Maybe there are other effects we don't know about, which increase as time goes on. Maybe Cleever knows about them and we don't. You said yourself that your eyes are burning more and more. I

111

don't feel that yet, but you've had the sight for longer than me."

"The burning in my eyes lessens if I switch focus. Even only for a second."

"It's like it's encouraging you to look. Weird. But I suppose you were breathing in the stuff for longer than me, so you might find it more difficult to control. Michael, what are you doing?"

Michael had risen from his chair, and was rummaging in the pile of unwashed cutlery next to the sink. When he turned round, he had a knife in his hand.

"You didn't see that soul, Stephen," he said.

"Oh, for God's sake." Stephen didn't want to admit it, but his brother's fear was infecting him too. He tried to concentrate on something positive.

"One real bonus, which I found out before you came back, is that you can see in the dark. I snapped it on in the bedroom. That's a beauty, isn't it?"

"I knew that already." Michael had slumped dismally back in his chair. Suddenly, he felt very tired.

"It's like it's infra-red, or something. We'll have to try some more experim—"

A tiny sound, as if of crunching gravel. Stephen stiffened. Michael froze. They sat motionless, every nerve straining out for noise. Seconds passed.

Michael looked at Stephen. Stephen shrugged.

"Can't hear anything now. Must have—Oh!" The bell sounded, a deep jangling noise out in the passage.

Stephen swung his legs off the table. "I'd better get it. Another ring and it'll wake Sarah. You stay here."

Michael said: "If he comes in here, I'll stab him, I swear it."

"Don't panic. Just wait here." Stephen padded out of the kitchen, closing the door almost to.

Stephen's footsteps disappeared up the passage. Michael was left in the kitchen. His eyes were tingling strongly again, and he felt hot and clammy. He fingered the knife in his hand. Breathe deeply. Keep calm. The back door was locked. The curtains were drawn.

There was a distant scrabbling as Stephen took the chain off the hook. A pause. Michael imagined the door swinging open. Silence.

Then Stephen's voice, veiled with mild surprise:

"Good evening, Mr Cleever. An unexpected visit."

Michael's stomach gave a lurch; his chest tightened, and he stood up clumsily, his hand tightening on the knife. And then his eyes flared with a sudden pain that made him gasp. Instantly, he refocused and the pain grew less. The room about him wavered and solidified again, daubed with a dull and reddish light. The knife in his hand leapt into sudden gleaming prominence, encased in a new, silvery aura. Metal pans and cutlery glowed in the dimness. Michael's head span; he leant on the table to steady himself, his head hanging downwards, trying to focus on the noises from the passage. He heard Stephen's voice again; unnaturally loud.

"I see. Yes, he said he'd had some sort of queer turn. No, he's gone out again now. He wanted to clear his head, he said."

The murmur of the other voice was inaudible. Michael's head was throbbing. His own hands, lying flat upon the tabletop, were indistinct and empty husks, and through them he saw the wood grains running. A sudden contempt for their lack of substance stuck in his heart. Only his knife was solid. Smooth hard metal. He gripped it firmly. Somewhere beyond, Stephen's voice maintained its flow, languid and assured.

"Well, I've no doubt he'll want to apologise on Monday. No, I don't know when he'll be back. That's very good of you. I'm very much obliged for your concern."

There was a long silence; Michael's head was hanging down over the table. He could see through his stomach to the cabinets behind. The silver buckle from his belt hung suspended in midair like a miraculous gem. It entranced him. In its way, it was as beautiful . . . and as mysterious, as any of the souls he'd seen. A quite marvellous thing . . .

"Michael." It was Stephen's voice, near and loud. "You were quite right. I've never seen anything like it. What a creature."

Michael snapped his eyes into the old focus, watching the buckle reluctantly fade to its old dull self. He raised his head wearily, afraid Stephen might draw attention to his condition. Somehow, though he didn't know quite why, he felt conspicuous and guilty, and had a reluctance to be questioned on the matter. But his brother's mind was elsewhere.

"I couldn't help it, Mikey; I had to look, after what you'd told me. But I waited until he turned to go, then took a quick squint at the side view. He never knew anything about it."

"I hope not."

"Well, it had to be done. Anyway, I got rid of him

114

pretty well. Gave nothing away, unless he read my mind too, and we can't contend with that."

Michael sat in a chair, heavily. "What did he say?"

"What you'd expect. 'Most terribly sorry to disturb. Rather worried. Unfortunate incident at my house. Brother seemed quite distressed.' That sort of thing. 'Just thought I'd call round and enquire.' He did it really quite well. If you hadn't told me, I might well have invited him in to check on you himself."

"Don't." Michael flinched.

"Anyway, then he said, 'Is Michael in? I'd like to see him,' and though it sounded friendly enough, I thought I detected a kind of catch in his voice, like something trying to break through. That was when I decided I had to take a look."

"I said goodbye, and as I was shutting the door, I made the switch. And – he's bad all right. It's not the shape that gets you, but the famine in the eyes. You have to ask, what has he done to become like that?"

He left a pause, but Michael said nothing. "You're right about the colour. And the teeth. As for the crocodile shape – well, I don't know, it doesn't seem quite right somehow. I'm not sure why. Crocodile heads aren't that curved, are they? They're flatter along the snout."

"What does it matter?" Michael's tension erupted savagely. "You saw it, you felt it. Is it evil or isn't it? And what does it want with us?" He threw the knife down on the table, and pressed his palms against his weary eyes. "Oh God, Stephen. What's happening to us?"

His voice trailed off. There was silence in the kitchen, and no answer to be had.

Soon afterwards, a silent, subdued Michael bade his brother goodnight and shut himself up in his room. Overcome with a weariness greater than any he could recall he went straight to bed, put out the light and lay on his back, staring up towards the ceiling. His whole body stiff with tension, he lay invisible in the darkness, too tired to move. Gradually, imperceptibly, over what seemed an endless time, his eyes closed, and he slept . . .

. . . long, deep, and deeply – but with a wakeful eye that never quite shuts out the light from far off places. It is dark all about, the darkness of great depth, but the thick earth to him is just like folds of glass or diamond. He pierces it with his sight and knows what lies beyond it; knows the rapid movements of clouds, the quivers of small green things rising and falling with the breath-quick seasons, the endless scutterings of the occupants of that airy place, as they wear their lives out and return to ground.

A slow breath in—

A thousand lives, each one a scintillating jewel, move on the surface, their movement catching light, refracting it in a thousand different colours.

A slow breath out—

They die; the jewels wink out. The dross returns to earth, sinks slowly to him though the glassy sediment, its value gone.

He stirs, restlessly, underground, and in the bed, Michael flings his arm across his face.

Dimly now, he perceives a paradox: the watcher cannot possess the beauty of the souls, though it sees them; the owners cannot see the beauty, though it is their own.

No one can bridge this gulf between possession and desire. Except, perhaps, the gifted few.

Michael, in his sleep, feels his new strength well up inside him – with a rush of pleasure which makes his head reel. Then a voice comes, calling him by name. He hides his pleasure – jealously, guiltily. On the bed, his cheeks flush red.

"Michael. The sight is not the only gift." The voice is high, close; it speaks of a secret long concealed.

In response, his eyes burn with an eager fire; but he does not answer yet.

"There are four gifts, Michael, of which the sight is just the first." The voice is nearer, it soothes him with a sweet desire.

In response, his heart beats faster; his legs stir on the bed, but he does not answer yet.

"It will take you years to learn the other gifts, Michael, if you struggle on your own. But you do not have to struggle. We can teach you secrets now, if you wish to learn them."

The voice is poised. On the bed, fingers twitch.

"Do you want to learn them, Michael?"

In response, his head moves, his eyes open; sightlessly they dart back and forth, here and there, across the room and the inner space, searching. His mouth opens wide: his voice is dry, but he croaks an answer.

"Yes."

Now the voice is very close. He feels a breath in his ear, smells a tint of metal, of some strong chemical . . . an acrid odour . . . Far away he feels a heat in the earth.

"Michael. There is something that you should know. Your brother is foolish. He has the power, but not the will – he will struggle to use it. But you can make it easy for him. You were there first. Lead by example. Then he will follow, and admire you for it too, as is your right. But do not tell him yet; power rests with those who keep a secret. He might try to take your leadership from you."

Michael's lips twitch in his sleep. This is only too likely. But he knows now. He will be careful.

"Michael. Come to me. Let me touch you. Then you will know the four gifts and what you might do with them."

Michael struggles upright, flings the covers from the bed. His eyes are sightless. Although the room is cold, he is perspiring with a distant heat. Midway between sleep and waking, he turns his head.

There is a figure there.

He rises; his feet feel stone beneath the carpet.

He walks towards the figure and the revelation.

20

Stephen sat with the light off in his window seat, his back pressed against the bedroom wall, looking out into the night.

The drive outside and lane beyond were pitch black; the yellow light from the Monkey and Marvel showed above the hedge, illuminating the outlines of the trees a little down the road. Away to the right, hidden by the darkness and the wall of the house, rose the low hard rise of the Wirrim. The warmth of the day still drifted skywards from the cooling ground.

There was laughter in the lane, of men passing homeward like shadows before the gate. It receded and was swallowed up. Stephen sat in the dark, letting the fears of the day spill out into his mind.

Even now, his heart tightened at the memory of the creature on the doorstep. And yet, although it had shocked him, it was nothing compared to what he'd seen in the kitchen, when Michael had raised his head with a face like old age. Something was happening to his brother, faster and stronger than to Stephen, and Stephen did not know what to do.

The night was an inky patchwork of shadows. Stephen flittered his gaze along the grey mass of the roadside hedge, until his eyes were resting on a deep patch of black directly opposite the cottage.

Suddenly, sharply, his eyes were filled with pain.

He screwed up his face with shock. It was what

Michael had described; his sockets stung and the lids felt hot and itchy. It was unbearable. But Michael had said that the pain lessened if you used the sight.

Stephen changed focus. Things changed.

The countryside appeared to him as if lit by a dull red-grey light. Everything was flattened, even the stars were gone, as if their life had been suddenly snuffed out.

And there was a watcher in the lane.

A creature stood against the hedge, looking up at the cottage. It had a reptile's head, blackish green and shiny, and its eyes were lost in the shadow of its muzzle. But Stephen knew that it was looking straight at him, that the darkness was no more perplexing to its sight than it was to his.

Then the creature opened its mouth in salutation and he saw its shining curves of teeth like the teeth of fishes, closely set, white and serrated with a wicked edge. Instinctively, with panic tightening in his chest, Stephen gasped and looked away – and saw the others.

Something with a reptile soul was watching from under the elms a little further down the lane. Its face was almost hidden beneath the lowest branches, but he caught the teeth glinting behind the leaves in the red-grey light. Another stood motionless in the centre of the field beyond. Even in his fear it struck Stephen how curiously indistinct the lower half of its body was. The head was sharp, the thick curved neck also, but below the chest the image faded out, until the lower half was almost imperceptible, even with the clarity of his eyesight, which brought the smallest midnight branches sharply into view.

After the first shock, he sat frozen, his heart palpitating. The beating of his blood echoed in his ear. Three figures, three reptile souls, and each one watching him.

Then a sudden anger rose in him.

"Who are you, you bastards?" he shouted, and his voice was swallowed by the night. The nearest reptile opened its mouth again; the teeth grinned a soundless reply. Stephen swore and forced his eyes to refocus, desperate to catch a glimpse of the human faces beneath the souls. His eyes swarm, and a burst of pain shrieked disapproval. Darkness smothered the view beyond the window and the stars sprang out again. But everything in the lane and fields was again blacked out. He could see nothing.

There was a rustling from the lane.

Stephen cursed and made the change again. The pale dead-light illuminated the landscape. The two most distant reptiles were moving now. The lower halves of their bodies were still invisible; they seemed to float through the air towards the leader by the hedge. As the one from the elms approached, the leader turned to it and opened its mouth. Stephen thought he heard a low whisper rise up from below – a human voice, strangely unnatural to his ears.

The sound sparked in him new energy, and an inspiration. Beside his bed, six feet away, was his cabinet, and in his cabinet was his torch. Army standard, high intensity, new batteries. Stephen would shine it on the watchers and reveal their human selves.

He began to swivel on the window seat. Instantly, the head of the first reptile soul jerked towards him.

He felt a pain in his head, a sudden sapping of his energy. A shout came from below, urgent and unconcealed. He thought he recognised the voice, but his thoughts were suddenly confused. The shape on the field began to run towards the lane, while the leader, without diverting his gaze from Stephen, gestured the third towards the driveway gate. Helplessly, Stephen heard the latch being lifted and saw the shape pass through.

On the leader's gaze, Stephen felt impaled like a fish on a harpoon. His muscles twitched spasmodically – once, twice – and suddenly, with a burst of willpower, he wrenched himself free. He threw himself backwards off the window seat and into the room, where he landed on the carpet with an impact that dazed him. When he opened his eyes after a moment, he was back in ordinary darkness.

The aching in his eyes had gone. Somewhere below him, in his garden or even in his house, a man or woman with a soul like a reptile was moving.

He got to his feet, and dived across the bed, crushing a pack of biscuits on the way. Then he was thrusting his arm into his bedside cabinet, rooting around amid the hankerchiefs, inhalers, tapes and tennis balls, while his other hand searched nearby for a weapon he knew was there. The torch was right at the back of the cabinet. He grasped it with a snarl of relief, and as he did so, his fingers closed upon his grandmother's walking stick, propped up against the wall.

Then he stood up straight and listened.

The house was silent. No sound came from beyond the window.

Stephen went out onto the landing and listened with

a frozen intensity. Silence. The stairwell was pitch black. Suddenly he had a terrible temptation to peer over the banisters into the dark pool of the hall below. He imagined with horror the figure that might be waiting, watching there . . .

No. He shook his head angrily, as if breaking a spell. Imagination would do him no good. He must forget their hideous souls, forget his fear of them. Above all, he must keep to his ordinary sight if he was to catch their human faces. They could see in the dark, but not round corners. So as long as he kept out of sight, they had no advantage over him.

The house was locked up; he had heard no sound of entry. There was time to rouse Michael first. For the moment, Sarah could wait. Holding the stick ready, Stephen walked soundlessly along the landing, past the door to the bathroom, past the door to their sister's room, down the passageway that led alongside the spare study to Michael's bedroom at the end.

At the door he paused. He looked back along the black passageway. The end of it was invisible, a smudge of blackness. Had there been a sound back there? He longed to use the sight, or switch on the torch – but he resisted the urge savagely.

Wait.

A tiny sound. A faint scratching. Nail on glass.

Sccrt, scrrt, scrrt.

It came from Michael's room.

Stephen cursed again under his breath. Quietly, quietly, swapping his torch to his right hand, he turned the handle and began to steal the door open. The door opened inwards, blocking his view into the room.

When there was space enough, he returned the torch to his left hand, then leaned forward and peered round.

The first thing he saw he took in with a glance. Michael's bed was empty, the duvet flung back so sharply that it was two-thirds on the floor. The bedside light lay beside it, switched on, but half rolled under the bed, so that a strange dull subterranean radiance extended weakly across the carpet.

The next thing he saw as he craned his head round was his brother. Michael was standing next to the window, his fingers pressed upon the glass. His neck was jutting forward, his forehead tilted against the pane. Although Stephen could not see his eyes, everything about Michael's posture suggested extreme concentration.

And there was something outside, just beyond the glass. A shape in the night, partially obscured by Michael's head, very dark and still. That something was scratching on the pane.

Scrrt, scrrt, scrrt.

With each scratch, Stephen's eyes throbbed with the desire to refocus. His fingers tightened on the torch.

"Michael." His voice was a violent whisper. "Get out of the way."

Michael made no sign of having heard. His face remained hidden, close against the glass. But slowly his hand moved, down and along, towards the window handle.

The thing beyond the glass gave a little quiver of movement. Michael's hand grasped the handle, absently.

There was an urgent movement from beyond the

glass. Michael's hand gripped tighter, and began to turn.

At that moment, Stephen stepped out from behind the door and turned his torch upwards and on with a fluid movement that stabbed a beam of light across the room, past Michael's shoulder and full into the window where the dark shape hovered.

Then several things happened all at once.

The beam seemed to explode against the glass, sending shattered splinters of light back into the room. Michael screamed; with his chin high, he was precipitated backwards away from the window and down against the side of the bed.

Outside the window there was a simultaneous cry. For an instant Stephen saw the beam light up a woman's face, contorted by rage and pain, then it too fell backwards into the night. There was a heavy sound somewhere far beneath.

It had not struck Stephen until that moment how impossible it was that there could be anything at all outside the first floor window. He lowered the torch and stood stupidly, looking at the blank square of the window.

"But we don't have a ladder," he thought.

Michael was lying on the floor. His chest rose with his breathing, rough and ragged. Stephen stepped over him and went to the window, the determination to see the face of his adversary still burning fiercely in his mind. The handle was already turned. Stephen pushed the window open and looked out, angling his torch onto the ground below. There was no ladder nor any other means of access to Michael's bedroom window.

Instead, lit in the theatrical beam of the spotlight, and struggling to rise from the rose bed, was a woman, her left arm crumpled up beneath her, and blood showing on her face. As he watched, she got to her feet and looked around, cradling her arm in her right hand. A sharp whistle sounded from round the house. Without a glance up at the window, she walked slowly off towards the corner which led to the side gate, limping and wincing with pain. As she disappeared from view, it swam into Stephen's head as if from a great distance who she was.

It was Vanessa Sawcroft, the Fordrace librarian, and with a strangely detached attention to detail, Stephen noticed that she was wearing her grey twill working suit.

DAY 3

PC Joe Vernon had just stepped out of the west door at St Wyndham's church, and was in the process of returning his helmet to his head, when Tom came hurrying up the graveyard path.

"Good morning, Reverend. I was wondering where you'd got to."

"Oh, morning, Joe." Tom came to a halt. "What can I do for you?"

If Joe noticed that the vicar was slightly flushed and out of breath, or that he spoke with an edge of impatience, he gave no sign. "Just wanted to speak to you briefly, Reverend. About yesterday's incident."

Tom hovered by the door. "Oh, right. Will it take long?"

"Only briefly, Reverend." PC Vernon removed his helmet and tucked it under his arm, in readiness for re-entering the church. Tom nodded.

"Of course. Come in, Joe."

He led the way to his study, unlocked the door and sat at his desk, placing a brown paper envelope on his in-tray as he did so. Sitting down heavily in the guest chair, the constable flicked erratically through his notebook, as if reminding himself of the key facts. Then he looked up and shrugged solidly.

"To be honest, Reverend, I don't think we'll have much luck with this one. We might come across it somewhere, by the side of the road; that's if it was just kids – you know, vandals – larking about. But if it was some collector, someone obsessed with a bit of old stone, who's to find it then?

"Not that we're exactly experts at stolen crosses, and I did contact Scotland Yard's Antiquities Division, but it was their opinion that the stolen fragment is very unlikely to be sold abroad, or even sold at all."

"I see," said Tom.

"If I were you sir, I should try and be content with what you've got." The constable stood up. "It's still quite a find after all."

Tom nodded. "I'm sure you're right, Joe. Thanks very much for all your efforts."

"That's all right, sir. Well, I'll see myself out."

As soon as the door closed, Tom reached out for the envelope in his in-tray. He prised off the sellotape which fastened the end, and drew out a grey booklet, bound and faded. The title was written on the cover in gold leaf.

THE BOOK OF THE WORM

by

A. J. WILLIS

Tom opened the blinds and let sunlight stream into the room. Then, pushing his chair away from the desk, he stretched out his legs and began to read.

May I cast light in a dark place

We do not set this book before you, reader,
to persuade you, nor to provide an exhaustive
account of the theories and learning of our
late friend, Mr Willis. Such a task would lie
beyond any man now living, for our friend
carried his work round in his head, and seldom entrusted himself to pen and ink. This
eccentricity, if such it was, was in part engen-
dered in him by the hostile reception given to
his ideas by certain prominent persons in the
field. To them we make no reply. To those
others who come upon this work, we say only
that it is incomplete, since disaster robbed
our friend of the power to pursue it to its
end. Only a day before his death, he entrusted the manuscript to one of our number for
safekeeping. That manuscript, together with
a few uncollected notes found on a separate
paper, comprises this book. We trust that it
may be of interest and stimulation. As to its
content, we, who are not experts in the field,
forebear to comment, only saying that we
always knew our friend to be a man of the
utmost honour and veracity.

> John Glynbourne
> Nathaniel Prior
> William Branch
> 1896

Introduction by the AUTHOR

I was born in Fordrace, and from my earliest childhood have been interested in the deep-rooted beliefs of my neighbours, which the years and the pace of change at the end of our great century have done little to diminish. From the start, however, I have had to fight against a very irritating disability in my efforts to learn about the local lore. My parents moved into Crow Wood shortly before I was born, and were still considered newcomers over thirty years later on the days they died. I early on discovered that being outsiders debarred us from the traditions of the local folk, and that though I might beg for details on certain subjects, my pleas were always quietly refused.

This difficulty, however, only made me more stubborn, and I have since found other ways to gain the information I desired. Perseverance over many years has paid off; I have discovered much, and if I have made some enemies in the process, I do not regret this.

For Reputation I care little. I only hope that by writing this account (and God grant that I might live to complete it) I may yet cast light in a dark place, where no light has shone for a long time.

Arthur James Willis
Crow Wood, Feb 1895

My first objective was always to discover what I could about ST WYNDHAM, the patron saint of the present church. Information about him is remarkably scanty. He does not feature in any of the official lists of the early church, and has no other churches dedicated to him. It was, however, clear to me that whoever this mysterious person was, he held a position of great importance in the Fordrace area, since no fewer than three farms, two copses and one stream contain his name in their title. It was also evident that his fame must have been widespread as early as the Conqueror's time, since a 'Wynndamms Church' is registered in the Domesday Book of 1067. The present church of St Wyndham was not built until 1086. This Saint, therefore, had to be Saxon or older. I began to search through certain monastic records, but for many years found no trace of him.

My searches bore fruit at last in Oxford. There, during my studies of the Welsh Triad poems of the sixth Century, I came upon mention of a certain Wyniddyn in a list of heroes. The poem includes this passage:

From the west Wyniddyn angered came,
Haw-frost hearted With oak and iron
He met that writhing Red-clawed thing,

Iron against fire Tooth against hand.
In that accounting Men became ash,
Our white wood blackened, Yet the band was
    drawn,
A band of stone, And the seal was carved.
So crept that famished fire A coward into the
    earth
And Wyniddyn rested.

What could we tell about this hero? His
fame lay in his victory over a terrible foe, a
foe whose weapons were teeth, claws and,
above all, fire. This enemy was subdued after
a ferocious battle in which many men were
killed, and white wood (trees? spears?) was
burnt. According to this Welsh source,
Wyniddyn fought his enemy with 'oak and
iron' – most probably a spear. The enemy
then disappeared into the earth, and it seems
it was forced to do so because of 'a band of
stone' and some kind of carved 'seal'. This
implies that Wyniddyn was a magician as
well as a warrior. Perhaps his magic was
strong enough to overcome the flames of his
adversary, but not strong enough to destroy
it.

Who was this enemy? Where had he fled?
What was the seal? There were many questions, but one was uppermost in my mind.
My suspicion was that this Wyniddyn was
none other than Fordrace's obscure St

Wyndham. Wales is not far from here, and there is a strong overlap in these parts between Celtic and Saxon heritage.

I had to wait a long time for confirmation. In 1892 I received permission to study the manuscripts in Hoston Priory, only 15 miles from Fordrace. Among them was a Prayer Scroll, tentatively dated to the Fourteenth Century, and one of its prayers contained a line which made my heart race:

Praise also to pale Wyniddham,
by whose seal the worm was cast down.

There was little doubt in my mind that the Wyniddyn of the Welsh poem and the Wyniddham of the Hoston Manuscript were one and the same. As well as the similarity between their names, there was the crucial 'seal' used to defeat an enemy. And now that enemy was identified – a 'worm' – the Old English word for dragon.

It took little daring to link this legendary hero with Fordrace's own St Wyndham. The very place names of our area point to the truth. Mr Limmins does not agree with me, and has seen fit to malign me in print, but who could deny now that Fordrace comes from Fyr-draca (that is, Dragon's Fire) and that the very name Wirrim, (how obvious it

seems now!), is a derivation of Wyrm – or
Worm.

What a breakthrough this seemed to me!
Light could now perhaps be cast on the thin,
persistent thread of folklore which runs
through the area, and which captured my
curiosity as a boy.

LOCAL LEGENDS OF THE HALL AND SEAL

In all my years of investigation, I have only
found one person prepared to talk at any
length about the Fordrace Legends. This
lady had lived under the shadow of the
Wirrim all her life, and indeed had never left
the county in her sixty years. It was in conversation with her that I received the first
proof that the old Wyniddyn legend was still
alive.

One day, we were idly chatting about our
childhoods, and childhood games. As a girl,
she said, she had learnt this following rhyme:

> Above the crag
> There bides the fire.
> Between the trees,
> There stands the hall.
> Beneath the hall,
> There lies the seal.

The good lady did not know what this meant;
she could only say that it was a common nonsense rhyme of her childhood, and that she

had sung it with her friends while skipping. They would sing it over and over again, faster and faster, until the skipping child caught her leg and fell.

The word seal again! I nearly shouted for joy! And fire – this was reference to the dragon or I was a Dutchman. But what did it mean?

Above the crag: there are many crags on the Wirrim – Raven, Dovetail, Old Toe, High Burr Span . . . It was impossible to know which was meant. But one thing was certain – the dragon was linked to the Wirrim, in this rhyme as in the place names.

I remembered then the significance of Wirrinlow, the old name for The Pit, that sizeable hollow high on the Wirrim. That this must stem from Wyrm-hlaew – 'Dragon's Mound' – is obvious to all except the foolish.

A pattern of belief was becoming clear to me.

Between the trees, there stands the hall: This was obscure. I felt this might refer to a hall Wyndham/Wyniddyn may have built. Maybe this was where he rested . . . Impossible to say.

Beneath the hall, there lies the seal: All the more likely then that Wyniddyn built the hall after his victory over the dragon. He buried the seal deep in the earth to protect it, and covered it over with his building.

Where could this building have been? I can only guess, and my guess leads back where we started from, at St Wyndham's church. We do not know when Wyniddyn was meant to have lived. It must have been before the Welsh poems, and therefore before the sixth century. There was a Saxon church on the present site by the Eleventh Century. Christianity would have arrived here centuries before. A hall or temple associated with the magician-warrior Wyniddyn would have presented problems to the Church. They would have been unable to destroy his influence on the people, and would have had to act quickly to link his old traditions with the new beliefs. The best way to do this was marry the two together. I think they set up their church on the site of the old pagan hall, and made Wyniddyn a local, unofficial saint.

Wyniddyn's seal, if it exists, is somewhere under the church, or within the church grounds.

What is this seal meant to have been? Who can say, but it evidently contains the magic the magician used to bind up the fire of his formidable enemy. No doubt it is best for Fordrace that it remains undisturbed!

WIRRINLOW
The 'Dragon's Mound' has a long history of folk tradition attatched to it.

[*There followed the stories of Marjorie Faversham, Meg Pooley and Mary Barratt which Tom had read in the library, the day before.*]

The good lady of the village admitted to me, after some hesitation, that The Pit was the setting for 'bad stories', though she refused to divulge them.

RELATED FOLKLORE

Interestingly, a good deal of more recent folklore surrounds one of the farms on the lower slopes of the Wirrim. Seen on maps from the Ordnance Survey, the Hardraker farm lies almost midway between Fordrace church and the Wirrinlow. It is an ancient small-holding, and seems at one time to have been prosperous, though it is now much restricted. A story my informant told me concerns an inhabitant of the farm several centuries ago.

'Bad John Hardraker was a Wizard. Tales were told about his dealings with fairies and worse. He put the eye on you if he caught you up on the hill. He flew too, high over the village church at night. One day a girlie was out on the hill after dark; she'd been fooling with her sweetheart in Stanbridge and was walking home late. She was getting pretty jumpy, what with the lateness of the hour and all, and she kept looking behind her as she went.

'Well, she looked back, and she looked back, and all at once she saw a man following her, a long way off. He was dressed in black and had a long cloak on. Well, she speeded up then I can tell you, but a little bit later she couldn't help herself, she had another look behind her. He was closer then, and he called out to her, "Slow yourself, Kitty, and bide a while with me!" She walked on all the faster when she heard that, but a little bit later she couldn't help herself, she looked behind her again. He was closer still this time, and she could see he had red eyes. And he called out again, "Slow yourself Kitty, and bide a while with me!" Now she began running, down the Haw path it was, down to the village, and her breath was coming in gulps. After a long while, she came near the mill stream, and she hadn't heard anything for a bit, so she snatches a quick look over her shoulder. And what should she see but him floating in the air not two feet behind her, with his cloak out and arms stretched and him smiling like a devil in hell. "Ah, you'll slow now, Kitty," he says, "and sure, you'll bide with me." And he makes a grab at her. But she gives a scream and makes one last effort, and she leaps over the stream, leaving a lock of her hair in his hands. And he can't cross running water, so he's left there, shaking his fist and hollering curses, but he can't do anything about it that time, so he has to go back up the hill.'

My good lady informant says that when she was young the children kept clear of the Hardraker farm and made signs against the evil eye when they passed close. I do not remember this in my boyhood. Nor have I found reliable records of this John Hardraker ever existing. Enquiries at the farm were not well received!

However, strong witchcraft traditions are linked to the Wirrim, and to Wirrinlow in particular. It may well be that the story of the ancient struggle between hero and dragon has left many magical associations in these parts.

(Our friend's continuous manuscript breaks off at this point. However, we include below a few disconnected notes, found tucked in his manuscript, which we suppose were to be worked into his book, had he lived.

J.G, N.P, W.B.)

Fire seems to crop up often in a lot of the tales.

July 1896: I have discovered that Meg Pooley and Mary Barratt were themselves Hardrakers!! They lived on that farm before their marriages in 1733. Perhaps this is the source of that farm's bad reputation? Perhaps not. Their brother, William Hardraker, lived on after them to a great age, dying in 1803.

Is it possible that the link to the past is stronger than I thought?

I have come across rumours – rumours only, mark you – which suggest that certain people in the village (I shall not write their names yet) have closer ties to the dragon legend than might be expected. Can there be a conspiracy? People will believe strange things. I must probe closer.

One boy says he saw something . . . He is scared, but I think I can offer him enough. All rumours. I must be careful.

In the Nineteeth Century!!

There is too much silence in this place. We shall see what is said when when the book is published. If it ever will be!

I must apply myself.

And there the book ended. Tom sat for a long time, deep in thought, with the faded pamphlet on his knee. Then he got up and went to look at the cross.

When Stephen came downstairs, Sarah was sitting out on the lawn drinking coffee and finishing off her grapefruit. She was in casual clothes, and there was an air about her of relaxation.

"You look dreadful," she said.

"Thanks."

Stephen sat himself in a garden chair. He surveyed the table. Raucous birdsong sounded from every tree.

"Oh. No cup," he said at last. He got up and wandered back into the kitchen.

"Sorry, I only made my breakfast this morning. You'll need a bowl as well, and the grapefruit's in the fridge."

"The cup will do."

Sarah appraised him as he returned. "Couldn't you at least put some trousers on?" she asked, surveying his boxer shorts and rumpled T-shirt.

"No." He poured out the coffee and looked over at the rose bed beneath the house. In the fragile sunshine of the early morning he could just see the marks where the soil had been rucked and flattened by a heavy weight.

Sarah blew her nose loudly. "It's going to be a bad day for hay fever," she said. "Again."

"This coffee's cold."

"Well, make some more. It's not my fault you get up late. Why are you in such a foul mood?"

Stephen made no response. He poured another cup of cold coffee. Then he said, "Are you going out this morning?"

"Well, no. I've got no houses to view till after lunch. So I thought I'd stay with you and Michael. I haven't seen enough of you lately." Sarah added a winning smile, but Stephen just looked sullen. She did her best to remain calm.

"Did you see Michael last night?" she asked, trying

to keep her voice cheerful. Stephen looked at her. He nodded.

"Was he OK? Only I sent him down to Mr Cleever's on a pretext. He was going to have a word with him, about – you know. I'm not sure it was the right thing to do, but it might make a difference . . ."

"It certainly had an effect."

"Oh. Good. I hope it was the right thing."

Stephen sat back in the chair and stretched his neck back to where it ached, looking straight up at the sky. He yawned savagely. Such sleep as he had had in the hours before dawn had done him few favours. His whole body was out of sorts.

He hoped Sarah would change her mind and go away. He had a few things he wanted to discuss with his brother.

After waiting by the window for a time, Stephen had tried to rouse Michael, but without success. His breathing had been slow and deep, as if heavily asleep; there had been a reddish tinge about his eyes, and his colouring was pale. At last Stephen had lifted him into bed, and gone downstairs, switching on all the lights and checking the locks. He had felt sick with fatigue and stress, but no longer sensed a threat from outside the house. The tingling in his own eyes, which had burned strongly ever since he saw the reptile souls, had subsided almost immediately after the incident at the window. The assault had ended. For the time being.

"There you are; at least one of you has the decency to put his trousers on."

Stephen had not seen Michael appear at the kitchen door, and he looked him over sharply. Michael was dressed and seemingly washed, and his face was perfectly dreadful. He had a dazed expression, and there was a blankness somewhere in his eyes which made Stephen squirm in his chair, even as he gave his brother a careless greeting. Surely Sarah would notice the eyes too, and think of Tom's accusations.

But Sarah seemed to notice nothing.

"The cups are in the kitchen," she said. "I didn't expect you down so early. There's grapefruit in the frid—"

"I couldn't get your pamphlets." Michael's voice cut in tonelessly as he walked over the grass.

"Oh, that's all right—"

"For the simple reason that they didn't exist."

"I don't—" Sarah turned the red of confusion. Stephen frowned. His eyes had tingled faintly.

Michael rested his hands on the vacant chair and considered his sister. "What were you trying to do, sending me to Cleever?" he said. "Did you think he'd give me a talking to? Did you think he might Do Me Good? I told you the truth yesterday morning, and it wasn't good enough for you, was it? Before the day was out you sold me for your peace of mind. Well, don't think you can pull the wool over my eyes. You can't any more. All I want to know now is—was it his idea, or yours?"

Stephen stirred in his chair. "Forget it, Michael," he said.

But Michael took no notice. "Was it his idea, or yours?" he repeated, raising his voice. "Was it his idea, or yours?" By now Sarah had had enough.

"It was his idea! Does that satisfy you? I was worried.

He said he would talk to you. If it was a mistake, I'm sorry. Can't you see? I was upset and it seemed like the right thing at the time."

"Fair enough," said Stephen. "Now do us a favour, Michael, and shut up."

But a sudden curtain of contempt had fallen across Michael's mind. Out of the confused images and feelings awash within him rose suddenly a clear picture of his sister's grotesque stupidity. Her miserable ignorance, her trifling weariness, her pathetic and shabby emotional games – all were suddenly made plain. Stephen, sitting next to him, felt the shift in the atmosphere, a heat grow in his own eyes. He stole a glance sideways at his brother and saw the eyes refocus, becoming distant and unreflective. He saw him staring at his sister.

"Michael," he said at once, "leave it. Leave it alone."

He stood up, but before he could act he knew Sarah had already sensed Michael's invisible attack. She shivered, and something behind her eyes seemed to crumple as if a sudden grief had come upon her. She looked like she was about to cry, and did not know why she did so, but instead she got up, whey-faced and shaking.

"What are you looking at me like that for?" she cried. "Stop it! God, you're sick! What's wrong with you?" Then she shuddered and half-ran towards the kitchen door.

Michael turned to follow her with his eyes. He didn't blink.

"Sarah!" Stephen caught up with her at the door, and hugged her. She was still shivering.

"He didn't mean it," he found himself saying

inanely. "He's a little confused." Sarah hugged him tighter.

"I felt—" she began, and stopped, at a loss for words. Stephen did not blame her.

"Go and see Tom," he said. "You need a break from us this morning." He paused, and looked over at the motionless figure by the table. "I'll deal with him."

Michael, at that moment, was filled with a ferocious joy. The colours of another's soul had been revealed naked before him, and where he had once been in awe of that hidden thing, his awe was now turned entirely in on himself and his own power. He had seen that slow and stupid dog-shaped soul quail before his gaze. He had seen its surface shudder, its outline weaken and its colours grow pale and indistinct. The flow of motion had slowed perceptibly, and the life-force in it had stuttered, and all of this because of his own clear gaze. All of this through fear!

Fear.

The soul had sensed it. The colours had revealed it. And Michael had fed on it in that moment with a wild delight, drawing strength on the fragility of his sister's soul.

He laughed to himself.

The soul was a pretty bauble, it was true. He had noticed that right from the start. Even his stupid sister's was exquisite, beautiful as jewels. But what right did she have to it? She would never see it, never weigh its beauty in the balance. Never know the subtlety and scope of its fluctuations, its endless vibrations which made the heart sing to see them. It was wasted on her.

Michael felt like a collector of great wealth and wisdom, who sees a priceless gem owned by an ignorant amateur, someone who would never truly know what she held in her hand.

And with that perception came a contempt for the owner, and all such owners like her, and a new distaste for the gaudy objects in their possession.

"You fools," he whispered under his breath, looking over at his brother and sister by the kitchen door. "You're poor sad fools."

It was only when she closed the kissing gate behind her and started walking up the path to the church door that Sarah began to feel better. Throughout the short drive down to the village, her hands had shaken at the wheel and her head had spun; so much so, that she had once had to pull into the side until her vision cleared.

Now, as she walked up past the gravestones, the memory of Michael's anger grew less acute and her spirits rose. There were answers to all problems, no matter how insoluble they might seem.

Sarah pushed open the door and looked inside. She could see Tom standing by the vestry curtains, looking down at the cross. He paid no attention as she entered and pushed the door to, nor even when she came up close behind him.

"Tom."

He visibly started. "Oh – Hi, Sarah! You gave me

quite a shock." He hugged her, distractedly. "Sorry about last night."

"That's all right. What are you doing? You were completely lost."

"I was thinking. Listen, Sarah, it's crazy, but you know what I was talking about last night? I think I'm on to something."

"It can wait, Tom. I need your help with Michael. He's just – done something which is really hard to explain, but it was bad, and I need your help."

"Of course. Sit down and fire away."

As Sarah spoke, she became uncomfortably aware that the morning's argument didn't sound nearly as horrid as it had actually been, and she was unable to express quite why it had upset her so much. But Tom listened carefully, and nodded as she finished.

"I'll come and talk to him. I should have done so yesterday. He does sound unsettled, and it may be that his talk with Cleever has made him worse. But Sarah, why on earth did you send him there? Cleever would infuriate a saint."

Sarah felt herself frown. "All right, it may not have been the best idea, but at least he seemed interested."

"Meaning I'm not? Well, let's not argue about it. I'll come back with you in a minute. But listen, Sarah, I've got to tell you something first. It won't take a sec, and it's too exciting to wait. I think I know what this cross is!"

He grinned with scarcely controlled excitement. "Look, you remember what I was telling you about yesterday? Well, read this. It won't take a minute. It's really short. And there are some strange things about it that you won't believe! Please, Sarah. Have a read."

He handed her a faded pamphlet. Sarah looked at it dubiously.

"Go on, Sarah. Please. You'll think I'm mad otherwise."

She sighed with exasperation. "All right, Tom, but I'm acting under protest."

"OK, OK." While she read, Tom hopped about her, seemingly unable to keep still. He looked over her shoulder, scuttled over to look at the cross, and came back again, all the time making little laughs of amazement to himself. Sarah grew extremely irritated. Finally, she looked up.

"All right, I've read it. Now what's the point? I want to go back home, and I want you to come back with me."

"In a minute. How did it strike you?"

"The ravings of a madman. Where on earth did you get it?"

"The Birmingham Research Library. I went up especially early this morning. Listen, Sarah, didn't anything strike you about it? When he talks about that Welsh poem, and the seal, the seal that he thought was buried on church land?"

"You think the cross—?"

"Is the seal. Yes. Yes I do. Come and look at it."

She came over, her interest jostling with her impatience. The stone lay below her, ornately carved and very old.

"It is a dragon, isn't it?" he said.

Sarah nodded. She followed the sinuous lines

around the interlacing body from the long thin head, with its rows of teeth, round the looping back, past the splaying claws and so on to the endless tail.

"And you think—" Sarah cleared her throat. Suddenly the air seemed heavy. She was not quite sure what she was going to say. "But this is a cross. Willis said that Wyniddyn was pre-Christian. He wouldn't have made this, would he?"

"Willis didn't know. He was only speculating. Wyniddyn might have come at the time when the first missionaries were reaching these parts. Maybe he was a partly Christian magician. Who can tell?"

"And this is his seal?"

"I think so. And Sarah – I dug it up."

"Yes. Oh, Tom – look." The excitement had won her over. She traced around the great circle with her finger. "A stone band, surrounding the dragon. Well, almost surrounding it."

Tom felt a sudden guilty pang. "I didn't break it," he said, more sharply than he would have wished. "It was broken already, when we found it in the ground."

"I know that, Tom. You don't have to shout."

"I wasn't shouting."

"You were. Anyway, forget it. It's a pity, but there it is."

"But Sarah, someone stole the arm, and you remember that last bit in the book, about people still having ties to the dragon legend? I didn't understand it quite, but he was connecting it to those stories of witchcraft long ago, and implying that some form of magic belief was continuing, behind all the fairy tales and nursery rhymes."

"Tom, he was writing a hundred years ago."

"I know, but if it survived till then, who's to say it hasn't survived till now?"

"Oh, come on, Tom. People aren't stupid. They wouldn't—"

"So why steal the cross?"

"Don't interrupt me! It's all very interesting, Tom, and may have some relevance to the cross, but don't try and take it too far. There are other things to think about."

"But I haven't finished, Sarah. Listen to what else I found out. On the way home I called in on the Stanbridge Herald and had a little browse in their archives. I read a couple of articles from 1895 about Willis's death – he died in a house fire – and there were rumours of foul play."

"So?"

"Arson was the theory. Only no one could work out how it had been done. Willis's house wasn't made of matchsticks. It was a solid brick affair. The weather had been wet. Yet the thing was an inferno in moments, according to witnesses."

"Probably just a study lamp knocked over, or a spark from his grate."

"Possibly. Except Willis had only just returned to the house after a few days' absence. He'd been in it for a matter of minutes when the place went up, according to friends who'd left him. Would he have had time to get a fire going?"

"Don't ask me. Now, Tom . . ."

Tom reached over and grabbed her by the arm. "But don't you see, Sarah? What if it all links together?

What if Willis's ideas about some sort of conspiracy weren't utter moonshine? What if he was closing in upon something which had been kept hidden for hundreds of years?"

"Tom—"

"They'd have been only too glad to shut him up, Sarah, don't you see? And think of all the talk of fire in his book, and how he died. Could that be a coincidence?"

"Yes," said Sarah. "It could. Honestly, Tom, you're beginning to sound like Mrs Gabriel."

"But that's the point. Arthur Willis has been forgotten, but the undercurrent of belief he was investigating hasn't gone by any means. Mrs Gabriel's tapped into it even now. That's what set me thinking in the first place. The cross is at the centre of all this, Sarah, and part of it has been stolen."

"So part of it has been stolen! Perhaps somebody somewhere hasn't let the old ways drop! Maybe! Or maybe it's all a series of coincidences and it doesn't amount to anything. You haven't proof either way, and I'm fed up of wasting time. Are you coming back to see Michael, or aren't you?"

"Just one more thing, Sarah, and I'm all yours. Listen, I got this book at Birmingham Research Library. I went there because Vanessa Sawcroft looked up in the Hereford and Worcester Central Library Index and couldn't find Willis there."

"I'm going, Tom."

"Wait. It turns out she was right. The one at Birmingham is one of only two copies in the whole country."

"Well?"

"The Research Library keeps records of who comes to take its books out. You have to join it, leaving name and address, and pay a membership fee. Well, I enquired whether I was the first to ask for 'The Book of the Worm', and it turned out I wasn't. The man at the desk even gave me the other person's name, so I could share my research with them. He gave me a name and address. Want to know who it was?"

Sarah looked at him stony-faced.

"Well, I'll tell you. Vanessa Sawcroft."

"So?"

"Sarah, she told me she knew nothing of the book! She lied to me! Or deliberately misled me, anyway. Why should she do that? And that's not all. Guess where she lives? Hardraker Farm."

"What?"

"Hardraker Farm. That was the address she gave the library. And you read what Willis had to say about that place!"

"Tom—" Sarah seemed to be having difficulty controlling herself. "Tom, I've listened to you for twenty minutes now. I'm not listening to you any more. You're not making any sense. The bit about the cross is great – I'm not surprised you're excited. But the rest – look, it's just nonsense. I don't know why Vanessa Sawcroft didn't tell you about the book. Maybe she forgot."

"Oh, come on—"

"Maybe she didn't. Maybe she's pissed off with you for going on and on about your obsessions and wanted to get you out of her hair. Who knows? But she doesn't live at Hardraker Farm, and I know that because only yesterday I was invited to look round it with a view to a valuation. It's empty, Tom. No one lives there. Stop trying to find patterns where none exists."

Tom looked doubtful. "Who says it's empty?"

"Mr Cleever. Remember him? Parish councillor, church warden – you know the one. He's the executor. Are you saying he's lying too?"

"Well, no – but the whole thing's too much—"

"Bloody hell, Tom!" Sarah was furious now. "That's it. Here's what we'll do. In two hours, I want you at my house for lunch, to talk to Michael. In the meantime, I'm going to do you a favour. I shall go up to Hard-raker Farm right now and take a good look round. And while I'm there, I shall keep my eyes open for flying wizards, lying librarians or cross thieves. OK? If I see any of them, I shall let you know. If I don't, perhaps you will stop wittering on about this bloody cross!"

With that, she turned on her heel and stormed out, slamming the door so hard that the nave echoed. Tom was left staring after her, still trying to think up what to say.

24

Stephen bided his time once Sarah had gone. He loitered inside the house, showering and getting dressed, and all the time keeping an eye out of various windows to make sure his prey made no run for it. But Michael seemed content to sit in the garden, drinking the remains of the cold coffee and gazing out into the hills.

"That's fine," thought Stephen. "Just stay right where you are."

By and by, Michael seemed to gain a slight lease of life. He stretched, yawned and walked back into the kitchen, where he opened various cupboards in an aimless fashion. But if he was hungry, nothing took his fancy. He stood undecided for a moment, a vacuous expression on his face. Then at last he made for the hall. As he passed a darkened recess, a silent figure stepped out behind him. An iron arm looped round his neck and began to throttle him, while another hand pulled his arm up behind his back in a policeman's grip. Michael struggled wildly, but the figure had no mercy and marched him up the stairs. When he hesitated, he was encouraged by kicks and twists of the arm; when he stumbled, he was wrenched onwards by the loop round his neck. In this manner, gasping and dishevelled, he soon arrived in the bathroom, where the shower waited.

"Right," said Stephen. "Time for a little chat."

Michael squirmed sullenly. "There's nothing to talk about. I'm tired. I want to sleep."

"Nothing to talk about? Oh dear, we are in a bad way." Stephen gripped still harder. "Firstly—" (Here he took Michael firmly by the neck and forced his head down into the basin.) "—we're going to talk about last night. Then—" (Here he turned the dial to freezing and took the shower head off the holder.) "—we're going to talk about what's going on in that stupid head of yours. Any questions, before we start?"

"Get off, you fool," came a voice, echoing up from the basin.

"Fine." Stephen turned on the water and stuck the shower head down the back of Michael's shirt. The water jetted down, briefly ballooning the shirt outwards before it erupted out at his waistline in an icy waterfall. His trousers were soon saturated, and a pleasing pool spread out on the tiles of the floor. Michael struggled manfully, but Stephen's years told.

"How's it going?" he asked pleasantly, after three minutes.

"You'll regret this, you bloody idiot," was the only reply, and for several minutes more the water gushed, until the back of Michael's clothes hung so heavy that his trousers fell down.

"Still not talking?" Stephen seemed regretful and surprised. The answer was forcible, and in the negative.

Stephen was thus pushed into more extreme measures, which were justified by the almost immediate response.

"All right, you bastard," said Michael. "You can stop. I'll talk with you, but it won't do you any good."

Stephen allowed his victim to return to his bedroom, dry himself and recline at leisure on the bed. He stood by the door, leaning against the wall nonchalantly in an effort to maintain the authority he had won over his brother in such a messy fashion.

"Well?" he said, finally. "What happened?"

In a sullen monotone, Michael told him what he could remember of his dream; the sense of depth, the perceptive eye from under the earth, and the beauty of the souls, which their owners could never comprehend. But he chose not to talk about the voice, and what it had told him.

"And why were you by the window?" asked Stephen.

"I don't remember." Michael's lie came easily, and he made a smooth change of direction. "You must see it too," he said, a touch of colour returning to his voice. "No matter how stupid you are, you must see what a tragedy it is. How can we respect them? They just don't understand what they have there, what they lose every time they die. But we can understand the value of it – at least I can."

"And what," asked Stephen, "is this value?"

"The beauty of the souls, of course – you must see that! The beauty of those shining things! They're like jewels."

"They don't look much like jewels to me. There's too much movement in them."

"The movement's not important. That's just caused by thoughts and feelings – it's bound up with the characters of the people who own the souls. Well, who cares about that?"

"Hold on, how d'you mean, 'own them'? They *are* them, aren't they?"

"Maybe, but it's not something we can understand, and the souls are far more beautiful than the people themselves, anyway. We've worried too much into what the shape and colour actually mean, but that's all pointless. It doesn't get us anywhere. The beauty is all that counts." Michael spoke slowly, carefully, as if remembering something he had learned long ago.

"The point is, with the sight, we can own the souls too. Switch them on just by willing it. Make them change colour, too . . ." A wistful note entered his voice. "I wish I could see like that all the time. It stops my eyes hurting." Michael refocused suddenly with practised ease. He gazed at Stephen for a minute.

"Even yours is precious. Even yours. Like something made of pearl."

Stephen felt a sharp pain in his forehead and a slight sense of nausea. He shuddered, but did his best to conceal it.

"Snap out of it," he said. "I don't like you looking like that at me."

Michael gave a snort of mirth. "I know. I can see that easily enough. Your soul's quivering like a leaf. Our stupid sister's quivered just the same. Strange, they're still pretty when they're scared. More than ever, if anything."

Stephen gritted his teeth and forced himself to look straight into the curiously swirling blanks of his brother's eyes. He felt a strong urge to make the change himself, but he resisted it. "That's another thing," he said. "What kind of worm are you, to turn on Sarah like that?"

There was a lessening of the pain; a flicker of concern passed across Michael's face. Then he laughed, and his eyes changed back. The pain in Stephen's forehead vanished.

"All right, granted," he said. "It was unnecessary. I just wanted to see what it felt like. I won't do it again, if you don't want me to."

"You'd better not, mate," said Stephen.

"Are you finished?" asked Michael. "I'm tired, as I think I mentioned."

"No." Stephen forced himself to think. What had he been saying?

"How come," he said at last, "you're suddenly ignoring the connection between soul and character? You were obsessed by that yesterday, when you saw Cleever. Remember that?" He looked straight at Michael as he spoke.

He'd scored a point, he could see that at once. A faint cloud crossed his brother's brow, a flash of a memory that had been pushed into a recess and forgotten. Michael spoke faintly, as out of a distant gulf.

"The shape . . ." He paused.

"Was a reptile," reminded Stephen.

"I was taken in by the shape. It doesn't matter what the shape is. I said that just now."

"That's not what you thought yesterday. It was evil, you said. And I agreed with you. It was."

"The dream changed all that. Evil, good . . . no, that's not what souls are about. They're about beauty, and if you've got the power, and the will, like I have, you can see that beauty whenever you want. You should know what I mean, Stephen. You've got the gift too. Perhaps you'll have the same dream tonight."

"I hope not."

"You will, I expect. You're a little bit behind me. It'll come."

Michael rolled over on the bed, and pushed his face into the pillow. His eyes were shut, and Stephen suddenly noticed, with a shock, the hollowness of his face. The cheeks were pale and the area around the eyes was chafed, as if he had been crying.

"And why were you at the window?" Stephen asked again.

"I told you, I don't remember anything about it. I just remember waking up this morning, in my bed. Now I'm going to sleep. I'll see you soon."

Stephen left the room. His head ached.

For an hour or more he lay on his own bed, where the need for thinking won over the desire for sleep. He could no longer ignore it: the change to his sight was beginning to affect Michael's mind, in a way which Stephen did not like, nor begin to understand. It was tied up with Cleever somehow and the woman at the window, and if Michael had forgotten the look of the reptile souls, Stephen had not. The hunger in their eyes . . . What were they after? What did they want?

Cleever . . . Ms Sawcroft . . . He groaned aloud. All the village might be in on it for all he knew!

Well, not quite all. Not Sarah. Not Tom.

Tom. He put the half-formed idea out of his mind. The man was a minister. If he heard one word of this, he'd bring out the bible, bells and candles and start an exorcism. Besides, he was biased against Michael, no question of that, and probably didn't want anything to do with him again.

So he was on his own. A thrill of anxiety ran through his body and his eyes began to ache. All of a sudden, he knew that whatever was happening to Michael was slowly happening to himself.

"It's no good," he said aloud. "We need help. We need help badly."

He went down to the kitchen, raided the pantry and opened two cans of spaghetti hoops. By the time he'd polished them off cold, with a fork, from the tin, he had made up his mind.

Before leaving, he looked in at his brother, and discovered him still asleep. His breathing was very slow and the room was thick and stuffy. Stephen opened the window, then thought better of it, and closed it again. He remembered his brother's last mumbled words. 'I'll see you soon.'

Not till I say so, you won't, thought Stephen.

Slipping his hand round the door, Stephen found the key in the lock. He withdrew it stealthily, shut the door and locked it. Then he put the key in his pocket and left the house.

When Stephen rounded the corner onto the green, and was faced with the brash, careless summer face of the village, his resolution nearly failed him. The middle-aged gossiped outside the grocers, Captain Cone sat in his van, handing out soft ice-cream to sticky children, and the sun beat down pleasantly on all ordinary things. How absurd it seemed, to bring forth into that ordered world experiences so confused and strange. And how much more absurd it was to imagine anyone would believe them. Stephen almost despaired. Twice he halted his bicycle on the edge of the green, twice he stood astride it, deep in thought, and twice he cycled slowly on. Absurd though it was, for the moment his hope was all he had.

As he passed into St Wyndham's churchyard, a sudden pain behind his eyes flared up and died away. With it went the feeling of suppressed panic at his own absurdity which had beset him since setting out. Behind his back, the bustle of the village grew dim, and the tumbled gravestones and bent yews beside the wall signalled an older scale of values, longer of memory and slower to judge or condemn.

When he entered the church, and felt the restful solemnity of cool grey stone all about him, his reassurance had grown still further. He found it easier to tell than he had imagined.

"Tom," he said, "I have something important to say, though you will think I'm mad."

Perhaps Tom could have suggested a reason for the reassurance Stephen felt on entering the church. But he did not think of it; he was too busy wrestling with the implications.

Stephen told him nearly all. He began by telling him of the Pit and what had happened there, to Michael and to him. When he said this, Tom took a sharp breath, but said nothing.

He spoke of the sight and what it could do. When he said this, Tom frowned and almost interrupted, but instead held himself back and stared intently at the diamond panes on the window above the chancel.

He spoke of Mr Cleever and the nature of his soul. When he said this, Tom started and cursed under his breath, shifting his gaze for a second to the cross, lying quietly in its corner.

He spoke of the assault on Michael's room the night before. When he mentioned the name of the figure at the window, Tom rose and began pacing the nave furiously, rubbing his head with his hand.

Finally Stephen told him of Michael, and his behaviour that morning.

"When Michael was at Cleever's, and first saw under the surface, there was something Cleever said to him. 'What you see, you will become.' And something is happening to him, something which is right up Cleever's street. That's why I've told you this, because I don't know what to do about it. Please don't think I'm mad."

He finished, almost hopefully, because Tom's silence throughout his speech had puzzled him.

Tom said, "I don't think you're mad, Stephen, although it's very hard to accept your story about . . . the soul. But other things . . . Other things are not as difficult for me to believe as you'd imagine."

Stephen sat stony-faced. "To be honest, I'd almost prefer it if you laughed at me. It would be a little more believable. I would in your position."

"On its own, your story about the sight, and the . . . attack would be impossible to believe. But I was with you when we found Michael. I saw his condition, and was with the doctor when he said he was stumped. But more importantly – I've been having some . . . problems of my own in the last couple of days."

"Like what?" asked Stephen.

He told him. It seemed the only proper thing to do.

"It isn't difficult," he said at last, "to see how people with the sight could mistake the souls they saw for imps and devils, and it isn't difficult either to see why others thought them witches."

Stephen flushed. "Oh right, so you think I'm a witch."

"No, but I'm saying this power comes from a very dubious source. And you've no right, either, to assume that what you see are souls."

"What else could they be? Don't get on your high religious horse about it!"

"I'm not!"

"You bloody are."

"OK, OK." Tom controlled himself with difficulty. "We're losing valuable time. Cleever poses some threat to Michael and we shouldn't leave him alone until we understand things better. Oh Lord! Sarah!" He broke off suddenly, horror-struck.

"What? What about her?"

"She's gone to Hardraker Farm."

"Is that a problem?"

"Cleever asked her to go there. And it was mentioned in the book. A bad place."

"What! And you let her go?"

"Look, I didn't know about Cleever then. All right, enough. We don't know that she's in any danger. Michael we know is. I say we get Michael here, to the church. Historically it must have the best protection, if it was Wyniddyn's hall."

"It didn't prevent them breaking in before," objected Stephen.

"Have you a better idea? We get him here, then we'll look for Sarah. Then we'll consider the position. I think we need that bit of cross."

"They've probably destroyed it," said Stephen, "or flung it down a mine."

"They may have done, but I don't think we should assume it. Something is going on which is making them get pushy. Why are they so keen on influencing your brother? What are they after, and why aren't they after you?"

"Don't forget, I only got a little dose. Michael might have been soaking it up for hours, for all we know. Maybe that makes him more useful."

"The question is, for what? But come on, let's get moving."

Tom's car was parked on the other side of the green, in a small lot reserved for the public servants of Fordrace. He and Stephen crossed over the road and headed across the grass, which was worn into an August yellow and flecked all over with toddlers and litter. A Punch-and-Judy man was setting up his booth in the very centre of the green, and a small excited crowd was gathered in front of the red and white striped awning in anticipation of a show. Nearby, queues had formed around Captain Cone.

They had almost reached the centre of the green when Mr Cleever walked down his garden path towards them. He walked swiftly, wearing a white suit and carrying a cane by his side. Stephen and Mr Cleever caught sight of each other at the self-same moment. Stephen saw the large head jerk forward suddenly, like a dog that has just picked up a scent.

Stephen started to utter a warning to Tom, but an explosion of pain erupted in his head and sent him reeling. As he cried out, clasping his hands over his eyes, he sensed something enter his mind; an alien presence, which moved clumsily here and there, filthy and searching. This trespass into his most private self was too much for Stephen. The heat flared within him, and with a furious thrust he drove the questing presence from his mind.

All this happened in the briefest of moments. Tom had barely registered the boy's discomfort by the time Stephen had driven the intruder from within him and began to run.

He ran at breakneck speed across the green, squinting between the fingers that shielded his burning eyes from the light. Conscious only of the need to escape the approaching enemy, he created havoc where he went, bowling toddlers over like ninepins, stumbling over prone couples, dashing ice creams from several hands, leaving a screaming, cursing, gasping stress of citizens in his wake. Twice he received kicks and punches of his own, as furious bystanders sought revenge, but he dared not stop. Indeed, he hardly noticed them, since all the time he was aware of a presence following him, circling his mind and probing for entry.

Off the green and over the road between the cars he ran, towards the Olde Mille Tea Room and its white chairs and tablecloths arranged in gleaming order on the tarmac. Three chairs he spun over, one old lady he caused to drop a sticky bun into her flowery lap, and one old colonel he inspired to lash out with a stick, before he had vaulted over the wall, and disappeared into the alley that ran down beside the Tea Room towards the mill stream.

As he disappeared from view, so he passed beyond Mr Cleever's range, and that gentleman was forced to turn his attention elsewhere.

The Reverend Tom Aubrey had been stock still, watching Stephen's erratic progress with an open mouth. Now he turned, and noticed for the first time the man in white approaching him.

Oh no, he thought. For an instant he was tempted to follow Stephen's example and run for it, but the image of the Vicar of Fordrace cantering across the green encouraged him to stay put and bluff it out. After all, he told himself, he doesn't know I suspect him.

"Good afternoon, Reverend." Mr Cleever was saluting Tom with a cheery wave of his stick, and smiling. "And what a fine afternoon it is. Encourages the young to unleash their energy, which does them good. Young MacIntyre can fairly pelt, can't he? Should get him in the Youth Athletics Team."

"Yes, quite." Tom searched desperately for some mundane piece of church procedure to discuss. To his horror, he found he could not remember which committees Mr Cleever was on, let alone any suitable details which could be used in conversation. What could he say? What—

A small, firm pressure, in the centre of his forehead, as if a stick was being gently pushed into his skull. And then—

Suddenly the pressure became a tear, and with a mental ripping, his mind was wrenched open and exposed. He felt something enter, and the force of it was so great that he nearly fainted.

A voice in his head. 'What do you know?'

He could not refuse. The occupying presence squeezed his mind and the information came vomiting out of him in gobbets of thought.

'The cross. I know you stole it. And Vanessa Sawcroft is in it too. I know because of Willis's book. She tried to put us off the scent, but I found out anyway. And I intend to protect Michael from you.'

A small girl with blonde hair, carrying an immense cone of melting ice cream, wandered between them. Some ice cream dripped from the cone onto the grass. She stopped and turned round to look at it, and some ice cream splashed on Mr Cleever's shoe. Both he and Tom were statue-still. A mother's voice called and the small girl tottered away.

'We don't know why you want him. But Stephen has seen your soul and that is enough. Also, I believe you are linked to the dragon.'

Mr Cleever's eyes never blinked. Tom looked into them and could not escape. Around them the hubbub of the village green was dulled, as if heard from under water.

'We are going to the cottage now, to pick Michael up. Then we shall find Sarah at the farm.'

For the first time, Mr Cleever's expression flickered. His eyes narrowed slightly.

'Hardraker farm.' Tom sicked the thought up.

Mr Cleever's head was bent slightly forward in an attitude of extreme concentration. All of a sudden, he straightened. Tom's mind juddered as the presence withdrew. His ears popped. He felt the noise of the green erupt all around him. Screaming, laughing, shouting, cars starting . . . Mr Punch was beating the living daylights out of Judy with a stout oak cudgel. "That's the way to do it!" he screamed in triumph.

"Thank you, Reverend," said Mr Cleever. "It's always a pleasure to talk with you. And very instructive. Goodbye." He gave a wave of his stick, and walked swiftly back towards his house.

Tom stood expressionless in the centre of the green, eyes wide with an inner horror.

Michael woke suddenly. He lay a while in the bed without moving, tasting a sharp acidic flavour in his mouth. The room was very hot; his pillow was damp against his face. He had been dreaming again; he knew it, although he could not recall anything about what he had dreamed. Only a faint writhing sensation in his stomach, just before he awoke. Strange: now it had entirely gone.

He sat up with difficulty, and looked at the clock, blinking to remove a slight film that had formed upon his eyes. It was 1.35. He had slept for four hours, longer than he would have guessed. He should have been well refreshed by now, but, as often happened when he slept during the day, he instead felt irritable and out of sorts. His body was raw and tingly, as if he had slid down a cheese-grater. And he was hot. The window was closed and the sunlight had pooled in upon the bed. He would have a shower.

Showering reminded him of Stephen, and a hot flush came to his face. There had been no call for what he'd done. Oh, he might strut and threaten, and use his size to bully, but he'd still wriggled and squirmed when he'd had the sight turned on him. And soon there'd come a time when physical strength would matter not at all.

Michael would have a shower, and then . . . he'd see.

He got off the bed and walked towards the closed door. Before he'd taken two strides, he noticed a tiny change in the familiar surroundings. The key had been taken from the lock. A sudden suspicion quickened his step. He rattled the handle.

Locked. And no need to guess who by.

For a moment, Michael could not believe it. Stephen had locked him in, in his own bedroom. His own brother. The shock of the discovery disorientated him. 'Am I my brother's keeper?', he thought, 'and is he mine?' With an upsurge of fury he kicked the door, jarring his toes and causing a further burst of rage. As he did so, his focus changed, drowning the room in red. Heat burst from his eyes; he snarled like an animal.

At that moment, in the distant hall, the telephone rang.

He froze in his anger. He knew it was for him, that he must answer it. The beating of his pulse in his forehead told him so. And he was locked in.

The telephone rang again.

Michael fell to his knees in frustration, his hands clenched, pointing towards the door that barred the way.

Stephen – I'll kill you when I catch you—

The telephone rang again.

—when I get out.

Somewhere in Michael's brain, his anger concentrated into a block so hot and dense he felt he had a burning coal lodged in his skull. His eyes had closed, but it seemed a red curtain billowed behind his lids. Across his body, every limb relaxed. His hands fell against the carpet, his back sagged slightly where he knelt. All the rage and tension rushed upwards into his head, to a hidden place, where it grew, with mounting speed, until the pain and pressure became unbearable and it seemed his head must split.

Then he opened his eyes.

And the door caught fire.

Michael did not see the flame come springing from the centre of the panel. For the moment he was blind; red shooting lines, like veins, crossed and recrossed along the surface of his eyes. His mouth hung slightly open, but no noise came out. The only sound in the room was the crackling of the timber and the popping of the paint as it shrank and blistered on both sides of the wood. And behind it all, the telephone rang on.

So intense was the heat concentrated on the door that within three minutes the centre of the panel had fallen away, and still the flames were licking outwards on all sides, a ring of fire expanding. Through the growing hole, the passage was filled with smoke.

All at once, Michael coughed, his lungs drawing in their first breath since he had sunk to the floor. His chest heaved and wracked, his lips drawn back like a beast's. At last, his eyes watered and cleared. His red sight had gone. He gazed ahead, uncomprehending, at the blazing hoop that had nearly severed his bedroom door in two. Beyond it, somewhere far away, beyond a corridor of smoke and scattered ash, a telephone was ringing for him.

He stood up, legs weak as water, and a new strength poured into them. With it, a terrible confidence awoke within. The fire was dying, having reached the fringes of the door. Only the corners remained, smouldering, attached to each other with thin blackened strips of wood. Halfway down, the rectangular metal lock protruded from the frame, naked of wood. It had warped under the heat.

Michael stepped up to the halo of charred wood and touched one edge lightly with a finger. It was warm, crispy. Then he stepped through the space, small flakes of ash settling in his hair as he bowed his head to pass beneath. He walked across a pile of debris and down the passageway, leaving a trail of grey footprints in the carpet. As he walked, he laughed quietly to himself.

At the foot of the stairs, in a niche beside the stick rack and the hat stand, the telephone was ringing. Michael picked it up.

"I'm glad you could make it, Michael," Mr Cleever said.

27

The Hardraker farmstead lay two miles from Fordrace, hunkered down on the slopes of an outstetched spur of the Wirrim. As Sarah drove along the untarmaced road, she passed endless small fields filled with pinched rootcrops, untended high pasture, and scrawny coppices of pine. These were the Hardraker lands.

Sarah knew a little of the farm. To her grandmother, the name Hardraker had been a byword for sloth and criminal neglect. The family had a bad reputation and they had let their farm drift to rack and ruin. Once it had been a viable estate – now, with the death of the last Hardraker, it was forlorn and deserted. In summer, no one worked the fields; in autumn, the rains turned the wild crops to green-black sludge.

Good, then, that it was coming on the market. Someone would turn it back into a working farm. Sarah spotted the huddled rooftops of the Hardraker buildings appear from behind the hill at last. By now, the road itself had disintegrated into a grassy track, pock-marked with stones and jagged pieces of old brick. It petered out finally on the edge of the grass-grown cobbles of the farm yard, under the black silhouette of the farmhouse. There, at the edge of the yard, she stopped.

The farm had once been huge. Its yard was bounded on three sides by stables and enormous barns filled with dust-covered debris. Beyond these, through side gates and covered passages, lay a maze of further barns, storerooms and animal sheds, thrown up on the hillside with no regard for regularity or form. The tiled roofs of most of the buildings were punctured with gaping holes, through which rafters jutted like black ribs picked clean of flesh.

Sarah tapped her fingers on the steering wheel. During the drive, her anger at Tom had subsided a little, and now she paused to take stock. Technically, she was now trespassing. Although Mr Cleever had invited her to see the farm, he hadn't said she could come up on her own at any time she pleased.

But it was hardly likely to matter. The place was clearly quite deserted. A quick look round would do no harm, and might force a little sense into Tom Aubrey's head.

Sarah stepped out of the car. The dust of the track scuffed round her shoes and the heavy pollen-laden air made her sniff and her face itch. She gazed round at the desolation.

"Oh Tom," she said to herself, "You are an idiot. There's no way Vanessa Sawcroft would live here. She's far too neat."

A sudden onslaught of pollen brought on a sneeze. Sarah dabbed her eyes with a tissue, and took her clipboard from the car. She would take a quick look only, and then head home.

Black windows stared emptily down at her from the dull grey front of the farmhouse. Instinctively recoiling, Sarah turned to the outbuildings. The main house could wait for another day.

The nearest outhouse was distinguished by a gaping

hole in the wall. Inside, it was empty, except for a pile of sacking in one corner. The next barn was filled with fallen timber and twisted ploughshares, although there was still a strong animal smell inside which made her nose tingle. She sighed, and made a few brief notes. Mr Cleever would have his job cut out getting much money for this.

Passing along the edge of the yard, she reached what had once been a side gate, although the wood had rotted on the hinges and fallen away. A flag-stoned passage ran down between two barns and turned a corner out of sight. She passed along it, noting the rough size and contents of the barns on either side: echoing cow sheds, cobwebby stores, piles of brick, rusted scythes, grain bags, mouldering heaps of meal, decay, decay, decay.

After a while, the relentless desolation began to oppress Sarah's spirits. She entered a cow house, moving quickly along past the empty milking stalls to the far end, where there was a dirty yellow door.

Idly, she tried the handle. It opened, scraping stiffly on the flagstones, and she stepped through. To her surprise, she found that the door opened not onto some further yard or barn, but into what was evidently part of the farmhouse. She frowned. The geography of the place had begun to confuse her. Still, she might as well look round, now that she was in.

The room was evidently a scullery. A large iron tub was suspended from a hook in the ceiling, and a wooden scrubbing brush lay on a counter, next to a tap. Stone steps led up to a low arch, beyond which Sarah caught sight of dark panelled flooring.

Beyond the steps, a long hall stretched ahead, losing

itself in the dusk of the house. For some reason, Sarah began to feel uncomfortable. There were too few windows in the hall, and too many black doors slightly ajar. The silence was oppressive. She really should wait for Mr Cleever before continuing her tour.

A door on the left, black with age, was open. Sarah looked inside, conscious for the first time of the sweat on her hands and down the back of her top. The house seemed to be acting like a reservoir of heat, though its thick old walls should have kept her cool.

The room was empty. An old carpet lay across the centre, studded with a few chairs and a moth-eaten sofa, and the windows were thickly curtained off, endowing it with the half-light of a sick-room. Sarah returned to the hall, at the far end of which was a huge door, almost certainly the main one which led to the yard. And on her right there rose a staircase.

All of a sudden, Sarah wished to be outside again, in the pollen-heavy air. The air here was too thick and stultifying. She would wrap up her tour early and come back another time. In company. Maybe just a speedy look upstairs, to check for rotting and structural damage. Then she would go.

The staircase rose with the steepness of a ladder, sandwiched on either side by the plaster wall. A narrow window high above gave it a mediocre light. After six steps it turned sharply at ninety degrees; six more steps and then another turn. So old-fashioned. The house must be hundreds of years old. The air was very hot, and grew more so with each step; it was like climbing the staircase in a hot house in some Botanic Gardens.

She stopped short. Had there been a tiny sound, a

quiet scraping suddenly cut off, from somewhere in the upstairs room?

Silence surrounded her. A voice inside her screamed out to turn and go, to escape into the fields and sunlight, but another stubborn voice said. 'Rats. I might have guessed.' Very, very quietly, Sarah went up the stairs, one by one, placing her feet on the edges of the wooden treads.

She climbed another step.

The board creaked; its sound had the impact of a knife in her back. Sarah froze, a heaviness seemed to weigh down on her spine. Don't be stupid. You're grown up now. Five more steps, and she reached the top of the staircase.

A landing. Through a nearby door there was a glimpse of a bathroom; white walls and a huge four-legged Victorian tub. A mirror too: curtained-off, except for a crack at the bottom, where its surface showed. 'Why a curtain over a mirror?' she thought. 'This place is weird.'

A quick look and then go. She strode across the landing, to where a brown and polished door stood wide open. The room beyond was bathed in sunlight, and there were white sheets of paper on the wall. Then she stepped through and saw the rest of the room, and her heart started pounding against her chest so hard that it seemed it might break through.

A chunk of stone lay on a white-clothed table, surrounded by a mess of pens and paper. It was rectangular in shape, smooth along every edge, except one, where the surface was rough and jagged. She knew it immediately for what it was, and also that she could never lift it by herself, for it was two foot long, and nearly a foot thick. A large greasy-looking sheet of tracing paper rested on the flat upper surface of the stone. Someone had carefully been tracing the outline of the carving on the cross.

For a moment, Sarah considered turning tail and running immediately. Then she stepped forward. She had enough evidence for the police, true, but not quite enough for herself. What was going on? This tracing . . . She bent over it and examined it closely. A head, crudely drawn, little more than a rough oval with two dots and a slash for a mouth.

Suddenly, she wheeled round: the sheets of paper pinned to the wall on every side were tracings and copies and photographs of the rest of the cross, magnified to all proportions, covered with annotations in red pen, diagrams, yellow highlights – and alongside them, older documents, sketches, and large scale Ordinance Survey maps of the Wirrim.

'Oh Tom,' she thought. 'You were right. But what on earth are they doing it for?'

One particular piece of paper caught her eye. It seemed to be a cross-section of a piece of ground. Stick figures stood on a rough curved line. Below it was stuck a photocopy of the creature in the centre of the cross . . .

A noise. From the stairwell. A floorboard creaking. Oh no.

Where could she hide? Out on the landing? No – they'd be round the corner in a moment. No. Another door – at the end of the room. Small. Perhaps a cupboard. Try the handle. Turns? Yes. Quick, dive through.

A small room. Dark. Sarah stood there, with her back against the door. Heat buffeted against her face: she felt like she was pressed against a radiator. An acrid tang bit into her nose and made her flinch.

Then her eyes grew accustomed to the dark.

The body of an old man lay on a bed.

It lay on its back, with its long thin arms by its side, stretched out like an effigy on a marble tomb. It was horribly thin; a white drape covered the body, but the sharpness of the ribcage almost pierced the cloth. The lips were drawn back and the eyes were closed.

And the great heat came from the body. It radiated out in waves which beat against Sarah's temples and burnt her mouth dry. She stood staring at it in mortal terror, unable to think, or act, or do. Her jaw sagged as the last vestiges of her will evaporated.

And then the body raised its head, and peered towards her with sightless eyes.

Sarah gave a cry of terror and made a wrench for the handle at her back, tearing at it and pulling the door open. She flung herself through and ran past the cross and out onto the landing. Somewhere behind her, there was a fast movement. Her breath came in gasping sobs as she leapt down the staircase three steps at a time. Halfway down the last flight she stumbled, and hit the remaining steps with the small of her back.

She lay for a moment at the base of the stairs, then forced herself to her feet. As she did so, a man came out of a room at the far end of the hall. He ran towards her. Sarah fled away along the passage, down the stairs into the scullery and out into the cowshed. Heavy footfalls sounded behind her on the flagstones. She dashed past the cow pens and out into the yard, along a side passage, round a corner—

Into an empty tool shed. She paused in confusion. She hadn't come this way. Turn round. Through that door. No. Locked. Oh God. Try this one. A barn. No way out. But a ladder . . . up into the hayloft. Quick. Softly now, avoid the rotten beams. Stand still out of sight. Did he see?

Silence. Sarah was a statue in the yellow-brown dusk of the hayloft. A scuffled footstep sounded outside. A muttered curse. Silence again.

Sarah stood there. The air was thick with haydust. A slight tremor began, high up in her nose. She twitched it, and closed her eyes in prayer. An itch began in her throat, water gathered in the corner of her eyes.

Oh God, hold it in, damn you.

The tremor gathered in her nose, and she pinched her nostrils together with sweating fingers. Her shoulders shook with the effort of repressing the coming sneeze.

Please . . .

Then Sarah sneezed. Twice. As quietly as she could.

Michael stood in the porch until he heard the car approaching along the lane. Then he walked down the drive to the gate. The car pulled in at the side of the road, and Mr Cleever smiled up at him through the window.

"Very good to see you, Michael," he said. "Care to hop in?"

He leaned over and opened the passenger door. Michael walked round the front of the car and got in. Mr Cleever reversed in the driveway and sped off along the green lane, past the Monkey and Marvel, and sharp right onto a rough farm track.

"A short cut," Mr Cleever said. "It's a little bumpy, but you won't lose your breakfast."

Michael looked out at a row of copper beeches at one end of the field, beyond which the tower of St. Wyndham's could just be seen. Then he said: "The Four Gifts. You said you'd tell me what they are. And how to use them." His voice sounded curiously flat and small, sucked away through the window into the blue immensity of the day. He disliked its weak and tinny sound, its irritating lightness. It would not suit him at all.

Mr Cleever gave a little laugh, and tapped a jig on the steering wheel with his fingers. "The Four Gifts," he said. "Yes, the Four Powers. Well, you've already used the first two quite proficiently. I hardly need to tell you what those are, do I?" He looked sideways at Michael, eyebrows raised.

"The Sight," Michael said. "That must be the first. And Fire is the second."

"It is indeed. And you can feel very pleased with yourself for demonstrating it so early. In some of us it took weeks to unleash the flame."

"I didn't do it on purpose. It just came."

"Fuelled by anger. Quite. It's a hallmark of all the gifts, Michael, that they are deeply given, and closer tied to our emotions than our rational minds. Although with practice, as you've found with the Sight, we can learn to control them. Whoops!"

One of the car's front wheels dropped into a tractor rut and they lurched forward violently. Mr Cleever struggled with the steering for a moment, then got them back on track.

"Four-wheel drive would be preferable for this route," he said, "but needs must. I don't want us to take the village road just at the moment. Right, you've experienced the first two gifts, and it might shock you to know that some of us never get beyond them. Paul Comfrey, for instance, good man that he is, has never got close to the third. Doesn't have the knack for some reason."

"You mean I might never— What are the other two?" Michael felt a shock of pride at the thought of any limitation.

"Oh, don't worry. I'm just telling you it's possible, that's all. Personally, I think you'll achieve the others in no time. You're very strong. The Third Gift, now that's in some ways the most delightful of all. It's flying, Michael; or Levitation if you prefer. That really is something."

"Flying!" Michael could hardly restrain his wonder, or impatience. "How high can you go? How long can you keep it up? That's . . ." Words failed him. "Wow."

"How high?" Mr Cleever laughed softly. "My boy, truly I do not think there is any limit to how high we might go. I say might, because of all things we must not be observed, and if you go above tree level in daylight, you will be observed by every man, woman and child in the whole parish."

"But at night though?"

"At night – yes, it's different then. Once, about ten years ago, when my gifts were young in me, I flew on a moonless night above Fordrace, as high as the Wirrim. I looked down on the orange lights and the dark rooftops, and using the Sight, I saw the owls floating below my feet. No one could see me; they were jewelled ants beneath my silent flight. Now say that is not a glorious power to have, Michael my boy! And here, we go right."

He turned through a gate, into another field, filled with sun-ripened barley. A narrow gap just afforded them room to drive along the edge, beside a shallow ditch. Michael's eyes were ablaze with a savage delight.

"When I receive that gift," he said, "I shall use it every night, and sometimes during the day. I can't think why you don't use it more often, or go further. I shall go to London, and cross the sea with it, and spy on people in their houses!" He chuckled with delirious glee.

Mr Cleever shook his head sadly. "Nice thought, but sadly, it doesn't work like that. There are limitations."

Michael frowned. "Such as?"

"Such as being unable to go too far from the Wirrim. And a worse one yet . . ." He let the sentence drift away, and seemed reluctant to discuss it further. Instead, he continued in a cheerier tone: "But the Fourth Gift, if you attain it, gives you the most power of all of them. I have this, and I use it as regularly as I am able. It's the power to enter people's minds, Michael, and encourage them to give up their secrets to you. You can do it in various ways, with various degrees of subtlety, but just imagine the power that gives!"

Michael said nothing. He was imagining.

"You have to be careful with it," Mr Cleever went on. "When done at full force, it leaves even the least intelligent person a little distressed. They take a dislike to you without quite knowing why. But used in discrete moments, once in a while, you can learn anything you wish, and with that knowledge, a lot of things can be achieved."

"But Mr Cleever," Michael said, "if you can read people's minds, you should be Prime Minister or something by now. Not just councillor of this crap place."

He was surprised by the force of Mr Cleever's reaction. The car stopped with a jolt in the track; Mr Cleever hit the steering wheel with the palms of both hands, and Michael's eyes flared with the pain of his reflected rage.

"You know nothing," Mr Cleever snarled, turning the force of his glare full on him. "Nothing but what I am telling you. How dare you doubt my abilities, when you, who have only discovered the Second Gift today, are being instructed in the powers by me, man to man? I have not done this with anyone before! None of the others has been so honoured. And I wouldn't do it with you either, if I didn't think your energy was vital to us! If you listen to me, boy, your powers will be truly limitless. But if you cross me, I'll leave you to discover your limitations entirely on your own. And you won't like them, believe me."

He turned away sharply, and started the car. It bumped along over the fields.

"I'm sorry," said Michael, though his heart raged within him.

"And don't lie to me either," said Mr Cleever. "You've forgotten already about the Fourth Gift. And it works all the easier with those of us with the Power. You should have noticed the bond already. The presence of one of us, and what we do, affects the rest, especially if we're close by."

"I've noticed. I felt it with you last night. And with Stephen."

"Ah, yes. Your brother. We're going to have to have a talk about him. But that can come later."

They were at the end of the field, which for the last few minutes had wound steadily uphill. Mr Cleever turned left through a gate fringed with dark low trees and almost immediately the hill steepened. The car advanced very slowly along an atrocious track. A bank of grass, caught in the shadow of the trees, rose on their right. All of a sudden, Michael saw a set of tumbledown roofs appear over the fringe of the bank.

"That's the Hardraker Farm!" he said.

"Got it in one." Mr Cleever fought with the gearstick to bring the car up the last and steepest incline. At length, they emerged at the top of the bank and trundled slowly over the field towards the buildings. "This is our operational HQ," Mr Cleever said as they turned into the central farm yard. "Right now, it's the base for the most important thing that's happened in these parts for the last sixteen hundred years."

He pulled over in front of the farm house and turned off the ignition. "And you, Michael my boy, are the most important part of all."

29

Mr Cleever led Michael up to the front door of the Hardraker farmhouse and rang the bell. Michael stood beside him, uneasy despite his semblance of calm. The mass of ruined buildings all around made him feel suddenly alone.

"Who lives here?" he said.

Mr Cleever gazed impassively at the door. "Mr Hardraker does."

"But I thought he was dead."

"He might as well have been, until now."

A sound of rattling bolts came from the other side of the door. "It's me, Paul," Mr Cleever said loudly. In another moment, the whitewashed door swung open and the way was clear to enter. First Mr Cleever and then Michael trooped inside.

"Paul, this is Michael MacIntyre; Michael, this is Paul Comfrey." A slight whey-faced man with fair wispy hair pushed the great door to and turned to face Michael. He seemed quite young, perhaps mid-twenties, and his expression was dull, sullen and a little stupid. He was very vaguely familiar and Michael assumed he had at some time passed him in the village. They looked at each other, unblinking.

"So, you're not running this time," Paul Comfrey said in a slow voice. "I nearly caught you at his house. You were fast."

Michael narrowed his eyes. "No," he said, "I'm not

running." He was thinking how foolish Paul Comfrey looked. 'I can well believe he hasn't made the Third Gift,' he thought. 'There's no competition there.' Then he remembered Mr Cleever's Fourth Power, and took a guilty side-glance at him. But Mr Cleever seemed to have noticed nothing.

"Have you had any trouble, Paul?" he asked.

"Yes. She came up, like you said." Paul Comfrey shifted uncomfortably, but made no attempt to explain.

"How far did she get? You can speak in front of Michael."

"She got upstairs." The man seemed most reluctant to give the details.

"As far as that? Dear me, that was remiss of you, Paul. Were you asleep?"

"No."

"Well. What did she see?"

"She saw the stone. And I think, maybe, she saw Mr Hardraker."

"She got as far as Joseph? Good heavens, Paul, that must have given her a shock. I hope for your sake that you roused yourself enough to catch her. Did you?"

"Yes. Had to chase her halfway across the bleeding farm. But she's safe now."

"Where?"

"The piano room. I put her car in the back shed."

"Who are we talking about?" Michael asked, having been bewildered long enough. His eyes were aching sharply and he wondered if he was responding to the tension between the two.

"If you're in discomfort, Michael, use your sight,"

188

Mr Cleever said. "It's good for you, because it trains your power.

"We have had a visitor," he went on, his dragon soul inky black and thickly flowing in the hallway. "And you may be a little surprised to hear who it is. But I won't keep it a secret from you, because you're so clever you'd soon find out. Your sister Sarah has decided to pay us a call. Yes," he continued over Michael's exclamation, "I'm afraid she has been poking her nose into your affairs again, and has seen things she shouldn't have seen. We will have to keep her here for a little while."

This was going too fast, even for Michael. "Hold on," he said. "What do you mean? You can't lock her up. Let her go." He felt his eyes flare with anger.

"Don't be weak, Michael. Don't forget how Sarah has tried to control you for years. Do you think she'd let you use your gifts as you'd wish? She'd do everything in her power to make you stop."

"I'd like to see her try. But that's not—"

"Exactly. You have moved beyond her. But listen, Michael. There are many things I must tell you shortly. If, when I have done so, you want to let your sister free, go right ahead. I won't stop you. Either way, she won't come to any harm. And soon, you'll be too powerful for her ever to control you again. What do you say?"

"I don't know . . ." Michael felt he was being weak. "Oh, all right, I'll listen to what you've got to say."

"Good. We have to be very careful, we special people. Nosy interferers like the vicar and your sister are constantly at our heels. And I'm afraid your own brother is involved with them too."

"Stephen? But he has the power himself! Well, a little of it." Michael corrected himself. "He didn't stay under long, you see."

The surface of the dragon soul broiled darkly. "I'm going to want details about how Stephen got his power," it said. "It was a very bad thing that he did so. I'm afraid your brother doesn't want to accept his gift. He's scared, and scared boys do silly things."

"Yes," said Michael. "He locked me in."

"Jealousy is a terrible thing, Michael."

"We've got to do it fast, George." Paul Comfrey spoke, and Michael looked at his soul closely for the first time. There was something strange about it. It was dragon-like too, but only in parts; the outline was smudged, as if another shape had been half rubbed out there. Nor was it quite as dark as Cleever's. Alongside the black was a strong hint of dirty yellow, especially around the edges. Then, for the first time that day, Michael remembered Mr Cleever's shout as he had run along another hall in terror the day before:

"What you see, you will become!"

There was something so confused, so mixed-up about Paul Comfrey's soul, that Michael now found himself wondering what the words actually implied. There was no doubt about it, Paul Comfrey's soul was in the middle of a change. It had been something else – possibly some sort of rat, or vole, judging by the shape – and now it was becoming reptilian. The awful implications settled like a weight in Michael's stomach. For an instant it threatened to disrupt his composure, then with an effort of will he brushed it from his mind.

What did it matter what had happened to this weak fool's soul? What matter if changes occurred to his own? He already knew the shape was unimportant. What mattered was that he was growing in power and setting himself apart from other men. Maybe Paul Comfrey was too weak to make the change properly. Well he, Michael, would be stronger, come what may.

"I quite agree, Paul." Mr Cleever was speaking. "Tomorrow night if all goes well. But there are things to sort out first. And introducing Michael to Joseph is foremost of all."

They had been walking slowly down the hall, and now stood before a large door, which Cleever opened but did not pass.

"Michael," he said, "I'd like you to wait here. Mr Hardraker wishes to meet you, but he will need assistance in dressing, so I may be a little time. When he does come, please don't be deceived by his appearance. Paul, go back and mind the door. Vanessa will be along soon, and Geoffrey can't be far behind."

He drew back, and Michael passed through into an immense living room, with high-backed sofas which were already old when his grandmother was young. There was ornate stuccoed plaster on the ceiling, and curly, twisting wallpaper unrelieved by any paintings or picture frames. The windows were covered with curtains as thick and heavy as carpets. He pushed one aside and looked out, and as the sunshine hit him, he realised the room must be in virtual darkness and that he was still using the Sight. It had become almost natural for him to do so, and the thought of turning back seemed strange.

The view outside was uninteresting, so he went to the sofa and lay out flat on it with his hands behind his head. He waited for a long while; how long, he could not have said.

Lost in grim thoughts about Stephen, he was caught by surprise when the door suddenly opened. He stood up in confusion. Mr Cleever entered and cast his eyes over him.

"Open one of those curtains, Michael," he said. "And if I were you I would stick to your ordinary sight while Mr Hardraker is in the room. It can be quite overpowering otherwise."

Michael pulled one of the great heavy curtains over, spilling light into the room. He adjusted his eyes dutifully, aware of a slight tingling across his body, which grew stronger by the moment; anticipation mixed with fear.

Then Mr Cleever stood aside, and Mr Hardraker entered. Michael felt a great wave of heat erupt through the doorway, filling the room in an instant. A shriveled thing sat in a wheelchair, pushed forward by Paul Comfrey, his face white and sweating. It was dressed in a pair of light blue trousers which displayed a horrible emptiness to the eye, and a thick pink woollen jumper, on which a head lolled. The bald skin was parchment-yellow and parchment-dry, and the two white eye-sockets glared from them unblinkingly. Michael felt a sick feeling in his stomach, but he quelled it, and stood firm.

The wheelchair came to a standstill. Michael waited.

Everyone stood silently around, impassive. The figure in the wheelchair made no move, no sign that it was conscious or indeed alive. Michael was searching for something to say when he felt a cold presence slip easily past his guard into his mind, and lie there a moment before being withdrawn. He could not repress a shudder as it withdrew, but he still said nothing. He felt his own power wax hotly in response to the easy entry, and lash out angrily across the room, flailing without any target or control. To his satisfaction, he saw Paul Comfrey wince visibly as the waves hit him, but a smile flickered on Mr Cleever's face, and from the figure in the wheelchair there was no response at all.

Enraged still further, Michael did his best to muster a proper retort. With an ease which surprised him, he framed his anger into a thin rapier-sharp bolt which he directed at Mr Cleever. As he let it go, he saw the same burst of fiery lines across his vision which had accompanied his escape from his bedroom, only this time thinner and more controlled. Then, for a moment, he felt himself amongst another's thoughts – random, alien, and strange. Mr Cleever's smile dropped away abruptly. The thoughts shifted from amused complacency to baffled alarm, and since Michael sensed a defence being mustered, he rapidly withdrew his mind from Mr Cleever's and turned back to study the group as a whole.

He fully expected some sort of mental attack in revenge for his aggression, but nothing happened. Mr Cleever's smile slowly returned, and some of the tension drained from Paul Comfrey's face. There was a movement at the door, and Vanessa Sawcroft appeared.

She wore a sling around an arm, and her face about her eyes was badly bruised. She gazed at him steadily, with her bruised face, but though when he had last knowingly seen her she had been checking out his books at the library counter, Michael was no longer surprised by anything.

Then Mr Cleever said: "Michael, Mr Hardraker is pleased to have met you. He wants to shake your hand."

The thought of touching that limp yellow claw, which poked out coyly from the woolly sleeve, was not the most pleasant Michael had ever had. But he was filled with a new confidence. In some way he had been tested, and his response had certainly surprised his new companions. He even had a notion that he had used the Fourth Gift on Mr Cleever, and this gave him a delicious thrill. So, trying not to notice the dead-fish eyes, he walked across to the thing in the wheelchair, bent down and picked up the hand.

The shock of it nearly killed him.

It was ice-cold, colder than ice, colder than the cold which bonds skin to rock and turns breath into frozen clouds of crystal shards. He felt the cold running up his arm, into his body, chilling, stilling, numbing him with the feel of death, thinning the blood and clogging his arteries with ice.

For a second, his brain began to grow numb too, but as his mind grew sweetly weary, his power responded with a desperate surge, and met the ice with fire.

Then there was an explosion all about him, a rushing of air and an orange light, and screams and shouts came from the doorway beyond. He felt his clothes ignite, heard the windows implode and the plaster on the ceiling crack. And, as if in a dream, he felt the energy within him raise him up, and his feet lift from the floor.

And in that moment of supreme delight, he dropped the hand which he held, and felt the energy fall back inside him. Then his feet returned to earth, hitting the charcoalled floorboards with a soft dry crunch.

The object in the wheelchair had not moved, except for its hand, which was palm up on the trouser leg like a great dead spider. Michael's own clothes were grey and smoking. He coughed twice; the noise was hollow in the ruined room. No windows remained, the curtains were gone. The walls were seared black and yellow with great scorch stains. The tall-backed chairs were skeletons, with wisps of fabric hanging from their bones. And of Mr Cleever, Ms Sawcroft and Mr Comfrey, there was nothing to be seen.

Michael thought that he had burnt them all to ashes, but then he heard the gasps and coughing starting in the corridor.

After Vanessa Sawcroft had recovered from her coughing fit, she helped Mr Cleever and Paul Comfrey carry the wheelchair back upstairs to Mr Hardraker's room. Her clothes, like those of the two others, were badly scorched, and with her arm hanging loosely in its blackened sling, she looked in pitiable shape. Paul

Comfrey's hands were shaking so much that Mr Cleever told him off sharply for unsettling the chair; and Mr Cleever himself, though he seemed to have escaped the worst of the inferno, was limping a little as he ascended the stair, and cursed more often than he was wont.

Michael followed along behind. He had a spring in his step.

Once Mr Hardraker had been removed to his room, Mr Cleever and the others took themselves off to wash and find what new clothes they could. Michael stayed in the room with the cross, studying the plans and sketches with a detached interest. He had no difficulty in recognising the Pit, but the reproductions of the cross's carvings puzzled him.

"Well, Michael." Mr Cleever had returned. He had on a new shirt and his face was scrubbed and beaming, but he limped as he crossed the room. "Would you have guessed you were capable of that, when you came with me this morning?"

"No. Of course not. Although I don't think it was all me. It was in response to— Mr Hardraker. It was a kind of challenge. If I hadn't—"

"And you responded admirably. Quite took us aback. We were expecting something, of course, but nothing that fierce, or we wouldn't have stood so close, would we, Vanessa?" He laughed, but Ms Sawcroft, who had just entered, did not. She sat herself down on a chair beside the table with the cross, and after a moment Michael and Mr Cleever did the same.

"Get on and tell him," she said.

"Just getting to it. Now – Michael," Mr Cleever

adopted a serious tone. "You were quite right to say that Mr Hardraker had a hand in that little effect, but not exactly in the way you think. In fact, the pair of you produced it together, through a mingling of both your energies and his will."

"I drew on my own energy to fight off his," objected Michael. "He didn't shape it in any way."

"Ah, but he did. Otherwise Vanessa and I would be black smears on the wall of that unfortunate room. Mr Hardraker shielded us from the full force of your fire. And more than that, it was only because of his direction that you were able to bring forth so much power in the first place." Michael frowned at this, and Mr Cleever went on, "Try it now if you want. You'll be able to set fire to things, but nothing like on that scale. I can see you're getting resentful, but you don't need to: you've far more power bubbling inside you than either Vanessa or I have, let alone the others. The point is that as yet you don't have the will to use it. Mr Hardraker does. The strength of his will you would find hard to imagine."

"So why doesn't he try out his special effects on his own?" Michael was quietly furious – the thought of being used by that horrendous old man set his teeth on edge.

"Ah, that question digs down to the heart of our problem, Michael, and it's your problem too, so try to keep a level head."

Michael breathed deep and sat back in his chair.

"We are all of us linked," Mr Cleever went on, "because the dragon has claimed us. And although for a time that makes us fortunate, it carries us into a kind of hell at last. Look at Joseph Hardraker. He was claimed when still in his teens, back in the days when bicycles were a new invention, and the first car had not been built. Oh yes, he's well over a hundred now, is Joseph, and who knows how long he might linger, in his living death, before his heart finally gives out. He doesn't move, he doesn't eat or drink; he doesn't need to any more. Time means nothing to him, he's past all that, reduced to a single flame of willpower burning endlessly in his head. Do you want to know why? It's because he has gone where the gifts must lead us all eventually."

"They make us immobile like our master," Vanessa Sawcroft said.

"They are a dragon's gifts. It gives us its sight, its flame, its flight, its power over the minds of men. For a while we can use them, as long as we stay within a few miles of the Wirrim. If we travel further, we grow tired, our eyes ache, pains wrack our bodies and we die."

"It happened to a man twenty years ago," Vanessa interjected in her flat, level voice. "I didn't have the gift then, but I remember the incident all right. He must have grown desperate, because he took the overnight express from Stanbridge station. That train doesn't stop till it gets to Paddington. And not long after they'd set off, other passengers heard scuffles and thuds from his compartment. They found him thrashing about on the floor with his hands over his eyes, and a minute or two later, with the train pulling ever further east, he was dead."

"How do you know he had the sight?" Michael asked.

"Joseph knew him. We always know each other for what we are. This man was getting on, maybe in his fifties, and he was slowing right down and losing his powers, so seeing the prospect of an endless old age trailing before him, he tried to break free. But it didn't work."

"You haven't told me why Hardraker is like he is. Why shouldn't he – why shouldn't we die like anyone else?"

"Because," Mr Cleever said, "with every passing day, we become more like the worm itself. We've breathed its breath in to us, we have its gifts, and so we change. And because it has lain silent and still under the earth since time out of mind, needing neither food nor water, nor air nor light, so our souls will grow still too. Our energy leaves us, first slowly, then more rapidly, until we are joined to the dragon in endless waking silence, where once we were joined with brilliance and power."

"When that happens," Vanessa continued, "there is no way out. You cannot even lift a knife to kill yourself, since all your energy has been lost. Only your mind lives on, trapped in your body, feeling the power there, but being unable to use it."

"Most people," said Mr Cleever, "choose to finish themselves before they reach that state."

"Or have their lives finished for them, by ignorant fools," said Vanessa.

"She means the witch scares, but that's all in the past. Nowadays, suicide is the most likely outcome."

"But not for Mr Hardraker," said Michael.

"No, not Joseph. Joseph is unusual, you see. He always was, perhaps because like you he received the gifts at an early age. From what he's told us, he had a wild disposition, and used his gifts unwisely. He had a particular fondness for the Second, which he would practise at night in lonely valleys on the Wirrim. Well, there was soon talk, of course; there always is, when someone uses the Second out-of-doors. It led to trouble, and to a busy-bodying fool butting his nose in, and in the end Joseph had to silence him, which he found easy enough to do. But it shows how careful we've got to be, Michael. Joseph's youthful exhuberance put himself – and others – at risk."

"And it hasn't stopped causing trouble for a hundred years," Vanessa added. "Tell him about Willis."

"It's quite irrelevant, my dear."

"Not according to the Reverend Aubrey it isn't."

"He is quite irrelevant too, Vanessa. We must not overburden the boy."

Michael felt this patronising. "What's Tom Aubrey been up to then?" he asked.

"Willis, the interfering nobody, who's been burnt and dead a hundred years, unfortunately left a few scraps of speculation to be published by the vanity press. They touch on the nature of the Wirrim and what lies in it. I'm afraid that the good Reverend has read it, and has set himself against us."

"He always was a meddling idiot," said Michael.

"However, as I say, that will prove irrelevant. To return to Joseph, he refused to cow-tow to his dwindling energies, and has remained here until his soul slowed to a standstill and his body has almost entirely ceased to function. He refuses to accept the inevitable, and so do I."

"So do we all," Vanessa Sawcroft said.

"How many of us are there?" asked Michael.

"At present only five. Vanessa, myself, Paul, Geoff Pilate—"

"Old Pilate! No way!"

"He's a cagey one, is Geoffrey. And very useful to us. Acts as our eyes and ears, sieving all the village news that passes across his counter. He's the fourth. And you're the fifth."

"And . . ." Michael was reluctant. "I suppose there's Stephen."

"I'm afraid we cannot count him, Michael. This afternoon I came upon him in the company of our dear vicar. They were on their way to take you from the cottage and imprison you in the church. If I hadn't phoned you, and you hadn't used your powers to escape, who knows where you would be by now."

"They wouldn't have held me."

"I'm sure they wouldn't, Michael. But I'm afraid your brother is a traitor to us. Why that is, I'm not sure. How did he come to be offered the gifts?"

Quickly, impatiently, Michael told him. He was reluctant to speak about it, partly because he did not want even to think about his wretched, cursed brother, but also because he was ashamed of giving the undeserving fool the power.

Mr Cleever listened without giving any indication of his opinion. His face was a mask.

When Michael finished, Vanessa Sawcroft said, "I don't understand. It's never happened so close together as that. First Michael, then – less than a day later –

Stephen too. And how could Michael see the gift rising? How could he predict where it would come out? We've never known when. Sometimes it's been fifty years before another person received the gift. That's why there are so few of us. It's always been pure chance."

But Mr Cleever's face was being split by a huge, slow grin, which widened all the time, until it seemed every tooth in his head was majestically displayed. Then he lowered his jaw and brought it up again suddenly, with a single sharp click.

"I've got it," he said. "All of a sudden, I've got it. And I know more certainly than ever that we are in business. We've got it right."

He leapt from the chair and began to pace the room, forcing Michael and Vanessa to swivel constantly where they sat. His great pink fist slapped against his palm as he spoke.

"The seal was split on Monday," he said. "On that afternoon, the cross was removed from the earth by our good friend the Rev. Aubrey, leaving one arm in the ground. On the same day, by chance, Michael was sleeping in the Wirrinlow, in the Pit. The master stirs, it senses that the seal is split and weakened. It sends forth its breath, which Michael receives, becoming stronger than any for many generations. All well and good. That night we take the remaining arm, breaking it for ever. Under the earth, the master responds. Michael is drawn to return to the Pit, bringing another with him. He sees the gift, he lets his brother receive it. But for whatever reason, for whatever personal inadequacy, Stephen rejects it. He only breathes in the barest fraction of what he could have had, if he had been wise."

He paused. The others sat there, drinking it all in.

"But what does this tell us? It tells us exactly what we hoped! That the master is ready for release. It only remains for us to break the bond, and we shall be freed too!"

Much of this Michael did not understand. Talk of seals and bonds meant nothing to him. But talk of freedom was important; his soul had been weighed down with the fate of Hardraker and those others who had gone before him.

"Do you mean that we shall avoid the slowing down of the soul?" he said. "The endless death that is not death?"

Mr Cleever sat down again. He bent forward with sparkling eyes, whose excitement stung Michael's own.

"For the last twenty years," he said, "I have experienced the joys of my gifts. I have lived as well as any man could dream of: all my appetites and desires have been fulfilled. But during those years, a nagging fear burrowed deep inside me. I knew that time was running out. Almost daily, I felt my energy sapping, my life growing rotten deep inside me, like a maggot-ridden apple that still looks good and shiny on a tree. I saw what had happened to Hardraker. I knew the limitations of our condition, our appalling fate. But I would not be quelled! I thought long and hard about what had happened to us, to all those poor, exalted, cursed ones who had been picked out over the centuries. I knew how close we were bound to our master under the Wirrim. And then it came to me. Its fate was our fate. If we wanted to live, live on perhaps forever, rejoicing in our power, going wherever we wished about the world – we had to release it from its prison in the soil. Make no mistake about it, that is why we have received these gifts. We have an obligation, which we must fulfil, and once we have done so, we will be well rewarded."

His voice was almost gone now, thinned out to the barest hiss which filled the room with a conspiratorial tremor. His face was inches from Michael's own. "To free ourselves," he whispered, "we must free the dragon."

Stephen had left the village by the allotments, running up the hill among the trellises and bamboo canes, until he found a small gap in the fence which opened out into the fields. He squeezed through, and lay in the dust-dry grass for a few minutes, peering through the hole back down towards the mill-stream with his heart racing and sweat dripping from the side of his face. No pursuit came, and there was no unnatural feeling in his head. Mr Cleever had lost him.

Once his breath had returned, he got to his feet and began to lope across the field, angling toward a thick scrubby hedge which ran away from him along the right-hand side. The land still rose upwards, and he knew he was conspicuous from the houses behind him and below, but once beyond the hedge a safe barrier would protect him from any watching eyes.

He reached it safely, and worked his way along it till he found a gate. On the other side, an enormous wheat field stretched along the rolling hillside. The chimneys of the Monkey and Marvel pub could just be seen at its opposite corner.

Stephen knew his way about this area blindfold. Two fields and fifteen minutes away was his cottage and his brother. He began to run, but immediately the stabbing pain of a stitch halted him. This reduced him to an uncomfortable fast walk, around the side of the shimmering wheat.

It was when he was halfway across the field that the road to the cottage came in view, and it was only a minute or so later that a large familiar car sped past the gap at high speed, and he knew that he would be too late. For the first time, he felt the tears welling, and a stinging hotness bathed his altered eyes. He tried to run again, but the pain lanced through his side, and, sobbing with frustration, he was forced to stumble along the edge of the field with the jerks and hops of a wounded bird.

"Tom, you fool, you told him!" He gasped the words out as he ran. "Couldn't you run too? Now we're done for, we really are!"

The field seemed to stretch out longer the more desperate he became. As in a dream, his movements became futile alongside the endless rows of corn and the vast impassive hill above him. Long before he reached the end, he saw the car pass back again towards Fordrace. Someone was sitting beside the driver.

He fell out at last upon the road, just below the pub. A goat-souled person was sitting on a trestle-bench beside the way, drinking a pint. It raised the glass in cheery fashion.

"Whoa, Stevie-boy! Steady on lad, where's the fire?"

Stephen switched his sight off for politeness sake – he had hardly known he'd made the shift – but didn't stop. He smiled as best he could with his tear-and-sweat-stained face, and passed on. A few more remarks fell against his back, but by then he was turning the corner and coming in sight of the cottage gates.

The door stood casually ajar. He saw the ash on the stair carpet. He caught the smoke on his breath. He climbed the stairs, going slowly now, and walked along the passage towards the bedroom door.

At first he thought it was open because of the light streaming through, but the shape the light made was somehow wrong. He soon saw why.

The ash was still cooling beneath his feet as he looked through the space, framed by burnt wood. He did not go in.

For a while he sat on the sofa and allowed himself a cry, but pragmatism soon returned. He went to the kitchen, drank three glasses of water and foraged out some food. After a few minutes of unenthusiastic crunching on a Tracker bar, he went upstairs and brought down his small rucksack, which he filled with bars, apples, crisps, chocolate and three roughly-cut ham sandwiches wrapped in cling-film. He added a bottle of water and stood back to consider it. Then he returned to his bedroom and rummaged through the clutter, unearthing a Swiss penknife, his pen-torch, and a thick winter jumper. These things were added to the sack.

Then he left the cottage, and locked the door behind him.

Goat-soul was still sitting outside the Monkey and Marvel, with a gleaming new pint before him.

"Hey-up!" he said. "You look in better nick now, lad."

"Jack, did you see Mr Cleever's car pass back this way?"

"Yes. But that was before you came this way yourself, huffing and blowing like a bull."

"I know. But did he have my brother in the car?"

"He did. You don't think our councillor's kidnapped him, do you?"

Stephen was beyond caring. "Yes he has. Did they head for the village?"

"Far as I know they did. But what's going on, Stevie? What's the game? Don't get hoity, lad. Answer me!"

Stephen walked on. He had not got much further when he was nearly run down by Tom's battered car, which was going much too fast. He leapt up against the hedge and waved his arms. Tom stopped ten yards up the road.

"You're too late." Stephen wasted no words as he got into the car. "You need to turn round. Didn't they pass you on the way?"

"Did who?" Tom looked dazed and ill.

"Cleever and Michael of course. I suppose you told him. Turn the car round."

"I'll find a wider spot." Tom drove on. Goat-soul watched them incredulously as they passed, turned in the Patrons' Car Park and sailed back towards the village.

Tom said, "He made me tell him. I don't know how. He just forced himself into my mind and I could hear my thoughts spilling out, telling him what we were doing. I told him about Michael, and about Sarah . . . God help me, I daren't think about it. I was sick afterwards."

"I'm not surprised," Stephen said. "And he's busted Michael out: the door's burnt down. It seems he can control fire too."

"They didn't pass me." Tom's foot was firmly on the floor. The village rushed towards them. "His car was gone, by the time I . . . felt well enough to drive, but I haven't seen it since."

"Any number of lanes they could have gone down."

"What shall we do, then?" At that moment, Tom was in no mood for decision-making. His head felt raw and bruised; it was difficult to think.

"We'll try Cleever's house. Just in case. Though I doubt he'll have gone back there. Then we try Hardraker Farm."

"Yes. Stephen, I'm worried about Sarah. I told him—"

"Yes, you said."

At the village, Tom parked on the edge of the green, outside Pilate's General Stores. He ran over to Mr Cleever's house, leaving Stephen waiting in the car. The green was quieter now; the Punch and Judy man was beginning to dismantle his stall, most of the children had gone, and the throng of cars had loosened around the grass's yellowed fringes. Fordrace was slowing down.

Stephen began to feel a deep misery and despair settling over him. Michael was gone, and there was nothing he could do about it. Whatever Cleever was, his powers were too great, and the changes to Michael too profound for Stephen to have any hope of reclaiming him. It was hopeless. Futile.

What was more, he was changing too. His eyes were always burning hot, and sometimes it took a great effort to stop changing focus for no reason. That struggle weakened him.

No, he hadn't the strength to go on with this. Let Tom do what he liked; he would leave him to it. He was so tired.

So tired . . .

– Wait –

Stephen had sunk down imperceptibly into a disconsolate slouch. Now he forced himself upright in the passenger seat, and shook his head violently like an animal which smells something bad. The weariness bore down upon him still, but he fought against it, knowing that it was artificial, and had been conjured in him by someone from outside. So subtle had been the attack that he had not noticed the delicate manipulation of his thoughts until he had almost succumbed to fatigue and despair. But the thought of just lying back and losing Michael had been too alien to accept.

And now he would fight back. First of all, he waited. Soon, little by little, he felt a delicate probing in his head. Something which had drawn back when he roused himself now came creeping in again, seeking to find entry into his mind. He let it come, trying to relax, all the time scanning the green for any sign which would reveal his attacker to him. People were walking here and there; the Punch and Judy man was sitting on a canvas chair counting his takings; a young man sat at a cafe table, looking moodily into a cappuccino. On his left, in the bowels of his shop, Mr Pilate was hunched up over the counter, reading a newspaper.

The thought probed a little deeper.

– so tired –

Stephen relaxed his mind, welcoming it in.

– so tired –

Then Stephen exploded his anger outwards, sending out a seismic shock of fury and defiance. He felt the trespassing thought shrivel before his onslaught and saw red bolts flash before his eyes.

The windscreen shattered.

In the shop, behind his counter, Mr Pilate staggered backwards as if he had been punched.

Stephen got out of the car, ignoring the startled faces on the green. The pavement was glazed with fragments of glass.

His sight had changed. He looked into the shop and saw, against the backdrop of soup cans and washing powder packets, a dragon soul hanging darkly. A red light throbbed in its eyes.

Tom came running over the green. He was still ten metres away when Stephen slammed back against the car with an impact that sounded like a metal crate being dropped. He fell on the pavement and tried to raise himself, kneeling on all fours with a dazed look on his face.

Tom skidded across the glass and crouched beside the stricken boy. Stephen's eyes were strange. In a whisper, his voice rose from his open mouth.

" . . . Pilate."

Tom looked up. Beyond the open doorway, beside the cheerful Wall's Ice Cream sign and the postcard rack, Mr Pilate was walking towards him.

And Tom's shirt caught fire. A flame rose up impossibly from his right shoulder, tickling the side of his face with its heat. With a cry, he dashed his left hand down upon it and snuffed it out, stinging his palm with the pain. Immediately, a new flame appeared on his sleeve.

Mr Pilate was standing in the doorway, looking down on Tom. Stephen knew that his attention was for an instant elsewhere. In a flash he had risen to his feet, and launched himself at the grocer's legs in a low rugby tackle. Mr Pilate was taken completely by surprise. As his legs were swept from under him, he toppled back against the postcard rack, going down in a whirl of multicoloured cards. The fire on Tom went out.

Stephen picked himself up and pulled Tom by the arm.

"Come on!" he shouted. "Go!"

From garden gates and windows, the villagers of Fordrace saw their vicar run pell-mell down the edge of the green, with Stephen MacIntyre at his side. They saw Mr Pilate get slowly to his feet and stare after them impassively, before turning on his heels and going back inside. The door was firmly shut and the blinds drawn. The 'closed' sign was flicked over against the window.

Outside Pilate's General Store, glass and postcards lay strewn together like a covering of snow.

It took a little under an hour for Mr Cleever to find them.

Stephen and Tom made for the Haw Road under cover of the summer hedges. Stephen was carrying his rucksack, and moved across the fields with a feral swiftness, his blood racing and his eyes bright. Contact with the enemy had brought new life into his bones.

Tom followed him, his shirt singed brown at shoulder and sleeve. There was a new determination in his heart. He did not have the advantage that Stephen had – he could not see Mr Cleever or Mr Pilate as they truly were. The difficulty of reconciling the ordinary appearance of things with what was under them had flummoxed him to start with, and made him slow to think and act. But the flames at his shoulder had changed all that forever. His old respectable trappings were flung off, and he ran low along the hedge lines with a single-minded speed.

They were bound for Hardraker Farm. Stephen and Tom had not discussed it; they had left the village in silence, knowing exactly where they had to go.

But the fields were blocked.

They had entered the croplands which meandered over the gentle folds of the Wirrim's lower slopes. Hardraker Farm lay somewhere above them. As they headed steeply uphill, surrounded by high grass and following a thick hedge studded with beech and oak, Stephen suddenly threw himself flat on his stomach. Tom followed suit, catching his first sight of a head moving just beyond the hedge on the top of the ridge. It was a young man's face, pale and thin. Tom squinted at it for a moment, then looked over at Stephen, who shrugged. Neither of them had met Paul Comfrey.

The head moved along to the furthest corner of the hedge, never once looking in their direction. At the corner, just when they hoped it might disappear from sight, it turned and began to retrace its path back along the skyline. Stephen swore softly.

"They know we're coming," he whispered. "He's waiting for us to show."

"How could they know? He might not be—"

"He's one of them all right. My eyes are tingling. I just hope his aren't too."

"But how could he get here so quickly? We've run all the way."

"Pilate's notified them somehow. They probably read his mind."

The head arrived at the nearest corner of the hedge and turned once more. Stephen drummed his fingers on the ground.

"He'll be here all evening. We'll have to try another way. Follow my move."

He waited for thirty seconds, until the head had left them behind again. Then he stood up, and ducked through the hedge, at a point where it was pierced by a tall beech tree. A moment later, Tom appeared by his side.

"Did he see you?"

"Not a chance."

They were on the edge of a giant wheat field, turned to a lazy gold by the late afternoon sun. A gate at the far side marked the beginnings of the Hardraker fields. Stephen considered it.

"That's our way through," he said.

But it wasn't to be. Before they had gone six steps, Tom caught sight of a figure standing beside the gate, leaning against the trunk of a tree. The face was in shadow, but the sun flashed white on an arm in a sling. Tom pulled Stephen down, knowing it was almost certainly too late.

"It's a trap," he said. "They're waiting for us to get too far in, then they'll cut us off. We've got to get away from here right now, and no arguments. Which way do we go?"

But Stephen was looking over Tom's shoulder as he said this. "Oh no," he murmured.

It seemed at first as if Mr Cleever was standing on the hedge behind them. He stood there like a giant white bird perched on an inadequate twig. His shoes were at least ten feet off the ground, resting on the uppermost branches. His hands were stiffly by his side. What's he doing up there? Tom thought. What's the point?

Then Mr Cleever stepped away from the hedge, and did not fall.

Instead, he raised a hand and pointed his cane

towards them. Stephen and Tom were up and crashing away from him through the wheat even as he did so. Behind them, the first heads of corn burst into flame.

Downhill through the wheat they ran, the bristles of the wheat heads slapping against their faces, their feet snapping against stalks, leaving a double trail in the surface of the field. Tom looked over his shoulder: Mr Cleever was not quite keeping pace with them. He moved slowly over the wheat, his face expressionless, his body rigid with tension. At his back, smoke curled slowly into the air. If they continued at the same pace, they might out-distance him. But there, behind him and to the right, Vanessa Sawcroft was coming through the air, her feet curled back a little under her body. And to the left, the pale-faced young man was running down the side of the field, arms and legs moving easily as he kept abreast of them.

"To the right!" Tom shouted. "They can't fly as fast as us, but he can run."

Stephen turned off to the right and headed off in a diagonal down the slope. He speeded up, nerves straining, eyes burning, the fire inside him wrestling with his common sense, demanding that he stand firm and fight.

All of a sudden, Michael rose up out of the wheat ahead of him. Stephen stopped so abruptly that he skidded and fell backwards into the wheat. Michael approached, walking nonchalantly a foot above the wheat heads and smiling as he came. His trainers were six inches clear of the topmost tufts, his arms swung freely at his sides. He stared down at Stephen with his head cocked at an angle.

"Stephen," he said, "you locked me in."

Looking up at him framed against the sky by the orange-brown wheat, Stephen used the sight upon his brother. A tremor went through him. Michael's soul had changed. It was darker, thicker; the little lights and sparks that had shot across it once were dimmed, and the currents which had stirred them were slowed. Far worse than this, the very shape of Michael's soul was different. The feline ears were less pronounced; like wax things they seemed to have melted into the head. Even as Stephen watched, they seemed to shrink and press up against the outline of the soul, which had narrowed hungrily.

Stephen could bear it no longer. He switched his eyes back.

"Oh, Mikey," he said. "You've changed."

"A lot of things have changed round here," said Michael, hovering above his head. "And it's not finished yet." He raised his hands. Stephen could feel the waves of anger washing down on him in fiery folds.

"Do it," said a voice behind him, and Stephen realised that Cleever had caught up with them. He could not see what had happened to Tom, and did not dare turn his face away from his brother. Michael was looking down at him with eyes which had suddenly become grave.

Stephen got painfully to his feet. Even now, his face was barely at the level of his brother's ankles.

"Do it, Michael," Vanessa Sawcroft said. Stephen did not turn round. He was squinting up at Michael, reading his uncertainty like a book, watching his fingers twitch nervously against his jeans, feeling the struggle in the malformed soul.

Three yards away, Tom stood looking around him on all sides. He and Stephen were hemmed in by the three, cocooned under a dome of heat which warped the trees at the edge of the field and gave the sparkling waters of the Race, which ran down the hill behind them, a hazy, lazy shimmer. Something tugged at Tom's memory; he stood there, trying to remember.

"You have the will to do it, Michael." Mr Cleever's voice shimmered like the heat haze, an unreal intrusion into a moment that stretched out forever.

Michael's gaze pierced Stephen like a sword. He saw the fire burning there, ready to erupt, and let a desperate plea form silently in his mind.

'Michael – I'm your brother.'

Michael looked at him. Then his eyes flared, but as they did so, they turned aside, away from Stephen, to the wheat stalks all around.

And the fire began. The wheat, rich, dry and golden-brown, had been almost motionless, only its whiskers waving at the sky. Now it changed – a shudder of movement rippled through the field, as each and every head of wheat around them danced for a moment to its own bright flame. Then, with an explosion of noise, a circle all about them was ablaze.

As the flames licked up, Mr Cleever and Vanessa Sawcroft instinctively rose out of their reach, but Stephen and Tom ducked down, below the blazing heads of wheat, and doubled up, began to push their way through the tinder-dry stalks which burned above them like a forest of giant matches.

"Make for the stream!" Tom shouted, above the crackling and the popping as the ripe corn burst and showered their backs with ash. Stephen did so, embers alighting in his hair and clothes, expecting at every moment the fatal burst of fire to come upon him from the sky.

But those above the flames had their own difficulties. The flames advanced as fast as a man could run, keeping pace with the fleeing victims, blocking a clear view of them with a blanket of smoke flecked with darts of flame. Mr Cleever hovered over their line of flight, looking to find an opening, but the black plumes engulfed him, and he was forced to wheel and retreat. Vanessa Sawcroft was driven back, coughing, to the edge of the field, where Paul Comfrey watched in horror as the crops that he had once helped sow were speedily engulfed.

Michael rose through the air, head reeling with smoke and anger. He had turned aside, at the crucial moment. He had been unable to make the strike. His will had failed him. Had Cleever seen that final failing? It would go ill with him if so.

But there was still time. They had not escaped yet.

Far off, four fields away, a cry went up. The smoke billowed into the cooling evening air, and cast a chill into the heart of Fordrace. Phones were rung, help was called, people ran out onto the green. Three miles away, in Stanbridge Fire Station, the first bell sounded.

Stephen and Tom scrambled down the slope towards the stream. Behind them, the path they cut among the cringing stalks disappeared into the mouth of the fire. There was a sighing in the air; a dark shape swooped down through the smoke and buffeted Tom on the back of the head. He struck backwards as he ran, and his fist hit something hard and solid, which cursed and fell away.

Before them, a space opened up. Wheat gave way to grass, which gave way to the line of trees. They ploughed through, as something struck against the branches high above them, and together half rolled, half fell down the slope into the waters of the Mill Race.

In the air above the stream, Michael found his power suddenly ebb away. He kicked backwards, losing height all the time, and made it to the safety of a beech tree, where he perched, his face black as an imp's, his breathing ragged, watching Stephen and Tom splash off down the centre of the stream, until the arching branches of the beech trees covered them from view.

There was a movement at his shoulder. Mr Cleever appeared, his face red, his suit stained with soot. Behind him, the field was an inferno.

"They're heading downstream," said Michael, as levelly as he could.

"Damnation," Mr Cleever said, coming to rest on a large branch. "We can't get at them while they're in the water. It saps the power."

"Will they head into the village, do you think?" Michael asked.

"Not by that tributary they won't. It goes to the Russet."

"Then we'll meet them there."

Mr Cleever studied Michael's face intently. "I know that you found it difficult," he said. "You've only had

219

the power in you for two days. But the power demands certain things. You must leave your brother behind you, and act against him, or he will betray us to the outside world again and again. If you had struck straight at him and not at the crops at his side, he would not have been able to resist."

Michael lowered his head. "I know," he said.

"Vanessa also knows, and she would act against you in revenge. She is strong that way, and stupid that way too."

Michael looked at him, then tried to look aside, but Mr Cleever held him with his eyes.

"Lord knows, Michael, I would kill you myself for your cowardice, but I know how we must raise the dragon. And without you it cannot be done. You must be strong."

"We must head them off," Michael said.

They left the tree, the leaves of which were already smouldering from the sparks of the fire below, and headed off along the edge of the field, following the route of the stream as best they could. Before long, Vanessa Sawcroft joined them. She was no longer in the air, but trudging on foot, and her eyes when she looked at Michael were evil. But she said nothing, and they passed beyond her over the hedgerows into the next field. Then Paul Comfrey met them.

'They're still following the stream,' said his voice in Michael's head. 'But people are coming.'

'Where?' Mr Cleever's thought cut across him like a knife.

'Down all the farm tracks. And over the Moss

Bridge. They're bringing things to fight the fire. The whole damn village is out.'

'Are they blocking our route?'

'The point is, George, we might be seen. We can't let that—'

'I know what the bloody point is, Paul. All right, we'll retreat back to the farm. Then we'll see. If they hole up in the Russet, we may yet be able to pin them down.'

Paul Comfrey's anxiety whined in Michael's head. 'But George, what if they go to the police?'

'They won't go to anyone, Paul. Animals are driven by fear into dark holes and lonely corners. And they are as isolated by all this as we are. What could they say to our simple Constable Vernon? – they wouldn't know where to start. No, their knowledge cuts them off, and they'll try to finish it alone. I felt their rage down there in the field. I saw their souls, hard as adamant and broiling with a single-minded purpose. We have things belonging to them, and that makes them dangerous.'

He glanced over at Michael, who was hovering above him, looking back towards the fire.

"But time is running out for them," Mr Cleever said aloud. "And we have our bargaining chips. If necessary, we shall not fail to use them."

He descended to the ground. There was shouting somewhere in the distance, and then the sirens began to sound above the burning of the fields.

DAY 4

The Russet at the hour of dawn was the colour of ink. The endless layers of trees were stained with shades of blue-black darkening into black, and the sharp chill of a summer's night lay on every leaf and trunk. Tom and Stephen, sitting against the mottled bark of a giant oak tree, had felt this chill for several hours, and even demolishing most of the chocolate and sandwiches from Stephen's singed rucksack had done little to keep it at bay.

Tom was sleeping, his head against the oak. Stephen had slept only fitfully, and was awake again. He faced the east, where a band of feeble yellow appeared beyond the most distant trees.

Mr Cleever had been right when he predicted that the fugitives would lie low and not seek outside help. The conflict they had entered now consumed them utterly, and events in the world beyond seemed meaningless to them. The elemental forces that sought to destroy them could not be countered by traditional means, by police or magistrate, doctor or journalist. They needed sanctuary, and the forest provided it: it had been as simple as that. They had made their way there, keeping to the stream, and had hidden themselves among the trees.

Half the night the fire had raged and the sirens sounded. Until well past three, the sky itself had seemed ablaze, and shouts and cries of exhausted farmers and villagers had echoed hoarsely on the air. The lanes around the Russet had been alive as never before, with cars, people, fire engines and an ambulance all negotiating the narrow bends.

Three fields had been gutted, and two others damaged. Tom and Stephen had witnessed the sorry struggle from the undergrowth close to the forest stream, watching always for signs of the enemy that followed them. Once they had seen what Tom swore was Mr Cleever's car, flashing past only metres away, but they had not seen its occupant, and it did not slow.

With the dying down of the fire, and the quietening of the night, they withdrew deeper into the forest fastness, and settled down beside the tree to rest.

But now Stephen was awake, his body riddled with chill, stiff as a corpse against the trunk. Something had woken him from deep sleep. What was it? On all sides the forest slumbered, cold and deep. The first birds had not yet woken.

'Stephen.'

Grimacing with the effort, he got to his feet and flexed his deadened limbs. He studied the emptiness around him on all sides, looking keenly into the dusk. Nothing, save the beating of his heart.

He walked a few steps, feeling his burns flare with pain as the circulation hit them. His feet made scuffling noises in the dirt. After a moment, Stephen looked back to where Tom slept on, a pale smudge against the dark tree. Then he turned and set off through the trees.

The daub of yellow in the eastern sky smeared itself wider and higher on the horizon. More and more of the forest became half-distinguishable, ancient trees leaning at odd angles in the blue-grey twilight. Stephen walked slowly, carefully, brushing his way past low branches heavy with leaves.

Then he was in a small clearing, where the ground was covered with ivy, and a huge dead tree, rotten with age, sprawled diagonally before him, across the centre of the space. Its crown was wedged somewhere in the foliage of the forest, its roots protruded like a mass of frozen serpents from the earth. Stephen halted. Sitting high above him, in a crook of trunk and branch, was Michael, still and watchful as an owl.

"Why not come down?" said Stephen, after several moments of silence. As it broke across the forest, his voice sounded curiously muffled.

"Where's Aubrey?" Michael said.

"Somewhere around."

"Don't play games with me. I can read your mind. But it doesn't matter. I would have known if he were close."

"Have you come to kill us, then?" Stephen asked.

"No – though I could, of course. I've come to warn you."

"Sure, like you warned us in the field."

"I didn't kill you then, and I won't now – as long as you're not stupid. If you want proof, chew on this: I sensed you almost an hour ago, when I entered the Russet. I knew you were asleep; I could have tracked you down while you slept, or brought Cleever to you. But did I?"

"I don't know," said Stephen.

"Don't be a fool!" Michael struck the bark with his

fist and the whole tree shuddered. "Listen to me for once in your life! What I've got to say is for your own good."

"Well?" Stephen stood waiting, his body tense, his mind as calm as possible, trying to be receptive to any psychic disturbances in the dawn forest around him. He felt no threat, no presence, save the emanations of anger and anxiety beating strongly from his brother. 'He's probably telling the truth,' he thought. 'For what it's worth.'

On his branch, Michael shivered suddenly, violently. "God, it's cold," he said. "Listen, Stephen, my power is stronger than theirs, though they only half realise it. They couldn't have picked you up in the forest, and even now they don't know I've done it. Probably, they'll never know."

He broke off, as if doubting himself. The darkness of the sky behind him was shot through with a pale light.

Michael's shoulders were slightly hunched as he spoke again. "I've come to you, Stephen, even though you didn't believe me once, even though you locked me in. Because we were brothers. So listen: something will happen today, and you can do nothing about it. It's a good thing, at least for us, and if you had any sense you'd keep quiet, wait the day through, and see what happened. But you haven't, so I'll be blunt. They know you're in the Russet, and will be watching the fringes."

"Why don't they come in and get us?" asked Stephen.

"There's been too much activity stirred up by the fire. They need to calm things down now, not set the woods alight. And anyway, there are more important things for them to do. So they're content to watch the Russet for most of the day, and the roads to the village, and if they see you, they won't rely on me to do things for them."

"The Russet is a big place to watch."

"True. But the other thing, which I doubt you'd have forgotten, and which I know the dear Pope won't have forgotten, is this: we have Sarah too. If either you, or Tom Aubrey, makes any serious disturbance today, she's the one who'll feel the consequences. Do you understand, Stevie?"

"Michael, you're talking about Sarah! Your own sister! My sister! What the hell do you mean 'feel the consequences'? Are you going to murder her?" Nothing that had happened so far had hit Stephen harder than this.

"Calm down." Light was pooling into the glade faster and faster. Stephen saw his brother's pale skin, his smoke-stained clothes, the red flash of his eyes when the light hit them. "Of course I'm not going to murder her. No one is. She'll be fine." Michael spoke quicker than before, more uneasily. "I'm just telling you what Cleever said. He won't do anything to her; we're just keeping her quiet till today is over."

"What the hell are you doing, Michael? You're all mad."

"Mad!" Michael raised his head and laughed, a high-pitched shrillness in the thin dawn. From somewhere far away, a cockerel answered him; the noises blended, until the laughter in him drained away. He sat still again on the branch.

"It's to prevent madness that we're doing this, Stephen. You don't know the price we pay for the Four Gifts. If you'd accepted the dragon's breath, as you were meant to, you'd know a whole lot of things you don't. But that's your stupid fault."

"I know about the dragon, Michael."

"In part. But not nearly as much as you think you do. You've taken an outsider's point of view, Stephen, ignoring the fact that you are bonded to it, and us, body and soul."

Stephen shifted from one foot to another. "You're no longer like me, Michael. In the field . . . your soul was melting. Changing shape and colour. Becoming like the others'."

"And what do you think is happening to yours?" There was a slow grin of pleasure; the eyes flashed. "It's only a small change so far, but the horse is no longer what it was, Stevie-boy."

Suddenly he leapt from the tree, came down to the ground fast, but still slower than gravity would have taken him. He was close to Stephen now, holding out his hand.

"Don't you feel the aching in your eyes, Stephen? Don't you feel the deep desire to change, to use the sight? Yes, I know you do. And soon you will want to use the sight forever, to pick out the jewelled souls around you, gather them to you, toy with them, discard them, feel the fire course through you and soar above the world like a bird in flight."

Stephen made to speak, but his brother cut in on him. "Don't bother to deny it. Your gifts are weak and you are weak with it, but you're fated to this. So listen, keep your head down today, and you might still profit by tonight."

"What's happening tonight, Michael?"

The smile flashed back. For an instant, even without the sight, Stephen sensed the tapering snout, the array of teeth. He shuddered.

"A liberation for us all," said Michael.

With a wave of his hands he was back in the crook of the tree. The glade was streaming with early morning light, but Michael, leaning against the toppled trunk, seemed curiously insubstantial, still cast in shadow.

"I'd better go," he said. "They'll be up at eight."

"What about Sarah?" asked Stephen.

"All being well, we'll let her go tomorrow. Maybe even later tonight. She'll be OK."

Stephen sensed a tremor in his head, a flinch in the shared wavelength, and knew that somewhere deep down, Michael was unsure.

He said, "I don't see any reason why I should trust you."

Michael made a dismissive gesture. He was looking up at the sky, sniffing the air. "Because I've risked myself to come here. You don't think they would trust me enough to send me, do you? Not after the cock-up in the fields? Sawcroft and Pilate would rather I burn!"

"In that case, Michael, why stay?"

"Because their fear is rather a compliment. And because they need me. But most of all because I need them. And so do you, Stephen. We're in serious trouble, you and I. But I'll cure it for us, you'll see."

He rose suddenly, into the space at the centre of the

glade. Stephen felt a rush of air as it was whipped upwards by the heat above him. There was a rustling. Michael passed in among the smooth, canyon-deep folds of leaves high above the earth.

His voice came calling back from nowhere: "Body and soul, Stephen, body and soul! You'll thank me for it – one day!"

The voice faded. Stephen was alone in the forest. All of a sudden, birds from every tree about him came screeching, wheeling, calling, erupting endlessly into the anxious sky.

On his return, Stephen found Tom still sleeping against the bole of the tree. He woke him unceremoniously, and told him of his encounter. Tom was alarmed.

"But if he knows where we are, what's to stop them attacking us?" he said, trying to get up, but finding his limbs dull, cold and unresponsive.

"He won't tell them. Mad as he is, he's still my brother."

Tom shook his head. The chase in the fields still preyed heavily on his mind. But he groaned aloud when he heard confirmation of Sarah's kidnap, and hid his face.

"We can't do much about it now," said Stephen. "But we may have a chance later. From what Michael said, they'll be too busy later today to keep an eye on us."

"Yes – busy." Tom raised his head back against the tree and sighed deeply. "Too right. Oh, what have I done?"

"You needn't get self-pitying. We don't know what they're up to, and it's hardly—"

"My fault? Of course it is! Who unearthed the seal? Who brought it out, leaving part of it in the ground, so that anyone could steal it? How long had it been safe there, until I came along and dug it up? Until I . . . came . . . along! Oh Lord!"

Stephen said nothing. He too had grasped what Tom knew only by intuition. 'A liberation', Michael had said, and at those words, the dragon in his soul had stirred. His eyes ached, a fiery pleasure seemed to flare within him. He longed to be free, to soar above the forest—

"What are we going to do?" whispered Tom.

Stephen blinked. "Um . . ." Guiltily, he thrashed around for something constructive to say. "That stuff you read – what did it say about Win – who was it?"

"Wyniddyn."

"Wyniddyn. You said some poem mentioned his fight with the dragon. What did it say?"

"Oh, it was only a fragment. I don't remember. It was typical Welsh stuff, totally obscure."

"You must remember some of it, something it mentioned."

"Stephen, I only read it once."

"Well try, damn it!" Stephen kicked out at the trunk of the tree and bruised his toes. He rubbed his foot, cursing. Tom seemed to take an interest in this; he watched him for a moment, then looked above him.

"That was one thing," he said.

"What?" Stephen was in no mood for politeness.

"Oak. That was in it somewhere. And stone."

"Oak what? Stone what? It must have been more specific."

"It wasn't, I promise you. What did it say . . .? Oak . . . stone . . . fire . . . I don't remember. No, wait! Iron was in it too."

"Iron what? – Swords? Spears?"

"Yes! Spears! Willis reckoned that Wyniddyn fought the dragon with a spear made of oak and iron. And there are spears carved on the cross, too."

Stephen walked around the tree, gazing up at the branches. "Spears . . ." he said. "I suppose we could make one." Tom got up and came after him.

"Make a spear? What good would that do? We're up against fire, for heaven's sake!"

Stephen turned on him. "Listen," he said. "We have little time, and less opportunity. Tonight, or sometime today, Cleever is going to try something which may or may not work. If it doesn't work, we are no worse off. If it works, and the dragon does come, neither you, nor I, nor anyone else in the wide world is going to have the faintest clue about what to do. That poem gives us a faint clue. We know it mentions stone: who's to say that isn't the cross? That's real enough. It mentions fire: we've seen plenty of evidence of that too. OK. So iron and oak make little sense, and sound too fragile to work, but they are all we've got to go on. We can't afford to ignore even the slightest chance."

Tom nodded. "All right," he said. "Here's an oak tree. We need a spear. How shall we go about it?"

"I have a penknife," Stephen said.

35

Dawn had come at last, and thin hard spears of light were piercing the cracks in the boarded windows, creating a ghostly half-glow in the shrouded room. Pale, hulking forms were illuminated on all sides, lumpen and mysterious, their identities concealed under dusty sheets. A grand piano, grey with sediment, occupied the centre of the room, and it was from under this, soon after dawn, that several sneezes erupted in quick succession.

Sarah had been having a bad time. Escorted to this room the afternoon before, by a silent nervous man who paid no heed to her cries of outrage, she had been forced to remain there ever since, surrounded by decades of allergy-inducing dust. She had made the mistake once of trying to lift a sheet that covered a sofa; the resulting plumes had made her eyes stream for an hour. After that, she avoided touching anything.

Her calls and cries had not been answered. The door was huge and thick; her beatings upon it had been weak and muffled. Through chinks in the boards she had seen the scrubby hillside behind the farmhouse, but her efforts to remove the barrier had only resulted in bleeding nails.

So she had lain in the centre of the carpet, under the piano, and given herself over first to despair, and then exhausted contemplation. Over and over again, through the evening hours, as the half-light faded and the room grew dark, she had tried to make sense of her kidnapping. Time and time again, the memory of Tom's assertions rose up: the cross, the folklore, the theft, the dragon. None of it made sense, but nor did her capture. What were these madmen doing?

What would they do to her?

She had not seen anyone, though food had been left for her just inside the door while she was in a doze. But she had heard things, things which increased her sense of unreality. There had been a loud bang during the afternoon, and distant sounds of coughing. Voices had passed the door occasionally, and she had definitely recognised Mr Cleever's voice more than once. Mr Cleever, the parish councillor . . . The world had gone mad.

Night had fallen, and apart from occasional footsteps on the floor above her, the farmhouse had been silent. Sarah had slept.

Now, with dawn, she stirred, and this set the dust rolling at her nostrils again. It took five minutes for her streaming eyes to open. When they did, her younger brother was standing in the room.

"Michael!"

Sarah struggled to her feet and rushed to embrace him. Michael stood his ground, accepting the hug without returning it.

"I can't stay long, Sarah dear. I just came to find out how you are."

"I'm fine. How did you get in? No, first get me out of here. They've locked me up."

"Yes. I've got the key. I've pinched it while they slept."

He held it up slowly, rotating it in his fingers.

"Quick then. Let's go."

"Sorry Sarah, you don't seem to understand. I'm not here to let you out."

"What? Don't fool around, Michael! We haven't time—"

"Shut up!" Michael's furious whisper stunned Sarah into silence. "I'm risking enough as it is. In twenty minutes they'll be up. So shut up and listen. You'll be all right. We'll let you out later."

"*We'll*?"

"Shut up, I said! We've got something to do today, and after it's done you can go free. Even go to the police if you want, we won't care. So just keep quiet."

"Michael, what are you talking about? Give me the key!" Tears of bewilderment appeared in Sarah's eyes. Michael flushed and stamped his foot in the dust.

"Don't give me any of that! It's your stupid fault, coming nosing about here. Trying to spy on me, and stop my power. It just serves you right, that's all! Why didn't you leave me alone?"

Sarah was crying now. "You're mad! I didn't come up here spying! It was my job! He told me the place was deserted! It had nothing to do with you at all. You're mad."

Michael narrowed his eyes. "What do you mean, 'He told you'? Who?"

"Mr – Mr Cleever."

237

"What! Don't lie to me." Michael was furious now. But Sarah just stood there, holding her head in her hands. Suddenly, she felt a sharp pain in her forehead, which flared up and just as suddenly died away. There was silence in the room. She looked up to see her brother staring at her with doubt and indecision on his face.

"Cleever *did* tell you about the farm. He didn't mention that to me." He frowned and clenched his fists. A wave of heat smote Sarah in the face.

"Come on, Michael!" she said. "Let me go. I don't know what you think you're doing, but it's wrong. Can't you see that? Please, whatever's going on here, whatever you've done, we can sort it out, only let me go. I can help you . . ."

"I can help myself!" Michael snarled. "You, Stephen, Aubrey, Cleever – I don't trust any of you! Well, we'll see who has the most power at the end of today. We'll see!"

"Michael, do you know how stupid you sound?" Sarah raised her dirt-and-tear-stained face. "You sound like a spoilt six year old. Just grow up and let me out!"

Michael's face contorted with rage. Then Sarah's disbelief turned to a desperate fury. She leapt towards him, stretching out for the key. But as she reached him, Michael slipped upwards, out through her hands, so that her clutching fingers brushed his shoes. He hovered above her, waving the key and laughing. Sarah gave a moan of terror and sank to the floor.

Her brother floated across to the door. Descending to the ground, he unlocked it and stepped through. He did not look back. The key was turned on the other side.

Sarah's head dropped to the carpet in despair. A halo of dust rose up all around.

It took a long time to make the shaft.

The oak under which they had slept had proven too old and and gnarled to provide anything straight or slender enough for their purposes. Close by, however, Tom had discovered a much younger tree, no doubt a direct descendent of the master oak, which had sprung up in a sunny spot. It had erupted in three or four places, strong, narrow and pliable; of these trunks, one, for perhaps two metres, was ramrod straight. Tom set about sawing this off from near the base, at a point where the wood became narrow enough to grasp firmly in the hand. Stephen held it straight, and busied himself snapping off small leafy offshoots. When Tom grew tired, they swapped roles, and after half-an-hour's sweat had run down their faces, the wood was severed.

The next stage was to chop the foliage from the end of the spear. They decided, arbitrarily, that the spear should be the height of Tom; at this place they made a nick in the bark, and set about carving through. The going was slow, for the penknife was by now growing dulled and blunt. It was while he was struggling with this that Stephen said, between curses, "You know, this spear will never be sharp enough to scratch anything."

"I was thinking about that. If you don't mind persevering with the knife, I thought I might test an idea."

"Such as?"

"Something I saw a day or two back. Don't worry, I won't leave the forest." He stood up. "Which way's the road?"

Stephen indicated. "Where are you going?"

But Tom was already heading off. "Oak on its own is not enough," he said over his shoulder. "I won't be long."

Stephen shrugged and turned his attention back to the spear. He was nearly half-way through, but the penknife was very blunt. Stephen flexed his aching arm, massaged his fingers and methodically began to saw.

There were always insects in Crow Wood. The strong sunlight, which flooded the ruins with a green-gold haze, was awhirl, alive with movement. Quick, delicate things passed by Tom's head, too swift to be sensed in full – a white wing-tip beside his eyes, a brief hum against his ear. But Tom walked unawares, stalking through the mortuary of bricks, his face turned to the ground.

A fluttering of birds in the topmost branches watched him pause in his stride, bend suddenly, straighten empty-handed, and walk on.

From narrow cracks under angular boulders of brick and mortar, lizards followed him with eyes that turned implausible degrees in oily sockets. Every now and again, at shutter-speed, their filmy lids blinked his image in the darkness.

Him scouring the rubble.

Him levering a beam free of the clinging weeds.

Him plucking a piece of blackened metal from the ground, scanning it intently, casting it aside.

Him kicking a charcoal beam in frustration, smearing his shoe black.

Him looking, always looking, as an hour passed.

Up on the slopes of the Wirrim, in the Hardraker farmyard, there was much activity. Shortly after nine, Paul Comfrey had entered an adjoining shed, carrying a toolbox and a saw. Since then, the sound of sawing had filtered through the half-closed door, punctuated occasionally by furious hammering.

Mr Pilate, teeth bared in a rictus of displeasure, had left the farm soon after, driving back to the village to open his shop and assess the implications of the previous evening's fire.

Mr Cleever had seen him off, then returned to the house with instructions not to be disturbed. He had not been seen since.

Vanessa Sawcroft, looking pale and tired, had then emerged, and spent a lot of time coming in and out of the main door, carrying several rucksacks. She had opened the boot of her car, and arranged the rucksacks there in a row, carefully checking and rechecking the contents.

Michael sat on an old grindstone, examining his nails. He had lied to Stephen about the watch on the Russet, which was indeed far too big for any feasible cordon to be erected around. In fact, the night before, Mr Cleever had dismissed the idea of pursuit. He had opted instead to ignore them, realising that their desperation cut them off from the world outside.

Even as he sat idle, Michael was reading the atmosphere of the farm, opening his mind to the Fourth Gift. From the shed he caught Paul Comfrey's excitement – confused and nervy – mixed with a plodding concentration at his unknown task. In contrast, Pilate's mind, as it had passed, was dark and furious, and Michael knew that Stephen was the cause. Geoffrey Pilate was not the kind of man to forgive an injury.

Vanessa Sawcroft, seemingly absorbed with the rucksacks, gave Michael the strongest readings. Her antagonism flowed out from her, washed against the walls of the farm-buildings and crashed back upon him from all sides. A day ago, he might have been inundated: now he absorbed it without effort.

Throw at me what you like, Michael thought. I am a rock.

He could sense Cleever too, somewhere deep in the house, a reading full of hard intensity of purpose. Michael frowned. Cleever had lied to him about Sarah. Though it was her own stupid fault for coming up here unannounced, it had been Cleever's invitation to value the farm that had got her interested in it in the first place. Cleever hadn't thought fit to admit this to Michael. Well, he would pay him back for that. Soon.

After a time, Michael grew aware that all these sensations were being swallowed by a subtler and greater presence, the source of which puzzled him. He could not trace it; it seemed to rise up from the dirty whitewashed stones of the farm-buildings all around – beside, behind, beneath him. It was almost as if it lacked a human centre, and that the ancient farm itself was alive.

Hardraker, thought Michael. It must be.

Perhaps the dreadful shrivelled body which had lingered long beyond its time could not encompass its own power. Perhaps that power had seeped out over the silent decades, to stain the stones of the farm around it, to sink in and lie there, awaiting the time when it could be harnessed again in full.

Michael felt the trickling movement all about him; sensed how every beam and stone was brim-full of a biding, dormant energy, and knew it to be true.

He's stirring, he thought. Ready for tonight.

For a moment, Michael knew himself to be small, bare and vulnerable. He closed his eyes, and a strange vision came to him. The farm was distorting, the barn roofs swelling and buckling in their centres, the beams breaking upwards through the roof in an explosion of spines and spikes. Lines of brickwork on every wall began to shift, and overlap each other like endless layers of scales. Whole rows of outbuildings twitched with a fitful impatience, and behind his back, the Wirrim rose to a colossal height, blocking out the sun.

There came the sound of a car approaching along

the track. Michael opened his eyes. Geoff Pilate's battered transit turned into the yard and stopped abruptly. He got out, and stood uncertainly beside the open door, sending out strongly anxious signals which Michael knew Mr Cleever would soon pick up.

Vanessa Sawcroft put down a rucksack she had been drawing to and fastening, and addressed the grocer.

"Well?" she said.

Pilate's brows knitted and he grunted dismissively. "It's bad," he said. "They're not up in arms yet, but it won't be long. I can't tell you when exactly."

"You should have stayed. Why didn't you stay longer? We were to call you at one." Michael noticed Vanessa Sawcroft's voice was shriller than normal, heightened with tension.

Pilate shrugged. "I had to close up almost as soon as I opened. Some of the old ones are coming over all enlightened, remembering things they heard when kids and had forgotten long ago. They began poisoning the others' minds. A few of the younger ones came in early on, but they soon dried up. I'm under suspicion too." His voice was low and dulled.

Sawcroft made no attempt to disguise her apprehension. "You're a fool," she said. "You can't be. We were well away from the field by the time they got there."

"It's not the field that did for me. It was that bloody boy. Yesterday, on the green, in full view of half the village. They don't understand the connection, but they know there is one." Suddenly, Pilate slammed his fist down on the roof of his car. The yard echoed with the sound. "That boy! We should have killed him!"

Sawcroft sniffed. "We could have. But we set the field alight instead."

"There's no we about it," Pilate snarled. "We were betrayed, by that little—"

"I'm right here," said Michael. "If you've got something you want to say, go right ahead. Or are you scared?"

Pilate's eyes narrowed and his fists clenched. He hesitated a moment, then began to move around the side of the car. Vanessa Sawcroft moved back slightly to let him pass. Michael sat waiting on the stone, watching him from the corner of his eye. He sensed a ripple run through the farm, whether of anticipation or anxiety he did not know.

Pilate stopped. Michael raised his mental guard, protecting his mind from any attack, ready to mount his counter-assault.

A sudden mental blow struck the side of his head, from a direction he could not have predicted. It was a cuff, a bit like the one his father had once given him, long ago. Both he and Pilate turned to the front door of the farmhouse. Cleever stood there, hands on the back of Hardraker's wheelchair. The occupant of the chair was now wearing a bright orange anorak and his lap was smothered in blankets. The head was hidden inside the jutting anorak hood.

"Geoffrey," Cleever said, "Mr Hardraker wants to know exactly what has made you leave your post."

Pilate, who had turned pale, stumbled through his explanation again. "It got so bad," he said at last, "that there were groups of them watching me from the green. Watching, and never coming in. All the time there were little parties of them hurrying to and fro, knocking on doors and huddling in groups. And several times I saw them going up to the church."

"And you think they are nearing the truth?"

"There's no doubt about it. That old hag Gabriel was being consulted by half the young men, sitting in state on the bench by the pond, warbling away, pointing at the church, and towards me." His voice took on an hysterical note. "I got out while I could. That's all there was to it."

Mr Cleever said nothing. Michael said, "But there have always been summer fires. It's the easiest thing in the world for one to start in August."

"Not within two days of the seal being found, raised and split," Cleever said.

"And not all of them result in a death either," Pilate added, and Michael felt a chill run through him. "They're angry about this. Vernon was marching about with a face like a beetroot."

Michael desperately wanted to ask about the death. Images of the fire flicking up from the dried wheat-heads came to him. But he knew the others would pounce on the question for a weakness, and with an effort he said nothing.

Cleever left the wheelchair on the step and strode down to the forecourt. "They suspect you, Geoffrey, because of the incident in the street yesterday. Which means they know Aubrey and the boy are mixed up in it. Good. Aubrey is doubly compromised. They'll be looking for him now."

"Why?" asked Sawcroft. The fear was apparent in the lines of her face.

"Don't be stupid, Vanessa. He's compromised because he's the one who raised the cross. Those of them who have half-remembered knowledge their sweet old grannies told them always knew he was reckless to dig it up. They just didn't know why. Now our fire will have triggered off a few connections. They probably blame it all on poor Tom."

"With luck," added Pilate, "he'll be hunted down and pitchforked before he can do any more harm."

"But what about us?" Sawcroft said. "We know they're after you, Geoffrey. Do they know about us?"

"It doesn't matter," Cleever said. "What they know won't matter a scrap after the summoning. We just need to get moving, that's all."

He cocked his head as if listening. Michael sensed a rustling in the stones and timbers of the farm. The figure in the wheelchair was quite still, but a breeze fluttered the fabric of the concealing hood.

"Mr Hardraker is ready," Cleever said. "It is time for Paul to bring out his transportation."

All eyes turned to the door of the shed, where for some time now the sounds of activity had been stilled. Michael felt Mr Cleever's mental summons pass; he waited for Paul Comfrey's response, but none came.

There was an embarrassing pause. Mr Cleever's tongue clicked. "Surely he can't be that incompetent," he muttered under his breath. The pause continued. Finally, Mr Cleever lost his patience, and surrendered his dignity to the walk across to the shed door. He rapped on it imperiously.

The door opened. Paul Comfrey's face appeared,

blinking at the light. "Oh," he said, somewhat startled. "Did you knock?"

"I did. Have you finished? We need to be going."

"Yes. I'll need someone to take the other end."

Mr Cleever looked over at Michael, who rose from the grindstone and came over to the shed. Uncertain of what to expect, he ducked under the low door and looked about him.

The shed smelt of woodshavings. Littered around on every side were the tools with which Paul Comfrey had worked all morning. In the centre of the shed, lit by the feeble light from the single window, was the contraption in which Mr Hardraker, the oldest and most powerful of the dragon's disciples, would make the ascent of the Wirrim.

It was a sedan chair. Of sorts. A huge, high-backed dining chair had been brought to the shed. Two incredibly long thin wooden poles had been attatched to its armrests, fixed so that the chair was at the centre of their spans. The ends of the poles had been wrapped with cloth to make gripping easier. Up the back of the chair ran several bamboo sticks, supporting the centre of a broad canopy, which Michael saw was made mainly of an old umbrella. This was a special addition Paul had just finished, and he was very pleased with it.

"Keep the sun off him," he said. "Keep him cool."

"Delightful," Michael said.

They each took up the supporting poles, Michael at the back and Paul Comfrey at the front. Then, at the count of three they raised the chair. The canopy waved and juddered alarmingly, but remained in place. With Mr Cleever holding the door open for them, they emerged out into the yard and proceeded uncertainly towards the porch. By the time they lowered it to the ground, Michael's arms were already aching.

'Why don't we just fly him up?' he thought to himself.

'Because—' Mr Cleever's voice sounded in his head, 'we need all our mental strength for the summoning. We shall carry him in shifts, and rest frequently.' Michael was shocked once more by the ease with which Cleever read his mind. He cursed his lack of protection and reinforced his defences.

Sawcroft and Pilate were staring at the sedan chair with little joy.

"This is it?" asked Pilate.

"It is, and you will help me transfer Mr Hardraker to his new chair." Together, he and Pilate bent to lift the fragile body. Michael watched curiously as they tensed and lifted, sweat breaking out on their foreheads, their muscles cracking. For something that was emaciated almost to bare bones, their burden seemed strangely heavy. It rose with painful slowness, both men gritting their teeth as they carted it across the narrow gap to the waiting chair. The breeze in the yard picked up and set the fringes of the canopy ruffling. Michael sensed movement everywhere. He heard floorboards groan and creak in the dusty bedrooms and iron cattlepens grind and scrape their joints in far corners of the farm. But at length, with great effort, the body of Joseph Hardraker was placed in the high-backed sedan chair, and covered over again with blankets.

Sawcroft now began handing out the rucksacks. Michael took his without bothering to open it. He was feeling surly and dispirited. After the glories of flight, the forthcoming climb promised to be a tedious and interminable one. The prospect of being pole-bearer filled him with a sour despondency.

But Mr Cleever's spirits were high again. He clapped Michael on the back as he passed him. "Everything's in place!" he cried. "The six of us, my friends, are setting off on the final journey we shall ever need to make on foot! Michael and I shall take the first stint at the pole. But first, we must bring out our fellow traveller."

He disappeared into the house on light feet. A moment later he returned, with Sarah at his side. She stumbled, blinking in the sunlight, her face grimy and tear-stained, her hands bound with a cord. When she saw the others assembled there, she called them all an evil name, then lapsed into a resolute silence.

Michael frowned. "Why's she got to come?" he asked. "Can't she just stay here? She might spoil things."

"Because, Michael, I want to keep a close eye on her," Mr Cleever said. "And besides, if she is with us, she can be set free the instant we have accomplished our objectives."

If Michael had been concentrating at that moment, he would have seen Vanessa Sawcroft catch Mr Cleever's eye and smile thinly. But he was too busy avoiding his sister's own gaze to notice anything at all.

"Miss MacIntyre can lead the way!" Mr Cleever smiled. "Vanessa, if you could walk with her?"

"Which way?" asked Sawcroft.

"Haw Lane is the only option. The others are too steep for Mr Hardraker's chariot!" His voice was wild with excitement, as he positioned himself between the front ends of the poles. "Let us go!"

Michael grasped the poles and took the strain. His shoulder and elbow sockets felt on fire. Feeling the jerk as Mr Cleever set off, he began to stumble forward.

With Sawcroft and Pilate at the head, Sarah between them, and Paul Comfrey trailing along at the rear of the company, the procession slowly left the farmyard.

All around them, the wind swirled with a high fever, and clouds scudded over the brow of the Wirrim.

It was almost one o'clock in the afternoon.

"Where the hell have you been?" Stephen was sitting against the oak again. Beside him, propped against the trunk, was the spear shaft, long, thin and straight, except for several woody nodules here and there, and a slight kink near the top.

"I got this." Tom held something up in his hands. Stephen took it, examined it, and swore.

"Ow! It's sharp."

"Exactly. I think it might once have been part of a candlestick. You see the curling bits there?"

"But do you think it's iron?"

"Look at the rust on it. Even for someone who knows nothing about metals, it's a safe bet."

Stephen considered it doubtfully. "Don't other metals rust?"

"No. Or if they do, I don't care. This is as good as we're likely to get."

"Fair enough. So how do we fix it to the spear shaft?"

"Jam it in, I reckon. Split the end and force the metal in. If we can get this long thin bit fixed, the jagged end will be sticking out in front. One spear."

This was easier said than done. The new, green wood was extremely reluctant to be split, and the penknife, by now on its last legs, was almost useless. In the end, Tom used the iron shard itself to cut its own slot, its serrated edge acting like a saw. Once a deep furrow had been made, they were able to pull the wood apart, and the metal was inserted as deeply as it could go.

The spear was made – over six foot long, with a rusted point jutting from its end. The metal was bunched in a molten clump just over the tip of the wood, with curving offshoots jutting back in the opposite direction to the point. It reminded Tom of a harpoon.

Get that inside someone, and they won't get it out in a hurry, he thought, and frowned at himself. Then he noticed Stephen sitting on the ground, with his head in his hands.

"Stephen?" he said. "Are you—"

"Hold on." A minute passed. Then Stephen looked up at last, and rubbed his face.

"There's movement," he said. "I just caught it five minutes ago. Something big is shifting. I felt Michael quite strongly, and maybe Cleever, but I think it's all of them at once. A long way off, but very strong."

Tom studied his face intently. "I didn't know you had a link with them," he said slowly.

Stephen looked at him with weary eyes. "That's how Michael found me in the forest. That's probably how they found us in the fields. I'm compromised, Tom."

Tom said nothing. He waited.

"But the thing is," Stephen said at last, "the thing is, those times they were after me specifically. Now – I think – there's too much going on. Too much racket. Their attention is directed up the hill. We have to trust we can get close, without them noticing me."

He stood up. "And I know exactly where they're going. Their whole souls are set to one single purpose. We can follow them easily."

In response, Tom shouldered the spear. Stephen collected his rucksack. They set off northwards through the trees, towards the nearest folds of the Wirrim. It was ten minutes past one.

39

A bitter taint hung in the air on Fordrace green, the after-taste of a bitter burning. It seemed to cling to every surface, working its way deep into the folds of clothes and skin, and like an invisible blanket subdued everything it touched. The green was almost empty. Several of the shops were shuttered, including Pilate's Stores, which was an unheard-of event in midsummer. The ice cream stall was empty, locked shut against the side of an outbuilding. At the far corner of the green, a small knot of villagers were standing together talking, pointedly ignoring the few puzzled tourists who stood uncertainly beside their cars.

From the shadows of the church gate, PC Joe Vernon surveyed the scene. Finally he walked slowly down to his car and drove off along the road towards the Wirrim and the MacIntyre Cottage.

After a whole night fighting fire, Joe Vernon wanted little more than to go to bed. Nevertheless, after hearing of the disturbance outside the General Stores, he had felt he ought to speak to the vicar and Geoffrey Pilate straight away. But neither were anywhere to be seen. Miss Price at the Church had not seen Tom all day, and Mr Pilate was not answering the door.

There remained only Stephen MacIntyre to try.

No one answered his ring. The front door of the cottage was locked, but the back door had been left open. Joe entered, and noticed immediately that the taste of smoke grew heavier inside, despite the coolth and emptiness. Then he saw the trail of ash leading up the stairs.

Five minutes later, Joe Vernon emerged from the cottage, and his face was grim.

On the way back, the road passed a bulldozed hedge. Behind it, a black wet mess of stalks and churned stained earth stretched to the hill brow, shining dully in the sun. Joe thought of Neil Hopkins, whose field this had been, and who had last been seen lying in an ambulance, covered in a white cloth.

Burning, burning . . .

A larger crowd had gathered on the green. The

entire fabric of the village's life was there. Young men and women, who should have been out on the fields and farms or commuting into Stanbridge, stood alongside their elders, those who ran the meeting hall, the bridge club and the Rambling Association. Ice-cream vendor and souvenir seller, farmhand and post-office lady, a multitude of Fordrace's inhabitants watched as PC Vernon stopped the car and levered himself slowly out of his seat. He leant back against the side of the car to face them.

"Any news then, Joe?" asked a young man on the edge of the throng.

"Little enough." PC Vernon surveyed the sea of faces with a slightly apprehensive air. There was an undue silence about them, an intentness which unnerved him.

"Well, Jack seen something," said the young man. "Get on and tell him, Jack."

A middle-aged man with a shock of sandy hair and a red and white complexion shifted from one foot to another and looked at the policeman through the corner of his eye. "It was yesterday afternoon I saw them," he said slowly, "about an hour before the fire."

"Saw who?" Joe Vernon asked.

"The MacIntyre boys, and the vicar. That's who you're interested in, ain't it?"

"It is."

"Well," said Jack, with the air of one who had told the story several times already that morning, "I was outside the Monkey, see, mid-afternoon, and George Cleever passed in his car, up towards the MacIntyre cottage. A bit later, he comes back again toward the village, with Michael MacIntyre beside him. Well, if it wasn't him, it was his twin, and I known him long enough to be sure. Anyway, soon after, maybe five minutes like, his brother runs out on to the road from the Harris field, and he's red and panting as if the devil were after him. He ran past me up to the house and was gone, all of twenty minutes or so, time enough to get myself another pint and do it some damage. Then he came back, walking down toward the village. And he says to me, "Jack, did you see George Cleever's car come by this way?" and I says yes I did. Then he nods and looks me in the eye and says "Jack, was my brother in the car with him?" and I says yes he was. Well, he looked so strange when I said that that I asks him whether he thinks he's kidnapped him, and him a councillor and all. And he says, and these were his exact words mind, "Yes he has," and heads off down the road."

The teller paused for breath and the crowd let out a collective sigh of appreciation at this mystery. Joe Vernon pressed his fingertips slowly and deliberately against the metal of the car door.

"Why didn't you tell me this earlier, Jack?" he said. "This might have a bearing on things."

"Clean forgot, Joe, what with the fire and all. Only remembered it when Lew said you were looking out for the MacIntyre boys."

"We're looking out for them all right," said a grim-faced woman. "After what they done."

Joe Vernon spoke quickly. "There's no proof of anyone doing anything," he said, "and I'll thank you all to remember that. We're following up those who've gone missing."

"Anyone seen George Cleever this morning?" someone asked.

"Didn't see him last night either."

"He passed in his car. I saw him. Took one look and drove."

There was a growl from the crowd, and a few curses. Sick men had risen from their beds that night and come with brooms and buckets to the fields. Joe Vernon made haste to interrupt.

"Jack, you said you saw the vicar too. Did you?"

"I did, and I'd tell you about it, if I could hear myself speak." A sizeable portion of the crowd, comprising many of the older villagers, were whispering loudly and urgently amongst themselves.

"Please! Mrs Gabriel, please!" Joe raised his voice to a previously unsuspected level. The whispering subsided. "Go on, Jack."

"It's just this. Stevie MacIntyre set off for Fordrace. No sooner that, than he was back, but this time in the vicar's car, with the vicar at the wheel. He must have met him in the lane. They turned in the Monkey's car park and were away again. Not ordinary goings on – eh, Joe? I had to have another pint."

The noise of the crowd rose again, discussing the revelation and its implications. "That would have been just before the fight with Geoff Pilate," someone said.

"Mr Pilate and Mr Cleever always were thick as thieves," said an old lady. "Mr Pilate was always going round to his place, spending half the evening with him."

"And where are they all?" an old man said. "Cleever, Pilate, those boys, the vicar. All missing, since the fire."

"It doesn't make any sense," said Joe. "We don't know that there's a connection." But his heart betrayed him. He remembered the fire-lashed earth in the church-yard trench.

"I'll tell you what the connection is." Mrs Gabriel, shorter than all, spoke at the very centre of the crowd, and the hubbub subsided. "It was the vicar who did it. He raised the cross and broke it. I told him the danger, but he wouldn't listen to me. Since then, what's gone right? The church has been defiled, and worse than that, a piece of the cross stolen: now fire has broken out again, and it won't be the last. The vicar's gone – perhaps dead, and the enemies are moving."

"Listen to me." Joe Vernon spoke, and everyone turned back to look at him. "We must remember that there is no proof that any of these things link up. It was a terrible night, but there is no proof that the fire was started deliberately. We have no proof at all. Remember that." He paused. The crowd waited.

"But I've just been up at the cottage. And there has been a fire there too, inside the house. That is itself a serious matter. Even on its own. So I want to speak to any of them – the MacIntyres, Mr Cleever, Mr Pilate. Urgently. And I want you to be patient while I try and find them."

He broke off, sensing a shift in the crowd's mood which he didn't understand. The whispering had started again.

"The fire is coming again," said one old man quietly.

"Above the crag," said another.

"And the seal is gone," said Mrs Gabriel.

Joe Vernon felt his command of the situation, if it had ever existed, had ebbed away entirely. Yet with his sense of powerlessness came a growing feeling of the need for action. He longed to give himself up to the mercy of events, to the momentum which was stirring in the crowd before him. He made one last plea for order.

"I shall first go in search of Mr Cleever," he said, "and see what light can be thrown on this."

"We shall all go!" cried an angry voice, and the crowd murmured in agreement.

"He'll explain himself to us," said another. It was the younger, and hotter-blooded voices that cried out agreement: the elder members of the crowd hung back, doubt and fear in their eyes.

"Find Pilate too, the swindling bastard," said someone at the back.

"He's shut up shop this morning," said someone else.

"Well, we'll knock on his door, then. He'll be happy to exchange a quiet word."

The crowd began to surge forward. Joe Vernon hesitated, then reached through the car window to take his helmet off the back seat. "All right then," he said. "Follow me, with the best of order, please."

Even so, he had to jog to keep ahead of the pressing throng. The younger villagers came first, then the elders at the back, shaking their heads, but seemingly unable to break away from the edges of the group. They crossed the green towards Mr Cleever's house.

In his garden, one or two of the younger men seized bamboo canes from the flower beds and held them loosely by their sides as they crowded round the porch. Joe Vernon rang the bell. A long silence flooded out over the quiet group. Joe rang again. Then the muttering of the crowd began to grow, swelling louder and deeper, until with a burst of rage, the first blow fell on the thick oak door.

On the steep summer-hard dirt of the winding track, studded with rocks and little gullies which caught the foot and twisted it, Mr Hardraker's chariot was a heavy burden. Its bearers had been changed several times: only two among the company had not borne it at least twice, one whose arm was broken, and the other whose hands were tied. At the halfway point, where the path turned sharply at the head of a precipitous gully, Mr Pilate and Mr Cleever were bearing the weight. They struggled on, heads resolutely downward, mouths agape, studying the remorseless movement of their boots upon the dust. Alongside them the others toiled, arms hanging wearily, brows drenched. Only Vanessa Sawcroft, whose injury had spared her a turn at the pole, had energy to spare, and she used this to keep a firm eye on the prisoner.

Sarah now walked behind the chair. At first leading, she had begun to outstrip the rest when the incline became severe, and had been ordered to follow directly behind the chariot among the others. Her face was impassive, but her mind was racing; she took in the details of everything around her.

After her night at the Hardraker farmhouse, and Michael's appearance and rejection of her, Sarah had passed beyond despair into a kind of desperate calmness. The nightmare that surrounded her was so grotesque that her commonsense had rebelled against it. She refused to be overwhelmed.

Just ahead of her, Michael was walking. He was not as weary as the others – his head did not hang so heavily – but he seemed nervy and agitated. Twice, when the chariot had stopped for a change of hands, Sarah had seen him start, and stepping to the edge of the path overlooking the gully, gaze long and hard into the haze of the distance. If he had seen anything down there, he gave no sign. For the rest of the climb, he watched his companions unceasingly, his eyes darting from one to another. But he would not look at Sarah; once only he caught her eye, and then he flushed and turned away.

He seemed older than she had ever seen him, older in the way he gazed at others, and there were lines on his face where there had been none before. Yet at the same time, in occasional movements or expressions, he was the same younger brother that he had always been.

Ahead of her, the hood of an orange anorak hung over the side of the chair, bouncing with a horrid heaviness. There was no sign at all that the body was alive, but Sarah had not forgotten her first meeting with Mr Hardraker.

The purpose to it: that was what obsessed her. They had been climbing all afternoon with slow and single-minded determination. Why should they do this – scaling the Wirrim, taking such trouble to bring the catatonic old man? There was no conceivable reason. And yet . . .

Sarah squinted against the glare of the sun up across the dark cleft of the gully to High Raise, the brow of which was pimpled with cairns and barrows. Then suddenly she thought back to 'The Book of the Worm,' the picture on the farmhouse wall, and the carvings on the cross, and deep down she knew what they believed.

And she was being taken with them.

With a sudden clarity, she saw again in her mind's eye the creature on the cross, with all its loops and coils and teeth and claws.

And a cold weight settled in her stomach as she guessed why she was there.

Tom and Stephen made their way along the course of the hill-stream, hopping from stone to stone, clambering across the tumbled boulders which were embedded in the long grass of the bank. Never, along all the meandering course of the stream, no matter how rocky the ground, did they stray further than three or four paces from the water's edge. Stephen led the way, Tom following, adjusting his balance to accommodate the spear which he carried in his right hand.

The sunlight of the afternoon no longer penetrated to the depths of the gully, and the steep walls of the Wirrim above were suffused with brown and blue. Somewhere high above, where the light still turned the grass golden and the air was hazy and indistinct, the footpath from Fordrace ran west to High Raise. Tom and Stephen shadowed its route, in the coolness of the gully, moving as swiftly as they were able, pausing here and there to check the skyline.

Once only Stephen had halted.

"There."

Up on the right, away ahead of them, where the incline was less steep than average, they saw a move-ment – a series of movements – near the hill brow. Tom caught a flash of colour, a glimpse of a little line of stick people moving slowly in single file before they disappeared around some turn in the path.

"It's them, all right," said Stephen.

"Did you see—?"

"I didn't see anyone. Clearly, I mean. But they're there. I felt them."

Stephen did not say what he had felt. Even as he had sensed his brother, he had felt a response, quick and precise, which had surveyed him in his turn and then drawn back.

'He knows,' he thought. 'I shouldn't be coming. But there isn't anything else I can do.'

Ahead of them, the slope of the stream quickly steepened, forcing itself down between great slabs of rock which had fallen from the crags above. The temperature of the valley was cold now, the air around the cascading stream especially so. They stopped beside a vast rectangular boulder, half covered in damp moss, and considered the position.

"We've got two choices," said Stephen, who had explored this way on several occasions in the past. "One is, we head to the left of the stream, which leads up into the crag – that takes us as straight for the Pit as makes no odds and we'll come out a hundred yards or so from its lip. The other is," he paused, and shielded his eyes against the spear-blue light above the hilltop, "to head right. The way up is easier, and we'll hit the path soon enough, but then we'll have to follow it along the level towards the Pit, and we'll be on the sky-line."

Tom grunted, scanning the austere face of the crag. It was deeply incised with great cracks and weathered screes. "How easy is it to climb the crag?"

"Difficult, not impossible. We were always warned it was too dangerous. One time Michael and I gave it a go, but we only got halfway, to where that scree starts, and we gave up. It was getting dark."

Tom made a face. "It gets us close to the Pit."

"Without being seen. I'd say we should do it."

"Then let's not waste time."

They crossed the stream. On a whim, Tom trailed the black, misshapen tip of his spear in the churning water. As they began to negotiate the tumble of stones at the foot of the crag, he looked back down the gully. Light was already draining out of it, while above them, sharp and pale, the sky showed eggshell blue. Traces of water glinted on the spear.

No trace had been found of any of the missing. Mr Cleever's door hung open, the window beside it smashed. Across the green, the entrance to the grocer's shop was gaping, villagers congregating on the pavement outside. Two car-loads of tourists, approaching from the direction of the A-road, slowed at the sight of the milling throng, took in the broken glass, the angry faces, and drove off fast. Joe Vernon emerged from Mr Cleever's hallway, blinking in the sunlight. He walked out onto the grass, to be surrounded by the excited crowd, anxious for a new clue before their collective daring drained.

Mrs Gabriel, who had refused to enter either building, had been speaking with Lew Potter, who had not. She turned to Joe.

"Mr Vernon. Lewis has reported what he has seen inside Mr Cleever's house. Images and engravings of evil things."

"Hardly that, Mrs Gabriel—" Joe's voice trailed off. He had been brought up at Fordrace, and even for him, aspects of the ancient sites of the Wirrim carried uneasy connotations.

"There is no doubt about it," she said, and Joe realised that the group was giving all its attention to her. "His obsession with dark things is all too clear."

"But he's not to be found," said Joe. "They've gone, and we don't know where."

"I think I do," said a tall gaunt woman, Mrs Plover from the Post Office. "Mr Cleever collects parcels sometimes, and letters, addressed to Mr Hardraker. Since the old man died, Mr Cleever has been his executor: he collects the post which builds up once in a while, signs for them, and takes them off. He still spends time up at the farm, he told me; he's going to put it on the market when the prices are more beneficial."

The crowd gave a mutter, whether of gratitude, eagerness or uncertainty, Joe Vernon could not tell.

"Well then!" One of the young men flourished his stick in the air. "To the Hardraker farm it is. We'll take our cars and see who we can root out. Come on!"

The crowd split into several knots, running towards their vehicles. Joe Vernon and Mrs Gabriel were left on the Green, Joe rubbing his wrist in indecision, Mrs Gabriel standing silent, brows furrowed, as if trying to remember something she had long forgotten.

"We seem to be the only ones who haven't got a lift," he said at last. "Would you care for a ride in a police car, Mrs Gabriel?"

The band of stone is broken.

(Time suggests itself once more. The pin-prick flares to an acorn's size, to that of a large pebble. At the centre is a white heat. It glows in response to the movement it senses, away and above, but growing closer. And to an intent which it recognises as its own.

The earth has grown deep now, compacted through millennia, yet the flame, though weak, remembers.)
Men dying
but among them a white arm raised, unburning, though the sky itself was scorched
and a force closed in, squeezing the scales till they burst and buckled with the pain of it.
Men died
but among them, one man laughed as the earth rose, shutting out the light
and the circle of stone lay like a dead weight all around. (So the worm reminds itself of the age with which it has been forgotten. Time impinges on its brain. Impatience flares. In the fiery heart of the blackness, it feeds quickly on its rage, and the heat grows stronger.)

The way up the crag was easy enough at first; an old scree, turfed over, which rose by gradually steepening increments, until it met the true rock face almost halfway to the top of the bluff. Thereafter, a series of irregular cracks and chimneys in the stone allowed Tom and Stephen to continue the climb, but the going was slow and difficult, particularly for Tom, who was carrying the spear.

Stephen was thankful for one thing. The crag

bulged to their right, cutting off all view of the top of the gully, where the true path ran. The vulnerability he had felt earlier faded, and he was able to concentrate on the practicalities of the climb.

After half an hour, he passed the point where he and Michael had given up their ascent. The going was tougher here, but by no means impossible, although the rock was brittle and occasionally treacherous. Once or twice, he took the spear from Tom to enable him to negotiate a tricky stretch. Each time, he felt the reluctance of Tom to part with it, and noticed how swiftly he took it back when the difficulty was over.

It's becoming part of him, he thought, and for a moment tried to recapture the picture of Sarah's Tom that he had known – was it two or three days ago? But that image seemed frail; it faded almost as he thought of it, to be replaced with the harder, more determined man scrabbling against the rock six foot below him. Sarah won't recognise you now, boyo, Stephen thought, and addressed himself to the next stretch.

A little way ahead, the rocks became slippery with water, which dribbled from a narrow fissure in the cliff. After warning Tom to take care, Stephen negotiated the wet stone until he was level with the opening. A sudden cry made Tom lift his head and squint upwards.

"What is it? What's happened."

"The water. Get yourself up here, Tom. Quick. And I can smell it as well."

Tom drew himself up. "What is it? Good Lord, that's sulphur."

"Yes, and feel the water."

"Warm!"

"Put your hand against the rock of the opening. Just inside the hole. Feel it?"

"Yes – the rock's warm."

"And this is right against the open air. There's something very hot in there."

They looked at each other for a moment. Tom said, "How much further to the top, do you think?"

"Not too far. You can see we're higher than much of the spur. The Pit can't be too much beyond that break in the rocks, though it's difficult to judge."

"When we get there—"

"We'll lie low and wait for our moment. There's no point in planning it. We don't know what—Christ!"

A short scream of despair sounded above them against the sky, then floated down the gully, echoing off the rocks on either side.

Tom's eyes were dark and staring. "That was Sarah," he whispered.

"You don't know that."

"Who else would it be? My God, I need your strength!" He sprang up against the cliff, and began to climb frantically, levering himself over hanging slabs, and gripping the spear with three fingers of his right hand.

"Go carefully, for heaven's sake!" Stephen set off in his wake, clambering as swiftly as he could, but all the time, in leaps and bounds, the straining figure above him drew further away.

45

Only another hour had passed, but to Michael, whose arms throbbed with pain and whose head was bowed, it had seemed an endless stretch. He had borne the chariot along the last section, across the undulating grassy spaces of High Raise, and though the sky spread wide above him, the air was stiflingly close. Sweat dropped from his face into the dust of the path. His palms were red and chafed – blisters were formed at the base of his fingers. At length a daze had come upon him; his sight changed, turning the earth to glass and opening a gulf beneath his stumbling feet. The sounds of the air were fading; with every step, he seemed to fall a little deeper. A distant noise came to his ears, a whisper carried along the tide of the rocks. He listened, but his blood beat too strongly in his head and drowned the whisper out.

"Michael." A voice. A hand on his arm.

"We've arrived," said Mr Cleever. "You can stop now. Take some water. You've done very well."

Michael took the bottle and drank. His whole body was wracked. For a minute or two, he could only stand and stare dumbly out in front of him; figures with lizard heads passed across his gaze, and the sky was an angry red.

Then he grew aware of his surroundings. They were at the lip of the hollow, where the ground was flecked with harebell, and a boy had woken blinded three long days before. The chariot was resting against the gorse at the side of the path; its occupant facing the Wirrinlow with its chin against its chest. The others sat or stood upon the path, each absorbed in their own thirst, taking focused gulps from the bottles in their rucksacks and studiously ignoring the sunken ground beyond.

Sarah was standing on the other side of the chariot. Mr Cleever, with his back to her, had taken too hearty a gulp and was coughing heavily. All of a sudden, she began to run, away from the hollow back down the path, her bound hands held tight against her side, her feet slipping on the stones. Vanessa Sawcroft gave a warning cry, Mr Cleever turned, and a column of flame erupted from the dirt track just ahead of Sarah, who screamed and fell back into the dirt. The column of fire dropped, and was gone. Mr Cleever walked heavily down the track and helped Sarah to her feet. Wordlessly, he escorted her back to the party and signalled a place for her. She sat there weeping, and Michael addressed himself to the last drops of water in his bottle.

After several minutes, Mr Cleever was refreshed, and went to stand on a sizeable stone overlooking the Wirrinlow. He took from his pocket a folded piece of paper, which he studied carefully, checking it regularly against the lay of the land below. The others waited in silence. Michael felt the tension radiate from all sides. High above, some white clouds were blown rapidly north-south along the line of the Wirrim, but down here the air hung heavily and still.

A sudden image of Sarah came into Michael's head,

unwanted and unasked for. She was standing in the kitchen of the cottage, smiling at him. He shook it away with a frown, and went to stand beside Mr Cleever.

"What do we do?" he asked.

Mr Cleever's eyes were half-shut; they looked out unblinking across the hollow.

"Yes," he said, as if he had not heard. "It is the right time. I can feel it, an imminence, all about us. And I am the first to feel this in as many centuries as you can count, Michael my boy. All those others whom the dragon embraced here, they all had the key to it under their noses and failed to find it. Their time has passed and fallen away on the wind. Now it is my time, and what beauty there is in it! That the old enemy should enclose the key to our victory in the very stone he used to trap our master! That the powers which he used to constrict, we should now use to release!"

He laughed and turning away from the hollow, signalled to the others to approach him. Paul Comfrey got up from where he crouched, nursing his bottle, and walked over. Michael saw fear in his eyes, and used the sight. Comfrey's soul – half-dragon, half-vole – was trembling. Its edges fluctuated, and the pale green surface jittered nervously. In contrast, Vanessa Sawcroft and Geoffrey Pilate's souls were inky dark and as sluggish as treacle. Mr Cleever's was jet black, with the hard confidence of granite.

"Keep an eye on the girl," Vanessa Sawcroft said. "We don't want her running away from us now."

"She won't," said Mr Cleever gaily. "She's tied in with the fate of things now! Can't you feel it? We won't leave the hilltop, any one of us, until this thing is done."

And Michael did feel it. A great pressure hung over them, as if a distant storm was coming, and it seemed to bear them down to the earth. The weight of it told in their eyes.

"My friends," said Mr Cleever, for all the world as if he were addressing a parish meeting, "I don't mind telling you I'm nervous. We're all nervous, because of what will come. But there is no point in waiting. We know why we must do this, and we know the rewards. The dangers we also know. The people of the village are stirring against us. Even now, they may be searching for some sign – of us, or Miss MacIntyre – ready to threaten us out of fear and ignorance. Well, within the hour, they will be nothing more than beasts in the field to us, nothing but cattle. Our time has come.

"Listen to me carefully. I shall speak with mouth and soul." His audience gathered closer. Michael loosened his defences, and saw a mental picture appear of the diagram on Mr Cleever's paper.

"The cross carried the essential pattern on it," Mr Cleever said. Between us, we shall recreate the pattern, and summon the master from his sleep. The carvings in the stone represent the Four Gifts. On the right arm is the eye – the First Gift. That shall be Paul's responsibility. The symbol on the shaft represents the Second Gift – Geoffrey, you have always been good at that: you shall conjure fire. The opposite, uppermost symbol, that is levitation – the Third Gift. Vanessa, if you would. I shall undertake the Fourth – the power of

273

mind, represented by the head. We shall stand in a circle . . . Michael, do you mind?"

"I'm sorry." Into Michael's mind unbidden had come an image of his mother, more clearly visual than any he could remember. Where . . .? It had distracted him, and Mr Cleever's razor sensitivity had noticed the slackening of attention.

"To continue." Mr Cleever brought the diagram back into focus. "We shall stand in the circle, and call forth these gifts at a given moment, using them to our utmost. Each has its role. The First shall see the dragon, the Second will awaken it, the Third will remind it of the joys of movement, and the Fourth shall summon it. All those impulses we will direct to the centre of the circle. At that centre shall be Mr Hardraker and Michael. Michael – listen carefully."

"Yes." Another picture had sought to break through his concentration, but Michael had thrust it away without being aware of its contents. He brought all his mind to bear on the implications of Mr Cleever's words.

"Mr Hardraker is the sump or storehouse of all our power, but he cannot use it without a trigger. The four of us will provide that trigger. Michael, who has the greatest raw energy, the greatest range of movement – you, Michael – must encompass the power that will erupt from Mr Hardraker, and direct it."

"Direct it, where?" Michael's voice was weak; he remembered his last encounter with Mr Hardraker's power.

"Downwards. Into the ground. We shall split the earth and bring the dragon forth. He is deep, but not too deep – and we could break the hill in two if necessary, and create a gap running from Fordrace to the Chettons!" He laughed again, and the image flickered.

"I'm not sure," said Michael, "that I could handle all that power."

"You are simply the conduit," said Mr Cleever. "It shall pass through you, providing you direct it. You are strong enough, believe me. If you don't direct it, well . . . there would be problems, of course. But I have confidence in you, Michael. You are a special man."

Michael felt the others' resentment and was gratified. "I'll do it," he said.

"What about the girl?" said Vanessa Sawcroft. Sarah was sitting several feet away with her legs drawn up, watching them with wild eyes.

"Well," said Mr Cleever. "I think Miss MacIntyre should sit within the circle. Out of harm's way. Once the thing is done, she can go where she wishes."

That was what Michael heard. In the others' heads, Cleever's voice whispered something more: *'Since we're lumbered with her, I think we may as well put her to good use. Just in case our master requires any special encouragement. He must be hungry, after all.'*

For a second, Michael was aware of a slight break in the mental pictures Mr Cleever was sending him, as if something was being edited out. He tried to navigate round the barrier, but then it was gone, and the picture of the cross diagram returned. A flicker of annoyance, which he quickly disguised, flared through him. What had he missed?

He shook his head, and the irrelevance fled.

"What happens then?" said Paul Comfrey. "Pardon me, but we need to know."

"We cannot know!" Mr Cleever gripped both Comfrey's thin shoulders and squeezed them reassuringly. "That is the peril and beauty of it! But think of sinking into the endless blackness of Joseph's old age, and tell me which is the better option. Eh, Paul? Exactly."

"I shall get out the things." Vanessa turned to her rucksack. Cleever nodded.

"We've brought some quartz brooches and flint knives," he said. "They may help to harness the power. Just a guess. Quartz and flint appear in some old stories, and it won't hurt to have them on us. Paul, take the poles off the chariot. We'll carry the chair down on its own. Michael, come with me."

He moved off to the edge of the depression, and ran down the grassy bank. Michael followed slowly.

At the very centre, Cleever stopped, and crouching, pressed his palm flat against the grass, motioning Michael to do the same. Michael did so; the afternoon coolness of the grass met his skin, and then a faint warmth, almost undetectable, rising up from the soil beneath.

"He's ready," Mr Cleever whispered.

Straightening, his voice thick with excitement, he called over to the others. "Come on, damn you! Paul, get those poles off, or I'll burn your hide. Miss MacIntyre, down here please!"

He marched away, and left Michael standing. All of a sudden, Michael knew Stephen was close. He sensed a movement, a rapid reconnaissance, darting out in

Cleever's wake. Somewhere nearby . . . Where? In the rocks of the crag perhaps, or in the gorse . . . The fool! He had told him to stay clear. It was lucky the probing thought was too weak for Cleever to notice in his current state, but that luck would run out soon enough.

'Go away.'

He framed the thought with deliberate care, directing it out over the rim of the Wirrinlow towards the East. A delicate thought, barely audible; even so, he shuddered as he glanced over at Cleever, who with Pilate was straining to carry the Hardraker chair down the slope.

'Go away. Or you'll die. I told you.'

The thought that returned, whether through intention or inability, was very weak. 'You have to stop this.'

'Get lost. They'll sense you and kill you.'

'What do you think they are doing with Sarah?'

'Go away, or I'll kill you myself. I won't let you compromise—'

"Michael!"

Oh no . . . "Mr Cleever?"

"Geoffrey and I need your help. Mr Hardraker's weight is too much for us here. We're at the epicentre of his power."

Michael was sweating uncontrollably as he ran over to the edge of the hollow. The shrivelled face of Joseph Hardraker had grown animated. It twitched all over with a sort of current.

"Take this side," said Cleever. "And use the Third if you have to. We're too close to split hairs."

The three closed on the chair and gripped. Michael smelt a strong odour – a mix of scented talcum powder and minerals. He wanted to be sick, but turned his mind to the effort of lifting. Only by all three directing the Third Gift upon the chair, did it consent to leave the ground. Michael suspected that at the present moment he would have had difficulty lifting either one of the frail wrists from the desiccated lap. Together, almost running in their desire to be rid of the burden, they guided the chair across to the centre of the Wirrinlow.

"Which way should he face?" Pilate asked.

"Doesn't matter. No, let him face me . . . align him roughly towards the west – that's it."

"The ground's hot!" exclaimed Pilate. "I can feel it through my shoes."

"Vanessa, bring the baubles over. Hand them out."

"Does it matter who has what?"

"Any will do. Give me that brooch. Michael, fix this on Mr Hardraker's clothes. Take this knife. You won't need it, but the stone blade comes from the earth of the Wirrinlow."

"Where do we stand?"

"Are we doing it now?"

"Where's the girl? Oh, I see her. Geoffrey, fetch her down. She can stand by Michael and Joseph. Right, Paul, you've got your stone? Good. You're to be opposite me. I'll be over on this side, twenty paces from the centre. I'll measure it out with the string. Michael, hold this end and stay here."

Michael stood by the chair, and pivoted the string, as the others began to align themselves in position. Sarah was brought into the circle. Her eyes glinted defiantly as Pilate motioned her to sit a little way from Michael's feet.

"Watch her," said Pilate, and turned his back.

Michael looked her over, sensed her readiness to run, to attack, to escape, and shrugged. Once he had gained his full power he might grant her mercy. Until then, she could wait. Somewhere inside him, a half-formed doubt cried out, but then some of the countless wrongs he had suffered at Sarah's hands came back to him and he crushed the doubt back down. He turned his attention to the others. They were a bedraggled lot, all hot and dirty from the day's climb; one pale and wounded, the rest flushed with apprehension. The sun was dropping swiftly now towards the west, and their shadows threaded long across the grass. Michael looked over towards the rocks to the east, but saw nothing, and his quick mind scan picked up no trace of his recalcitrant brother.

A thin unfamiliar voice beside him. 'If he meddles, he will die.'

Michael turned in shock. The limp body was motionless, the white hairs on the skull twitched not an inch. Had it spoken? Had the voice sounded in his head? Impossible to tell. He looked across the hollow, but Mr Cleever was busy marking distances. Already Comfrey and Sawcroft were standing ready, and Pilate was adopting his position to the North. He felt a sudden urge to run, but as soon as he made a step, Mr Cleever felt the string go slack and waved him back. His jaw locked, his hands damp, Michael resumed his place by Joseph Hardraker's side.

At last, Mr Cleever fixed his own place to the west of the Wirrinlow. He marked it with a stick and walked over to Michael, rolling up the string and grinning amiably.

"I hope you are ready, Michael," he said. "When you feel the power around you, focus it downward into the earth. We keep it up until we get results, which judging by the heat of the ground, won't be very long. Good luck."

He turned away. "Good luck to you all!"

The same salute was echoed from every side.

A whisper from Sarah. "Michael. Don't do this. They're mad. You're not the same."

And at that moment, an attack from Stephen – a childhood scene, a family, his mother . . .

"Shut up," Michael said. "Both of you, just shut up."

'Michael,' said the thin voice in his ear, 'hold my hand.'

'Don't be a fool,' said Stephen, faint and far away, and Sarah ground her nails into the hot earth with the agony of her pleading: "The dragon is evil, Michael, can't you see it? Look at these creatures! Do you want to become one of them?"

"I am one of them, goddamit!" Michael snarled. "It's too late!" And the thin voice said again, "Hold my hand, Michael, and feel our power."

"If you are all ready," called Mr Cleever, "we shall begin."

'Michael—'

"Michael—"

'My hand, Michael.'

"Oh God—"

Then he reached out and took it, and the calling of the voices faded into nothing.

It began with a flicker, which Stephen, crouched among the rocks and gorse of the head of the crag, felt like a tap at the base of his skull. It was fearful in its gentleness; it seemed to have no source and no direction, but at that moment he was swept away from his brother's mind as if carried by a great wave. For a moment he was dizzy and confused. Then consciousness steadied itself, and he raised his head and looked down into the Wirrinlow.

From the platform of the rocks, he had a view into three-quarters of the hollow. The young willowy man with the sandy hair stood nearest. His back was turned, his shoulders hunched, and his head, which radiated a baleful concentration, was bowed towards the earth. Stephen did not have to see his eyes to know that he was using the sight, sending it downwards at an angle under the hollow.

A moment passed. The vibration of the sight spread around the circle. The other participants, rigid with attention, waited in silence. At the centre, beside the chair, Michael stood as if carved from stone.

Now a new vibration, discordant with the first, sprang up. Its source was Geoffrey Pilate, the Fordrace grocer. His hands were together as if in prayer, but with their fingertips pointing outwards, towards the centre of the circle. As Stephen watched, the tips rotated down. Then, with a violence that stung the air, a silent flame of dark orange sprang from them. A few tendrils leapt eagerly inwards towards the two figures at the centre, but Pilate, his face white, eyes turned upwards, seemed anxious to keep the fire under his control. It remained steady, flickering about his fingers, while the frequency of its note passed around the hollow, rebounding off rocks and earth walls and growing in strength. Stephen rubbed his ears, which were growing sore, as if he was diving deep into a bottomless pool.

A little further forward, squeezed down between two upright stones, Tom lay on his stomach with the spear pressed close beside him. One rust-covered curve of the spear-head was so near that it brushed against his cheek; he smelt the sharp metal tang, saw its unfocused reddish-blackness in the corner of his eye as he looked down on Sarah crumpled fifty yards away on the floor of the hollow. His heart thudded painfully against the ground, his mouth was clagged with dry spittle.

Oh God, help me, he thought. Tell me what I must do.

His head moved slightly. The old iron pressed against his cheek, marking it with a brown scar.

Now the note of the Third Gift echoed round the hollow. Vanessa Sawcroft, standing opposite the grocer with his hands on fire, stiffened where she stood. Her bad arm was pressed against her chest, the other was rigid by her side. Slowly she rose from the ground, at first with a fluid ease, and then with sudden checks and judders. Stephen noticed a spasm of pain break over her face, and felt her thought suddenly lash out across the gathering music of the circle.

'George,' it said. 'Quickly. The pull is terrible.'

Immediately came the response. The Fourth Gift, the internal eye, was all around them, seeing into their every doubt and fear, rolling over the pain of their effort and reassuring them with its presence. Mr Cleever's energy was unleashed. He flooded the hollow with it, immersing and cradling each one of the other three, nursing their reserves ready for the final summoning.

Tom felt the iron burn cold against his cheek, and at that moment, Mr Cleever's presence passed over him between the stones, ignored him, and was gone.

Stephen was taken unawares. He had no time to mount a defence, and it would not have done him any good had he done so. He ducked, instinctively and vainly, but Mr Cleever's eye fell hard upon him. There was a raging and a buffeting all about him; he cried out in terror and despair – then the fury receded at a great pace, and Stephen, to his own amazement, was left alive, sprawled back among the boulders of the crag.

In an instant, Tom was with him, bounding back between the rocks with spear in hand.

"Stephen – what's happened?"

"It was Cleever; he was all over my mind. No, I'm all right. He pulled back, for some reason. Didn't he see you?"

"No. But if he's spotted you, we'd better move."

"There's no point – we're not the issue any more. Can't you feel it all around us? It's like a song."

"I don't hear anything."

"It's not a song in that way – but all the powers, used at once. I can't think straight. And it's getting worse – Oh God, too loud—!" To Tom's horror, Stephen fell back, clutching his head in clawing fingers. There was a sudden sound behind him from the hollow. Unwillingly, Tom turned.

The first stage was over. The gradual build up, of gift upon gift, power upon power, until the sky and earth were ringing with them, was now complete, and Michael knew his time had come. He had watched impassively, with a tiny voice always speaking in his ear, readying him for the task ahead.

'Yours is the finest of all powers (said the voice), equalled only by mine. Why do I whisper? So that George Cleever does not hear us. He is too busy concentrating, setting us free – we must not disturb him. Kind George. Brilliant George. I applaud his insight. But his power is dirt and dust and broken things before yours and mine. Ah, Michael, I have hung on waiting for you for such a time. My road was squeezed into a thread by the cursed trundling of those damned seasons. Bones and hide, I was, bones and hide. Softly – can you feel it? The woman struggles, George joins the harmony. Now, tighter, hold my hand. Empty your mind of all things. We must break the earth, Michael, you and I. Empty your mind. We shall receive all, and pass it to him.'

'Now— (Mr Cleever broadcast his thought)— All

four of us – direct everything to the centre, and do not stop until I tell you, or be damned to hell. Curse Vanessa (this to himself); if she ruins this through her cursed weakness—'

Sarah saw the fire erupt with a savage joy from the grocer's fingertips. It crossed the circle directly over her in a yellow arc which sputtered tiny ropes of flame. Down into the centre it poured, and in an instant, her brother was consumed. She hid her face.

The fire was only one of the four powers which hit Michael at that moment. All four entered him, he felt himself a vessel, a hollow thing, which was being filled. Flames licked all around, the world scorched, but the cold hand in his own protected him. In the middle of the inferno, he shivered.

The vessel was filled. It burst. Michael's gaze, his mind, his soul was directed on the ground. All four powers tore into the earth. From beside him, unannounced, came a tremendous energy which joined the others, and augmented them, and seemed to Michael to have no limit.

The ground was ripped asunder.

At the Hardraker farm, the first stone fell from the topmost chimney. All along the sagging roofs, slates and tiles shuddered against each other, setting up a gentle chattering which echoed round the yards. Old doors, jolted off latches, swung themselves open with sudden violence. The people of Fordrace, who were clustered in the central yard beside the solid reassurance of their cars, were filled with panic, and moved closer to each other.

"An earthquake!" said one man, his voice hushed with awe.

"Don't be stupid – you don't get earthquakes in England," said a woman.

"It could be the wind," a large man added, in a small voice.

"We must go now." Mrs Gabriel spoke from the seat of the police car. "The place is giving us warning."

Some of the people were so much in agreement that they opened their car doors. But others looked worried.

"Joe and Lew are still inside," said one. "We can't go without them."

"Don't you believe it."

"Well, you go then. I'm staying."

There was a sudden shudder across the whole surface of the yard. Cobblestones here and there were shaken loose from centuries of dirt, and half rose from the ground.

"Christ, that does it!" said the large man. "I'm going." He sat heavily in his driving seat. "Anyone who's not stupid, get in."

More than one made ready to join him, but a young man raised his chin and shouted out at the top of his voice. "Joe! Lew!"

The farm took up the shout: mocking echoes resounded on all sides. A wooden cross-beam, somewhere in the great barn behind them, fell thirty foot with a cresendo of crashes.

A white shape moved in the gloom of the hallway.

"It's Joe!" cried a woman, "and he's carrying—" She broke off in bewilderment. Joe Vernon, his face suffused with red blotches of effort, appeared at the door. Behind him was Lew Potter, also staggering under the strain of the weight they carried.

"The cross!" said someone. "The missing piece."

"Help us take it!" Joe Vernon's voice was a croak. "We can't carry it any more."

A dozen hands reached forward. Joe collapsed to the side. Behind him, in the darkness of the hall, was a sudden roaring.

"Dear God," said Lew. "The walls—"

Mrs Gabriel was suddenly amongst them. "We must take this back!" she cried. "Right now, back to the church. No argument. Sean, William, whose is the car with the door at the back?"

"What about the boys?" said a man. "They might be—"

Joe Vernon interrupted. "There's no one in there," he said. "We must leave. Now."

Three windows on the first floor shattered. Glass shards sprinkled down upon the courtyard. The crowd melted into their separate cars, and doors were slammed fast against the farm's destruction.

The fire bit into the earth. A cleft of flame and billowing smoke had been opened where Michael and Joseph Hardraker stood encased in flame. The black chair had turned to ash; now Mr Hardraker hung suspended like an unused puppet at the centre of the fire. His legs, arms and head were limp, his feet trailed over the deepening pit. Michael stood on a jutting promontory of soil, eyes closed, head bowed.

The earth below was turned to glass, which bubbled, hardened, cracked and shattered, then fell away in quick succession, consumed by the furnace-heat. Michael looked below it. His sight was clear beyond anything he had imagined; he saw diamonds and quartz stones, emeralds and lodes of gold, all at unknown depths and distances.

And there, right below him, the worm in the earth. Coil upon coil, motionless, trapped in its pore. He called out to it, looking for a response – but the stillness of centuries had to be unlearnt and the coils had fused.

So Michael summoned it with the third and fourth powers. He rose into the air, lifting the spindly Hardraker doll with him. 'Look up!' he thought. 'Remember the sky! The most marvellous of your gifts!' He directed his mind downwards, towards the mass of scale and spine. 'Look up!' he called. 'We have heeded you at last!'

On the edges of the circle, Mr Cleever, sensing the moment of crisis, exhorted his flagging troops to one final effort.

Among the rocks, with his hands to his ears, Stephen opened his mouth with a soundless cry. There were flecks of blood between his fingers.

The cords that bound Sarah's wrists blackened and snapped in the heat. Now she was on her feet, running away from the column of fire which extended into the sky. The soles of her shoes melted as she ran.

Tom began to run down the slope towards her. He held the spear up near the head, and the base of the handle bumped against the ground.

Then the dragon moved.

And with that movement, the power of all those linked to the dragon by its gifts was multiplied. For so long dependent upon the worm's remembered energy, its sudden real activity flooded new life into their fading souls, creating a profound effect: of dizziness, confusion and drunken joy. This was the greater the longer they had been linked, the longer their powers had waned and shrivelled towards the deathly stillness of their master. For Michael, three days linked, the effect was minimal; he felt he had been dealt a buffet to the head, he staggered in the air and steadied himself. Paul Comfrey felt tipsy, but the sharpness of his First Gift waxed – he caught a glimpse of the coiling thing below him, and broke his sight off in fear. For Vanessa Sawcroft and Geoffrey Pilate, the effect was more pronounced. They reeled where they stood, as years of gradual dulling and slowing of the mind were reversed in seconds. George Cleever's was the most severe experience. He screamed in pain. It was as if a knife were scouring him from the inside; he tottered and half fell, and as his controlling intelligence was broken off, the summoning powers rolled upon the burning grass of the Pit in disconnected ecstasy.

But Joseph Hardraker was engulfed by a blue fire. His hand was whipped away from Michael's, and he was curled and uncurled in mid air, surrounded by licking tongues of flame which obscured him from the sight of those below.

I come.

A new strength entered Stephen from outside him. The pain in his head subsided and he got groggily to his feet.

Michael looked down into the gulf, from where there came a crashing and a rending of rocks displaced. The fire conjured by Geoffrey Pilate had vanished with the breaking of the circle, but now a new fire, issuing from the ground, rose to replace it. Behind it, rising slowly, was a whiteness. Michael felt a surge of triumph; he hovered in the smoke and surveyed his companions, who rolled like swine upon the ground. He was the only one still upright, the only one fit to greet their master.

There was a movement at the edge of the hollow – something was trying to climb the slope. He narrowed his eyes and looked through the flames. A jewelled soul shaped like a dog's head was scrabbling on the soil, slipping backwards as it tried to ascend. Michael could not remember who this might be, and he found he could not refocus to find out. There was something else there too, just above the dog-shaped jewel; another jewel, shaped like a deer's head. It was bowed close to the other, as if in an embrace.

*

Beside him, the body of Joseph Hardraker jerked and contorted in its own blue nimbus. The fingers clenched and unclenched, the face blurred and changed.

On the lip of the Pit, Tom grasped Sarah by the hand and pulled her towards him up the slope. Both tried to speak, but the roaring of the flames smothered their words. Tom pointed back towards the path and pushed her away, but Sarah resisted, holding her ground. Then suddenly he had hugged her and was gone, down into the hollow with the spear head flaring against the fire.

Now Stephen entered Michael's mind again, stronger than before. The dragon's strength had surged in part to him. His voice carried above the gale of energy, pleading with him, but it was a hopeless plea, without any belief or fervour. Michael saw Stephen among the rocks now, a misshapen soul, in which the dragon was sullied by the stubborn nag. Michael approached him through the air and came down to land beside him. 'I told you it would be worth it. Even you are stronger now.'

'Michael, your face—'

'You're not still fretting! Look at us! The world ends all around us, and here we are still arguing! Everything has changed. It isn't Cleever any more. It's me – and maybe Joseph, if he lives. Well, I know you understand this; I felt you give up just then.'

'I just haven't got anything to say.'

'Your trouble, Stephen, is you're not one thing or the other.'

Then Michael caught in Stephen's mind a fleeting pang of hope and fear. He saw through his eyes an image; a man running over burning ground, carrying a spear. For a moment the dislocation confused him, then he understood, and turned, in time to see the jewelled deer-soul moving fast across the hollow towards the rupture in the earth. Although with his sight he found the spear was invisible to him, he knew it must be there. He started forward, but at that moment, his brother's weight fell on him from behind, and he was borne down under a hail of blows.

As Tom ran he felt his feet blistering from the heat through the soles of his shoes. He passed Paul Comfrey, who had risen and was looking about him in leaderless confusion. On his right, Geoffrey Pilate was also stirring. For a moment, Tom was tempted to deal with him before he recovered, but his priority was clear. The edge of the Pit was charred black; it shook, and lumps fell away into the void. Tom approached, holding the spear steady in both hands. The expectation of his own death hung heavily on him, weighing down every step. He hoped against hope that Sarah would have had the sense to get away, but he knew in his heart that she was still close by. Smoke billowed from the Pit. A hissing noise sounded above the rumbling which came from just beneath the lip.

Tom crouched close beside the hole, just beyond the reach of the flickering heat. The spear was curiously cold in his grasp, and its rusty head showed black against the fire.

Then a pale thing rose at the heart of the flames,

oval in shape and swaying, a dull white sheen surrounded by blue fire. A poison plume of sulphur belched forth with it, blinding Tom for a moment and wracking his lungs. There was a high-pitched screaming which deafened him. His grip on the spear weakened, then grew tight again, and he tried to focus on the distance between him and the slender shape which still swayed sightlessly before him.

A scream of hate from above. Down from the smoke came an unknown youth with jet black hair and eyes of fire, naked except for the charred remnants of an orange garment around his shoulders. His thin lips were set in a smile of madness. He gestured – and Tom was afire.

Beside Joseph Hardraker, the dragon's head thrashed back and forth with spasmodic fury as it struggled to free its body from the earth. One great white claw lunged in the smoke and smote the ground. Cracks ran outwards across the breadth of the Wirrinlow.

Sarah stood on the ridge surveying the chaos below her, consumed by indecision. Terror told her to run – run and not look back until her sanity was restored. Yet, even in her fear and amid the confusion of smoke and flames, which belched forth from holes and craters across the hollow, she could pick out three people with crystal clarity.

Her brothers, rolling in the ashes, punching and tearing at each other like dogs. Tom crouching by the Pit, a silhouette against the flames. Then he was on fire, and something erupted in Sarah unlike any anger she had ever known. A madness had consumed her family, and everything she held dear was being destroyed. Enough. It would not continue. Propelled by her fury she was halfway back across the Pit before she quite knew what she was doing.

Outside St Wyndham's church, the people watched the smoke rise from the Wirrim. They were entirely silent now, except for desultory moans whenever a new flare showed against the darkening sky. Only Mrs Gabriel, orchestrating her helpers with terse commands, ignored the spectacle.

"We shall use the main door. Is it open?"

"I'll see." Joe Vernon ran across. "Yes."

"Quickly then, pick it up. Carefully! We mustn't chip it. Are you ready, Lew? Right. As fast as you can. Keith, you hold the door. Now one at a time – you first Joe. Mind your backside."

As they entered the church, a muffled explosion sounded from high up on the hill. The nave was lit with freckles of colour from the windows. Silently, with only puffs and wheezes from the men, they passed along the aisle to the vestry, where the curtain was already drawn back. The Fordrace Cross lay there on its trolley, its broken face towards them. Mrs Gabriel surveyed first it and then the single arm with a decisive eye.

"Can you hurry, please?" Lew Potter begged. "My arm's killing me."

"It looks all right," said Mrs Gabriel, ignoring him. "It is a clean break, thank the Lord. And positioned in the centre of the trolley. Right. Lower it down then – no, Joe, move around, can't you see you've got the top bit? That's it. Gently. As near flush as you can. Fingers out? Good. Now Joe, push it into place. Give him a hand, William. Well done."

"Christ Almighty! What was that?" cried Joe. With drained faces the men looked at one another, and then as one they ran back down the nave, leaving Mrs Gabriel alone by the united cross. Without haste, she sat herself down on a nearby chair in the vestry, and pressing her lips together, began her vigil.

The worm had not yet freed itself fully when the stone bond was renewed. As it felt the pressure return, a red line, studded with spikes, opened in its head and let forth a scream of rage which broke against the sky and rebounded across the Wirrim's slopes as far as Stanbridge and back again. Its newly waxing strength was weakened, but it had its response ready. Quickly, it drew on the reserves of its nearby cohorts to win free of the ground. Everyone, from the numinous Hardraker hovering in the air, to Stephen, who lay unconscious beneath his brother's furious onslaught, had their power sucked from them.

The fire that spun about Tom's body was snuffed out, as Hardraker's will was distracted. At that moment, Sarah appeared beside him.

"Tom!"

She rolled him over. He was still breathing, but his hair had gone, and his face was wealed. The fingers of his right hand still clenched the spear.

Michael got up, his head reeling. The dragon was almost out of the ground. The long neck merged into the slender body, dull white like maggot's flesh. A sudden nausea came over him as he looked at it, in sudden knowledge of its alien nature and the malign will that had kept it alive and waiting for untold centuries out of the sun. He knew, in that instant, how cursed they all were – he, Cleever, and even Hardraker, to think that with their petty powers they could hold themselves up before the worm and expect its thanks. He felt it draw on his strength even as he stood there, and the hopelessness of the situation gouged his heart.

Then Michael, with a sudden painful return to his human sight, saw his sister, kneeling by the prone body of – who? He didn't know. She was wresting something from his grasp. Mr Cleever, his energy exhausted, eyes bulging, mouth agape at the horror issuing from the earth, was nevertheless moving round behind them. Even with his power weakened, Michael sensed his cold intent. And he had a knife in his hands.

"The spear—" Tom's lips moving.

"I'll take it. Loosen your fingers. Come on – loosen them!"

The spear was light in her hand. Miraculously, the heat had left the oak shaft quite untouched, but the rusted head seemed forged anew. The rust had vanished, and in the dragon-light it gleamed. Sarah looked towards the dragon.

Only the back haunches were still left in the pit. The tip of the tail raked against the edge. As Sarah stood there, watching the head swaying this way and that, she realised that the dragon was blind.

Then Michael passed her at a run, and Mr Cleever,

who had stood behind her with his flint knife drawn, was knocked sideways to the lip of the Pit. The knife fell from his fist and vanished into the void.

Now the youth with raven hair who flew beside the dragon caught sight of her with a terrible cry. Instantly, the blind head turned in her direction and swept downwards, the mouth opening impossibly wide. A hundred stiletto teeth cut the air. Sarah raised her arm to protect herself, and the iron spear, which now shone brighter than the flames beyond, was thrust into the blood red mouth and down into the throat.

At this moment, many things happened.

Sarah felt the spear whipped from her hands and up into the air. A blaze of heat drove her backwards with her hands over her eyes, and she collapsed alongside Tom.

The dragon tried to scream in rage, but it could not. The spear was stuck fast in its broiling throat, and the iron was melting, pouring down its gullet faster and faster, until the space was clogged. It thrashed its body back and forth in its pain, and its tail, still trapped below, broke the earth around it.

Mr Cleever, lying on the edge of the Pit, found the ground shifting. He tried to rise, but a whole section of the lip gave way and he was precipitated bodily into the flames.

Michael, a few feet further back, leapt for safety as the earth collapsed about him. He landed beyond the lashings of the tail and rolled among the stones. As he did so, he felt the entirety of the dragon's gifts snatched from him with the speed and absolute implacability of a death.

The youth in the air gave a despairing scream. He dropped from the sky, shrivelling as he went, ageing, cracking, shrinking with phenomenal swiftness, until, as he disappeared into the inferno of the Pit, he was once more old Mr Hardraker, a broken puppet, a dragon's plaything.

From their various places in the hollow, where they had wandered in the madness of their powers' rise and fall, Vanessa Sawcroft, Geoffrey Pilate and Paul Comfrey experienced the sudden loss of the thing that had moulded their souls over years of bondage. Only Paul Comfrey, whose mind was not entirely shrouded by the dragon's gifts, escaped insanity.

A mile away, and hundreds of feet below, the Hardraker farmstead collapsed in upon itself, wall upon wall, roof upon brick. Visitors the next day found not one outhouse standing.

The dragon's head and legs beat against the ground, but it was already dead. As the last vestige of life faded, it fell back into the pit, bringing vast slabs and chunks of earth down with it. One single jet of fire, which was seen for miles in all directions, erupted in its wake, but the crack had closed beneath it even as the gobbets of yellow-orange flame were completing their final fizzling arc over the Wirrim.

When Stephen woke, he found the Wirrinlow had changed. A great mound of black-streaked earth rose up in the centre of it, half as high as the slopes at its side. All the grass was gone; the earth was churned and broken, and bodies were scattered here and there. Those of the Fordrace grocer and librarian were deathly still, but Paul Comfrey was twitching and groaning. Slightly to one side of the mound, Michael sat, hunched over, staring into space. Close by, Sarah was cradling Tom's head in her lap and refusing to allow him to rise.

Almost unconsciously, Stephen tried calling to Michael with the Fourth Gift, but with a shock he found his voice echoing back ridiculously in his own head. He tried using the sight, but discovered he was merely squinting. Where the gifts had lodged, there was now nothing but a hollowness in his head; a faint impression of something that had floated out of reach and been forgotten. There was no doubt about it: the powers had gone.

He looked at his brother again. Michael was squinting too, frowning, and shaking his head in puzzlement. Stephen sighed. What on earth would he be thinking now? What could he ever say to him?

Then he caught Sarah's eye. She was stroking Tom's forehead, and talking to him, but as she did so she looked up and saw Stephen and smiled. Stephen smiled back. He got up painfully, and began to walk towards his brother and sister across the ruined ground. Hot ash crunched beneath his feet, and the first stars were visible in the sky.

In the church of St Wyndham, in the darkening vestry, Mrs Gabriel was awakened from her sleep of exhaustion by a great rustling cascade, like a lorry-load of gravel being emptied right beside her. She sat in the twilight blinking vainly for a moment, then got up and felt along the wall for a switch.

After a minute's fumbling she found it: the bright orange light illuminated a huge pile of stone-grey sand, which spread out in all directions from the buried trolley, and almost entirely covered the vestry floor.